UNDER
THE GUN

UNDER THE GUN

JOHN VORHAUS

PINNACLE BOOKS
KENSINGTON PUBLISHING CORP.
www.kensingtonbooks.com

PINNACLE BOOKS are published by

Kensington Publishing Corp.
850 Third Avenue
New York, NY 10022

All Kensington titles, imprints, and distributed lines are available at special quantity discounts for bulk purchases, premi-
ums, fund-raising, educational, or institutional use. Special
book excerpts or customized printings can also be created to
fit specific needs. For details, write or phone the office of the
Kensington special sales manager: Kensington Publishing Corp.,
850 Third Avenue, New York, NY 10022, attn: Special Sales
Department; phone 1-800-221-2647.

This book is a work of fiction. Names, characters, businesses,
organizations, places, events, and incidents either are the
product of the author's imagination or are used fictitiously.
Any resemblance to actual persons, living or dead, events, or
locales is entirely coincidental.

ISBN-13: 978-0-7860-1994-6
ISBN-10: 0-7860-1994-8

First printing: September 2008

10 9 8 7 6 5 4 3 2 1

Printed in the United States of America

To my mom.

CONTENTS

ACKNOWLEDGMENTS

Fiction writers, like poker players, tell lies for a living. But even fiction must stand on a platform of fact, and I want to thank the people who helped shore up mine, most notably Annie Duke and Jack McClelland, for their thoughts on tournament structure, and Tony Guerrera, for backstopping my math, as usual. Thanks to P0kerH0 for lending his catchphrase— I'd also like to thank the Internet in general, whose teeming anonymous informants provide an indispensable source of, if not fact, at least consensus reality. For everything from the name Sivapathasundaram to the going rate for rhodium, I wonder how any writer ever got along without it. Thanks to Greg Dinkin and Frank Scatoni at Venture Literary and Richard Ember at Kensington for letting me walk this road. Thanks to Maxx, who kept calm faith as I battled through endless hedgerows.

PART ONE

The Gamble in Him

Fate is what life hands you.
Free will is what you choose to accept.

1 Apostrophe Catastrophe

The IM that Guy Harris sent Hal Harris that Friday told his brother to drop everything and come to Las Vegas right away. It didn't say "*and bring money*," but in Hal's long experience with Guy that was pretty much a given. Hal ignored the message. He figured if it was truly urgent—or even if it wasn't, for Guy was no take-no-answer-for-an-answer guy—there'd be a follow-up phone call. Sure enough, ten minutes later the phone rang, and Guy's manic voice came down the line, boasting how by dint of skill, native intelligence, and "balls the size of boxcars, Hal!" he had won something to do with some big-deal poker tournament. This was, Guy assured his brother, an event of such cosmic consequence that it definitely required glorifying in high Vegas fashion, which for Guy Harris usually meant too much to eat, too much to drink, and a liberal application of strippers.

"Come to Vegas now, Hal. You've got to help me celebrate."

"Guy, I've got a ton of work to do."

"So do I, man. I'm supposed to be playing poker."

"That's work?"

"You know it is. It's my job. But look"—and here his voice changed—"we really need to talk."

"So talk."

"On the phone? Screw that. I miss your shining face, sunny Jim."

Hal sighed. Peel back the histrionics and you arrived at the same old subtext: *bring money.* "Look," he said, "if you need cash . . ." He didn't know what he was going to say next. *Call Western Union? Get a real job?* He used to could tell Guy to hit up their parents for it, but with them long dead, *the only soft touch left dangling on the family tree is me.*

"I don't need money, Hal. I need to fucking celebrate!"

Once, long ago, Guy had tried to explain to Hal about tells, the mysterious psychic (or merely observational) means by which poker players detect lies in one another's play. Like how they act strong when they're weak, or weak when they're strong, or how they'll look you in the eye in a threatening manner when they're bluffing and don't want you to call. "Sometimes," Guy would tell him, "it's like this rift in the fabric of space. You just know they're not telling the truth." A rift in the fabric of space? Like almost everything Guy ever told Hal about poker, it went in one ear and died there. But for some reason, just now Hal thought he heard something in Guy's voice that, well, felt like a rift in the fabric of space.

"Guy," he said, "are you scared?"

"Scared? Why should I be scared?"

"I don't know. You sound weird."

"Just come to Vegas, will you?"

"I can't, Guy. Really. I'm in the middle of my crunch."

"Oh, yeah, that's right: taxes. Feeding the maw of Uncle Sammy."

"Hey, just because you don't—"

"Don't start with me, Hal." This was a well-chewed bone of contention between them. As an accountant and what Guy called, with no little contempt, *a citizen*, Hal scrupulously declared every cent he earned, whereas Guy, by his own admission, took a more "creative" approach to tax filing. How he'd never gotten audited was beyond Hal's comprehension, but it was only ever a brother's love that kept Hal from personally dropping a dime.

So Hal didn't start. Then there was this long silence, like Guy was searching for another avenue of attack but coming up empty. At last he said with kind of a shrug in his voice, "Whatever, bruz. Look, I have some things to take care of. You change your mind you know where I live. I'll leave a key under the mat."

"Why would I change my mind?"

"Ah, you won't. You're in the middle of your crunch." He fired off an angry last word—"This wasn't about money, Hal"—and then hung up.

Hal Harris had no illusions about his brother. Guy was selfish, manipulative, narcissistic to an extreme degree, genially corrupt and gently degenerate, a fan of every casual vice from masturbating in the dark in the room they shared as boys to smoking the kind of noxious cigars that make people gag. He was utterly without self-discipline, other-awareness, or the vaguest sense of social responsibility. But he could charm the pleats off a Girl Scout's skirt, and he'd get your back in a bar fight. And he wasn't afraid. Of nothing was he ever afraid. He said that's what made him such a good poker player. More than once Hal had watched him shove wads of hundred-dollar bills into a pot while smiling over his shoulder at Hal and saying, "What are they gonna do, kill me?"

So though Hal tried to forget about the phone call and bury himself in his work—even as it threatened to

bury him in it—he kept coming back to the sound of
Guy's voice on the phone. No matter how many coats of
bravado-colored paint Guy slapped on, Hal could still
see the fear bleeding through. He knew it was real.

What are they gonna do, kill me?

Hal kicked himself for his stupid sentimentality,
but what could he do? Blood was thicker than rational
thought. So he blazed through a bunch of returns,
farmed the rest out, booked a flight online, and cabbed
it out to the airport in time to catch a six o'clock nonstop, Pittsburgh to Vegas. With the time change he'd be
there before eight, in plenty of time to . . . well, in time
to do what? Even as he boarded the plane he wasn't
sure why he was going or what he thought he was going
to do or find. He supposed Guy was having some sort of
a meltdown, and the white knight in him—there was a
fair bit of white knight in Hal Harris—maybe hoped
this was a chance to drag Guy out of chaos and into
some semblance of a regular life. He knew that Guy had
no patience for dull normals, and Hal frankly couldn't
imagine Guy holding down a job like his, or even any
job of any kind, not if it meant reporting to someone or
showing up on time or doing things by rote. But maybe
Guy had gone so thoroughly broke that he was ready
for the narrow and straight at last.

Probably not, thought Hal. *Probably he's just figured out
a new way to play me.*

With a brother who lived there and denizened its card-
rooms, Hal was no stranger to Las Vegas. He'd served
his time in casinos. He knew them well enough: the sat-
urated colors and overloud sounds, the cocktail waitresses with the low-cut this and high-cut that, the grim
grins plastered on the gamblers' faces as they watched

their stake slip away, the way everyone affected the devil-may-care attitude of happy sailors dancing on a sinking ship. For his part, Hal had always held the city of sin at arm's length. He'd long ago figured out that if you could actually beat Vegas, Vegas wouldn't be there, which realization dimmed his actuarial enthusiasm for craps, slots, blackjack, all of it. As for poker, he was a dead loss there. Hold a gun to his head and he could recite the ranks of hands:

high card
pair
two pair
three of a kind
straight
flush
full house
four of a kind
straight flush
royal flush

But that's about as far as it went. Some people have card sense and others don't, that's all. Or rather, some people have the gamble in them and others don't. Hal never did. While Guy was pitching nickels with his thug buddies against the back wall of their junior high school, Hal was nerding off in the library or doing supplemental sets of math problems for extra credit. Math always came easy to Hal, like gambling came easy to Guy. "They come, they go," Guy would say. "Fuck it." And then hit up his bruz for a loan. Which, of course, he never paid back. It had occurred to Hal that he probably chose a career in accounting just to get some control over numbers, since he could never get control over his brother, who had no control at all. It may also have been why he never learned to play poker. Guy always wanted him to, so he'd have someone to play against when he'd busted everyone else, but Hal never took the bait. Either he was playing dumb or just was dumb, but he figured if Guy couldn't get decent competition out of him, he'd leave him alone about it, and eventually Guy did. So Hal's understanding of poker never extended past what beats what, and whenever he watched Guy play he let his mind wander to other things.

After a turbulent childhood and adolescence during which their divergent worldviews ground against each other like tectonic plates, Hal and Guy had settled into an amiable "you go your way, I'll go mine" adulthood and saw each other sufficiently infrequently to keep their clashing passions on low boil. While they viewed themselves as chronic opposites, in fact they complemented each other quite well. Being with Guy was a high for Hal: pleasant enough in measured doses but not to be overdone. Hal in return gave Guy the sort of plain, gray background against which bright colors shine in high relief. Measuring himself against his brother's straightforward (and to Guy's eyes bland) way of life made Guy feel superior and sharp. In the sense that each other's flaws just reinforced their own cherished beliefs, they were perfect companions. Opposites don't merely attract; they validate and confirm.

They were now in their late twenties, and the shape of their lives seemed to be set. Hal, thirteen months his brother's senior, had taken his accounting degree and immediately put it to work in the sort of company where sensible sensibilities were positively reinforced and wearing a Hawaiian shirt on Casual Friday was the acceptable limit of outrageous behavior. Guy, meanwhile, had given college a scattershot failed attempt; kicked around for a while, burdened neither by focus nor fixed address; and finally come to rest in Las Vegas. When he discovered cardroom poker, he knew he'd found his home.

Romance had eluded both Harris boys, for Hal was too cautious to give his heart away without a clearly calculated and gauged return, and Guy kept renewing his girl-of-the-month club membership for mortal fear that the subscription would lapse. Hal supposed the time would come when he would marry and breed according to the well-defined suburban script. Guy had no such illusions. There was no settle in him, as anyone who'd ever watched him fidget in his seat in a poker game would quickly attest. Hal worried for his brother: for the poverty of his spirit, for his wastrel ways, and for his tangible lack of desire to build something lasting in his life. But whenever he voiced these concerns to Guy, his brother would fire back with an existential, "What's the point, bruz? You can't take it with you." This passed for thoughtfulness in Guy's don't-ask-don't-tell philosophy and was the seawall upon which the waves of both Hal's logic and his compassion inevitably broke.

The plane descended toward the setting sun, with the mountains on fire behind and the city in shadows and loud neon below. In the seats around him Hal could feel the quickening pulse of anticipation. Soon these eager revelers would be scattered around town hunting and chasing the Vegas buzz wherever they could find it: in the free drinks that the house so generously provided; in the stage shows presenting larger-than-life spectacles at larger-than-life prices; in the "escorts sent directly to your door"; in the all-night pub crawls that held out the tantalizing promise of real human contact (or anyway sex) but ultimately seemed to deliver only a big bar tab and a hangover of storied proportion. Vegas was like that. It stole so much: sleep, discipline, sobriety, time, common sense. And after it softened you up, it picked you clean. What got Hal was how they never stopped coming back, no matter how many times they went home broke. Insanity, he'd been told, was doing the same thing over and over again in hopes of a different outcome. He didn't think they were all insane, just victims of selective memory—*gamnesia,* Guy called it—a bettor's confirmation bias that filters out the losses and overstates the wins.

Then again, here he was, landing in Vegas again, trying to save his brother's lost soul again. Insanity, they say . . .

Hal thought he would cab it to Guy's apartment, but Friday night at McCarran Airport was impossible for cabs, with a line that snaked through switchbacks like Disneyland on Labor Day. He didn't feel like waiting, so he went to the rentacar desk with the shortest queue and paid way too much for one of those new cheap Chinese imports, a subcompact Song Serenade with fine vinyl seat covers and all the pep of a narcoleptic riding mower.

Guy lived in a rundown housing complex called the Evergreen Apartments, a name that always amused Hal because there was never ever anything evergreen about the apartments or grounds—except possibly the pool, which was ever green with algae—or the surrounding avenues and streets. It took Hal an hour to get there, a slow, aching grind up the I-15 in an accordion crush of trucks, commuters, minivan cabs, and out-of-state platers. Frazzled and edgy by the time he arrived, he parked behind Guy's building and made his way up the outside stairs to the second-floor rear corner flat that Guy called home. He knocked on the door but got no answer. Not that he expected one. Guy had said that he had some

things to take care of. Hal took this to mean harvesting
the poker tourists, whose toxic cocktail of eagerness,
impatience, and jet lag made Friday Guy's big-money
night of the week. He had, he told Hal, made a study of
this and found Friday more profitable than, say, Saturday, because Friday was when most tourists blew into town
and hit the poker tables all overamped and underskilled.
By Saturday the good ones had found their feet and the
bad ones had gone broke, leaving the tables top-heavy
with locals who, like some latter-day Donner Party, spent
the evening more or less gnawing on one another's legs.
Floridly put, but Guy was florid like that.

Hal lifted the welcome mat to find Guy's key. On the
mat he read the words *The Sivapathasundaram's*. He
couldn't imagine where Guy had gotten this cheesy artifact—probably stole it off the Sivapathasundarams'
doorstep—but he knew it was the gratuitous possessive
that tickled Guy. Words were to Guy what numbers were
to Hal. They moved and delighted him and sang to him
in a way. But he was indignant about ignorant assaults
on the language. As outlaw as Guy was in his lifestyle, he
had a mocking contempt for anyone who couldn't follow simple rules of grammar, and apostrophe catastro-
phes were his pettest pet peeve.

"Yoo-hoo! Mr. Sivapathasundaram? Anybody home?"
Hal stepped across the threshold into a living room littered with beer bottles, chips, coins, cash, playing cards,
porno magazines, and promotional discs for online poker
sites. An Australian flag draped over the back of a threadbare brown couch served as . . . what? Upholstery? Style?
Above it hung a frameless print of dogs playing poker,
staple-gunned to the drywall at an odd angle. Guy had
taken a Sharpie and given the dogs dialogue balloons.
"That's not a hand, that's a paw!" said one. "Call if you
don't like kibble," said another, and, "Shut up, bitches,"

snarled a third. Through an open archway Hal could see the kitchen, cluttered with the flotsam of Guy's bad food habits: empty pizza boxes, a can of aerosol cheese . . . and a giant bag of dry dog food? Hal didn't know Guy to have a dog but couldn't imagine his circumstances to have been *that* reduced, so he assumed dog, somewhere.

Hal went into the bedroom. On Guy's night table stood an empty bottle of Jack Daniel's with a candle jammed into it. This, along with a John Coltrane CD case and some empty condom wrappers, suggested a night of, *well, I suppose you'd call it romance.* Per the condom wrappers, Hal didn't search too hard for further evidence.

There was a bathroom off the bedroom, and as he hadn't had a pee since Pittsburgh, Hal decided to avail himself. A sign on the door—another purloined apostrophe catastrophe—proclaimed this the "mens' room." Hal walked in and squared up in front of the toilet. As he unzipped, a rustle of shower curtain caught his ear. Given the tiny, close nature of Guy's flat, Hal couldn't credit a refreshing cross breeze. Curious, he turned toward the sound—just in time to take a thick brick of crystal to the face.

He went down like a drunken coed, smashed his head against the sink, and remembered no more.

2 Minty McGinty

Hal woke up facedown on the couch. The smell of ancient dust and stale spilled beer made him gag. He rolled over, opened his eyes, and saw poised above his head the fuzzy outlines of the same crystal slab, now shot through with fissures. He flinched, bracing for another blow.

Instead, he heard his brother's voice.

"Look what you did to my trophy, man." Guy's face replaced the trophy in Hal's haloed field of view. "You cracked the shit out of it. You're one hardheaded bastard."

Hal groaned and sat up. "What the hell?"

Guy regarded the wounded artifact mournfully. "I won this, you know. I played my ass off to win this." He thrust the trophy in Hal's face. Between the crazing in the crystal and his own furred vision, Hal could barely make out the words etched into it:

Sun King Poker Challenge
No-Limit Hold'em
1st Place

"That's from the Sun King, man. I had to iron out over four hundred slackjaws to win that thing."

Ignoring the lament—or boast—Hal asked, "Why did you hit me?"

"I thought you were a prowler."

Hal rubbed the rising welt behind his right ear and then the other one above his left eye. "I called your name."

"In fairness, you called Mr. Sivapathasundaram."

"You didn't recognize my voice?"

"It's been a long time since I've heard it."

"Guy, we spoke on the phone this morning!"

Guy squeezed his eyes shut for a moment, a gesture Hal had long since come to recognize as one of faux remorse. "Oh yeah, that's right." Guy set the trophy down on the coffee table. It stood at an odd angle atop a bottle cap. "What can I tell you, Hal? Things have been weird around here."

"Weird enough for you to lurk in your own shower and whack your unsuspecting brother upside the head?"

"Almost exactly that weird. Although, again in fairness, I think it was the sink that did most of the dam—"

Over the years Hal had found that it sometimes took direct action to drag Guy back from the fantasy plane upon which he spent so much time, so he grabbed his brother by the shirt front and pulled him down on the couch beside him. Guy landed with a *whoof*, and a gout of dust puffed up. He looked at Hal with doe eyes. "What?"

"You hurt me, bruz. Apologize."

"I barely tapped you. Geez, you're thin-skinned."

"Guy . . ."

"Okay, bruz. I'm sorry. Mea fucking culpa. Okay?"

"Okay. Now tell me what's going on."

"What's going on," said Guy brightly, "is we're getting

a beer. Let's go." Guy bounced to his feet and helped his brother to his. As if seeing Hal for the first time, Guy broke into a broad grin. "Not for nothing, man, but it's good to see you. I'm glad you came out." He hugged Hal and clapped him on the back. Hal endured the hug but didn't really return it. Guy was the huggy one. Hal had never developed the knack.

They went outside. "How's your head?" said Guy. "You okay to drive?"

"You want me to drive?" asked Hal. "What happened to the Hawk?" The Hawk was Guy's cherry red El Camino, his pride and joy, one thing in his life that he would neither hock nor lend.

"Yeah, that's part of the story," he said. "Where you parked?" Hal pointed out the Song Serenade and Guy's face fell. "You couldn't rent a real car?"

"It's what they had. So what? It drives."

"Well, we'll work it out."

"Work what out?"

By way of answer, Guy put his fingers to his lips and rendered a sour, flat version of the famous first notes of Beethoven's Fifth Symphony. As Hal winced at the sound, Guy threw open the passenger door and flipped forward the passenger seat. Before Hal could even ask why, a great hulking beast, like a sheepdog with dreadlocks, only bigger, much bigger, hurtled toward them at speed. In response to Guy's command, "Saddle up, Minty!" the huge dog poured into the backseat, filling it completely. "Hal," said Guy proudly, "meet Minty McGinty."

"Oh my God, Guy. It's a horse."

"Nah, come on. He's barely a hundred pounds."

Hal peered in at the astounding creature, whose long, white, corded hair covered and obscured all his features—eyes, legs, mouth—such that he looked like nothing so much as the business end of a giant mop. Suddenly, without warning, the dog's tongue leapt out of the hirsute tangle and slathered Hal's face with a long, slurping, and altogether affectionate kiss. Hal recoiled in disgust; the dog obviously wasn't called Minty for his breath.

"He can't come in the car, Guy. It's a rental."

"Don't worry. He's a Komondor. Komondors don't shed."

"Shedding I'm not worried about. Shocks and springs I'm worried about."

"Well, you worry too much. He's a beautiful dog, and sweet as flopped quads. Let's go."

They left the apartment complex and angled north on a grotty boulevard until they reached a rundown roadhouse opposite the North Las Vegas Air Terminal. There they parked in back among a dissolute array of motorbikes and beaters. As they got out, Guy reached back to fondle Minty's ropy forelocks. "Be good, Minty," he said. "Anyone hassles you, you eat 'em."

"You sure he won't eat my car?"

"This piece of shit?" said Guy, smacking a fiberglass quarter panel with the flat of his hand (and leaving a shallow dent). "Who cares?"

Hal beeped the car locked. They went inside. Hal found a table while Guy bought beers, which they worked in silence for a while. But silence was not Guy's strong suit. He could never just sit and be, and soon he began to fidget, playing with his beer mat, the sugar packets and condiment bottles, anything he could get his hands on. He took a quarter and started rolling it across the back of his hand, flipping it from finger to finger in a practiced way that betrayed all his idle hours at a poker table. Hal could tell that Guy was working himself up to tell his story. He didn't rush his brother but did wonder how long this was going to take and how much damage to his rentacar, and thus security deposit, Minty McGinty could do in the meantime.

At last Guy spoke. "I won a poker tournament last week. Great big motherfuckering one, too."

"Well, congratulations."

"Didn't win a dime, though."

"Okay, Guy, I admit I don't know your business, but isn't the point of these things to, you know, win money?"

"Not if it's a satellite."

"A what now?"

"Satellite. Like a qualifying match. Winners advance to the next round." Guy explained that there were two types of poker tournaments: ones where you won money outright and ones where if you won, or finished high enough, you earned a buy-in to a much bigger event. When he started talking about how poker satellites leveraged bankrolls, amortized prize pools across much larger playing populations, and provided small-timers a shot at big payouts, Hal's eyes started to glaze over. But that didn't stop Guy or even slow him down. He meandered through a long, discursive monologue on how poker, with its roots in riverboat gambling and Old West gunslinging, had long been held in public regard somewhere between petty crime and cockfights; how in recent years, thanks to the twin engines of internet poker and televised tournaments, it had enjoyed an explosion of popularity and acquired a surprising glaze of respectability. This was especially so on the tournament side, where a certain contest of prestige leapfrog was currently under way, pushing entry fees for the most glamorous top tournaments through the old ceiling of $10,000 to $25,000, $50,000, and beyond. The fallout from this buy-in inflation was increased reliance on the satellite system as a means of feeding players into the game. Since only the most well-heeled players could afford the astronomical direct buy-ins, satellites had become the norm. "All of which brings us," Guy said at last, "to the Poker Apocalypse."

"Of course it does. Why wouldn't it?"

The Poker Apocalypse, Guy explained, was the brainchild of one Kai Cortland, a famous name in Las Vegas casino development, and "a major fucking ego, even by local standards." He was always trying to one-up the other guy, even if the other guy couldn't give a rat's ass what Cortland was up to.

"Hence," Hal hazarded to guess, "a poker apocalypse."

"No, *the* Poker Apocalypse. 'The biggest poker tournament in the history of ever.' "

"What's the buy-in?"

"Hundred grand."

Hal spat a little beer. "A hundred thousand dollars? Who's got that kind of money to enter a poker tournament?"

"No one," said Guy. "That's why there's satellites. And satellites into satellites. And satellites into satellites into satellites. Ten bucks gets you into this one, a hundred into the next, a thousand into the next. Keep winning, you keep advancing. Or if you have the scratch, you can jump the queue and play in the supersatellite that feeds right into the main event. That's what I did. That's how I won this." Guy reached into his pocket and pulled out a glittering silver disc about a third larger than a standard poker chip. He slid it across the table to Hal. Hal turned the coin over in his hand, noting an engraved silhouette of a man—presumably Kai Cortland—on the front, and the words *Poker Apocalypse* scripted on the back. "This will get you into the tournament?" he asked.

"Yep," answered Guy. Then, after a pause, "If I live that long."

Hal knew all about Guy's gift for hyperbole. In Guy's universe, nothing was good if it could be great or great if it could be off-the-charts spectacular. Nor was there ever anyone quicker to turn a hangnail into a potential amputation. *All manic all the time* was the audio logo for Radio Guy (except when manic crashed to depressive), and Hal was inclined to dismiss this self-described threat on Guy's life as so much white noise between frequencies.

Except for one thing.

"Guy," Hal asked, "what happened to the Hawk?"

"Oh yeah, that." Guy looked pensive, an expression so foreign to his face that Hal could literally not remember ever seeing it there before. "Okay, it's like this. I win the satellite and collect my tournament entry chip, right?"

"If you say so."

"So now I'm heading out of the casino, fighting my way through the swarm of rail stoats—"

"Rail stoats?"

"Weasels. Mooks. Mooches. You win a big tournament, they come out of the woodwork, like, glad-handing you and telling you what an awesome player you are, how they were sweating you the whole way, and by the way since they're running a little lean right now and being as how you're so flush could you maybe cut loose a little surplus fundage?"

"I understand," said Hal pointedly. "It can be so annoying when people borrow money."

Guy shot him a hooded glance. "You want to hear my story or not?"

"Go ahead."

"I'm just about out of there when this skinny Vietnamese kid comes up to me—"

"How do you know he's Vietnamese?"

"Duh, he looks Vietnamese. Besides, you see an Asian poker player these days it's five to one he's Vietnamese."

"Why?"

"I don't know. They got the gamble in 'em. Anyway, here he comes: dyed blond hair, miles of attitude. I figure he's another mook, but no: he wants to buy my jeton."

"Jeton?"

"Chip, Hal, tournament entry chip. Try to keep up. So this mook offers me face value for the TEC. Cash, right now. I tell him no. So he offers face plus ten."

"A hundred and ten grand? Why would he do that?"

"No fucking clue. Maybe he just hates money."

"I assume you took the deal."

"Hell, no. I told him to blow me. Hal, one thing you learn in this town, someone offers you a deal that seems too good to be true, it is. I figure he was trying to con me or date me, but either way fuck him, right?" Guy took a long swig of beer and wiped his mouth on his sleeve. "So now I'm driving home, right? Me in the Hawk, cruising along. I reach this construction zone where they're putting in a flyover, so there's dirt and gravel and shit all around. This Lexus cruises up alongside me. And who do you think's behind the wheel?"

"Asian dye job?"

"Bingo. And the dipshit tries to run me off the road! In a Lexus!"

"What did you do?"

"Well, unfortunately, I went off the road. Caught some gravel, rolled the Hawk, fell down an embankment. Next thing I know I'm crawling from the wreckage."

"Were you hurt?"

"Not a scratch, but"—Guy raised his bottle and offered a toast—"shed a tear for fallen comrades, bruz: the Hawk is history."

"What about the Lexus?"

Hal shook his head. "The next car I saw had flashing lights. They gave me a field sobriety test and sent me on my way."

"Did you tell them what happened?"

"I don't talk to cops, Hal. Nothing good can come of it."

"How'd you do on the sobriety test?"

Guy gave his brother a hard look. "I hadn't been drinking."

"Okay, if you say so. But you must've been pretty pumped, though. After your win, huh? Little dopamine in the ol' bloodstream?"

"Not enough to hallucinate, if that's what you mean."

"And you're sure the driver was the same guy?"

"Of course I am. How many Asian dye jobs do you see every day?"

"How many could you recognize in a moving car late at night?"

"So now you're saying I'm paranoid? I made the whole thing up?"

"Maybe you just overreacted."

"Oh yeah, yeah, that's the way it happened. I'm driving down the road minding my own business, la la la, when suddenly for shits and giggles I decide to freak out and roll my truck." Guy shook his head. "Damn it, Hal, I thought you'd understand. I hoped you'd help me figure this shit out. I haven't even told you about the other guy."

Hal was on the point of asking what other guy when

suddenly something big and hairy and exceedingly stinky stuck a tongue in his ear.

"Minty!" shouted Guy. "You rascal! What are you doing here?" In no universe could Minty McGinty be considered a lapdog, but in that moment he made every effort to try, thrusting his paws and massive chest up on Guy, tilting him back in his chair. This placed his business end in Hal's face, and Hal discovered that Minty was no mintier back there.

"How did he get out of the car?" Hal asked, doing his best to shove the dog's massive ass aside.

"Oh, he can open doors," said Guy. "I tell you what, this is one smart fucking dog. You should see him play poker."

"He plays poker?" asked Hal.

"Yeah," said Guy, with a wink. "But he's got a tell. He barks when he's got the nuts. I'll go put him back."

"Won't he just—"

"I'll tell him to stay. Like I said, smart dog." Guy led his monstrous dog out the back of the bar. The bartender gave Hal a dirty look. Hal just shrugged, like, *What do you want from me? It's not my dog.*

Hal sat there musing, trying to sort out all his brother had said. Had Guy come completely unhinged or was he really in danger? Either way, how could he possibly play in this Poker Apocalypse thing with a clear head? *And who gets involved with something called Apocalypse in the first place? Isn't that sort of an obvious warning sign?* Hal decided to get Guy out of town, chill him out somewhere for a few days. Try and reroute the deranged train of his brother's life.

Then he heard Minty bark.

Hal was not a dog person. He'd never had one as a child and had had only casual contact with them since.

But Minty's bark, an odd, aggrieved sort of half howl, struck such a discordant chord that Hal didn't think twice. He leapt to his feet and ran for the door, pocketing the tournament chip as he went.

He raced across the parking lot to his car. The passenger door was open and the seat was tilted forward but Minty was nowhere to be seen. "Minty?" Hal said. "Guy?"

"Over here, bruz," came a wan reply. Hal followed the sound of the voice and found Guy some yards away leaning against a dumpster with his hands folded over his belly like the Buddha.

"Guy, what's going on? Where's Minty?"

"Ran away. Got scared."

"Scared of what?" Then Hal saw it. The dark tar oozing between Guy's fingers. "Holy fucking shit, Guy! You've been stabbed!"

"You think?"

"Hang on! I'll get help!"

"Too late for help, bruz. Where's the chip?" Hal hauled it out and gave it to Guy, who turned it over in his hands until it was covered with blood. "Ain't this a bite in the butt, huh? Just when I was going big time."

"Who did this, Guy? Asian dye job?"

"No. Some other guy. Big. Beer gut. Fucking ugly." Guy looked at the chip through half-closed eyes. "He wanted this. I told him to blow me." Guy pressed the jeton into Hal's hand. "Take it," he said. "Enter the Apocalypse for me. Win the motherfucking thing."

"I don't play poker. I don't even know how."

"You've got a month to learn." Guy coughed weakly, spraying a fine mist of blood on Hal's shirtfront. "Slaughter Johnson will help."

"Slaughter what?"

Guy's eyes fluttered. He struggled to keep them open. "And take care of Minty, will you? He's a smart fucking dog, but he needs a lot of love."

Then Guy Harris died, and his brother stood alone beside a dumpster with a hundred grand's worth of trouble in his hand.

3 Mayonnaise Motherfucker

The detective who questioned Hal was named Danny Ding. Hal thought it must be something of a curse to go through one's professional life as Detective Ding, but a Dinged-up childhood had probably been no picnic either. Hal could relate: when he was young they had called him Hal O'Peño and Hal Itosis. *It's not easy being a kid no matter what,* thought Hal. *You think you've got a mockproof name, something like Jack Rich, they'll be calling you jock itch by lunchtime.* He found it odd to be thinking of such things at such a time, but he understood that in his current state he wasn't thinking straight, and any thought was possible.

Ding was a ponderous little man with a round face, beady black eyes, a desperately wannabe goatee, and a thinning tonsure of straight black hair. His shirt was old enough to have defeated its promise of permanent press, and his herringbone jacket looked like the only one he owned. He wore scuffed brown brogans and affected an air of bored indifference as he said, "So, a guy knifed behind a bar, huh? Where the fucking news crews?" He asked Hal some desultory questions but seemed not at all interested in the answers, including Guy's description of his assailant.

"Aren't you going to write that down?" Hal asked.

As if to indulge him, Ding mimed writing in an imaginary notebook and said, "Victim whacked by ugly troll. Secondhand account of attack narrows suspect field to every mayonnaise motherfucker in Las Vegas." Ding flashed a creepy smile, showing a set of the most acutely akimbo teeth Hal had ever seen. "Witness descriptions are crap," said Ding.

Not that Ding needed witnesses, particularly. To his jaundiced eye, this was just a drug deal gone wrong, with the perp long gone, and a laughably slim likelihood of justice. So he asked Hal a lot of lifestyle questions about Guy and pointedly ignored any answer that didn't fit into a degenerate druggy profile. After listening to Ding play "blame the victim" for a while, Hal decided that Guy was right about nothing good coming from talking to cops. Eventually Ding got tired of the sound of his own voice and said, "Right, I'm done with you. You can go."

"Do you want me to not leave town?"

"Did you kill him?"

"What? No! Of course not."

"Then what the fuck do I care where you go?" Ding walked off to harass some rookie cop for not stringing hazard tape right.

So . . . where the fuck do I go? wondered Hal. *To a hotel? Back to Pittsburgh? Follow Guy to the morgue?* Then he remembered. *Shit! Minty!*

He looked around the parking lot. The dog was nowhere to be seen, so Hal mimicked Guy's off-key whistle, quietly and self-consciously at first, but then with more vigor. The cops gave him strange looks, like, *Well, they deal with grief like they deal with grief.* Then Minty came blasting out of some bushes where he'd been hiding or digging or eating whatever unspeakables made his breath so redolent. He raced to Hal, reared up on his massive hind legs, and nearly knocked Hal over with the full force of his hundred-pound love. While the cops snickered, Hal shoved Minty into the Serenade and got the hell out of there.

He drove back to Guy's apartment, where he fed Minty a mountain of dog food and made a meal of heated canned whatever for himself. In the back of his mind it occurred to him that he was having an absurdly normal moment, considering the absurdly abnormal circumstance. But the front of his mind was still in shock, and in times of shock he defaulted to habit. Such as: *I always read while I eat.* So he went looking for something to read.

On Guy's bookshelf, amid the clutter of manga comics and science fiction novels, a battered hardback caught Hal's eye. The cover, in lurid black and pink, featured a falcon or an eagle of some sort diving down on a poker table with a clutch of cards in one talon and chips in the other. The whole presentation screamed *self-publish,* but what struck Hal was the title, *Swoop and Pummel: A Guide to Tournament Poker.*

And the author.

Slaughter Johnson.

Hal flipped the book over and saw a picture of the author, a weathered, angular man with an untamed nimbus of white hair who looked like nothing so much as Albert Einstein on crack. Hal took the book back to the kitchen table and skimmed the introduction while he ate. "The first thing you need to know about poker tournaments," wrote Johnson, "is that most people lose most of the time. If you can't stand disappointment, you don't stand a chance." Johnson went on to run the numbers, demonstrating how the average tournament paid 10 percent of the field or less, and so the average player—average by definition—had very nearly no chance to win. "Not *no* chance," the author assured:

> If you get lucky and lucky and lucky again, and if you never get unlucky when it counts, then you get to stand at the top of the pyramid, and from that lofty height you can piss on the folks below. They won't care. They'll be so busy licking their miserable wounds they won't even notice. But remember: Absent a game plan, and absent massive amounts of experience and skill, your chances of winning a poker tournament, especially a big one, are essentially the same whether you enter it or not.

Good times, thought Hal. Here Guy had charged him with nothing less than winning "the biggest poker tournament in the history of ever," yet according to an expert's (or at least an author's) assessment, this was about as likely as hitting a hole in one on a golf course blindfolded and drunk in the midst of a blizzard. Plus, he had his life to get back to. The taxes couldn't wait. His clients couldn't wait. More than once he'd heard Guy say, "There's two kinds of problems in this world: my problem and not my problem." *So how is this my problem?* wondered Hal. The more he thought about it, the angrier he got. Where the *hell* did Guy get off dragging him into this mess in the first place? Guy was the one with the freestyle lifestyle, not Hal. All Hal ever wanted was peace and quiet, and a job to do that was reasonably engaging and not too hard. Now all of a sudden he was supposed to drop everything except the lance Guy used for tilting at windmills, and turn himself into some sort of incipient poker pro? Nonsense. Gogglebox nonsense.

He read another passage from *Swoop and Pummel*:

> Your enemies want something of you. All their bets, raises, chat, body language, and psychic energies are directed at getting you to do what they want. Maybe they want you to fold. Maybe they want you to call. Maybe they want you to stand on your head and shoot ping-pong balls out your ass. But you can be sure that whatever they want is for their benefit, not yours. Success in poker is therefore quite simple. Just figure out what your enemies want, and then don't do that.

Yeah, simple. Like alchemy is simple. Just figure out how to turn straw into gold and then do that.

Best just to walk away.

It wasn't that Hal didn't love his brother, wouldn't love to avenge Guy's death in some samurai sense. But there was very little samurai in Hal—none, so far as he knew. And he prized sameness over change. He regarded his brother's passing as a tragedy but, if he was to be completely honest with himself, something Guy had doubtless brought on himself in one way or another. So Hal went to sleep that night determined to get back to his own life as quickly as possible. It was no flashy life, but he knew it and felt comfortable in it, like the one winter coat he'd worn for years and saw no reason ever to replace.

For reasons both sentimental and hygienic he couldn't face sleeping in Guy's bed. He found some reasonably clean sheets and blankets in a closet and made himself a bed on the couch. After everything he'd been through, he thought he'd have trouble nodding off, but as the heated canned whatever made its uneasy way through his digestive tract, and the residual adrenaline leeched out of his system, a great weariness took hold and he sank into a dark, solid slumber.

Sometime during the night he had this dream where Guy was grabbing him by the neck and throwing him to the floor.

Only it wasn't a dream.

And it wasn't Guy.

He belly flopped with a thud and looked over at Minty, curled up in an unconcerned shag ball nearby. *Some kind of guard dog you are,* he thought. Then his assailant was on top of him, straddling him, whacking away at the back of his head. "Guy Harris, you rat bastard! What did you do with my dough?"

Hal offered the only defense he could think of. "I'm not Guy!" he shouted.

After a moment, the blows stopped. Strong hands grabbed him and flipped him over. He found himself staring into the liquid blue eyes of a sturdy young woman with copper-colored hair, wildly out of control. She wore tight jeans, cowboy boots, and a blue satin jacket with the word *Vinny* embroidered in yellow over the left breast. For a moment she kept her fist cocked, as if she wasn't entirely convinced that he wasn't Guy. Then the evidence of her eyes sank in.

"You look like him," she said. "A little."

"I'm his brother, Hal."

"You a scum-sucking douche bag, too?"

"I'm . . ." Hal was at a loss for words. "I'm an accountant," he said at last.

After a moment, the woman nodded and got up. She walked over to Minty, who had roused himself into a languid stretch, and scratched him behind what were probably his ears. "Hey, Minty," she said. "Who's a good boy?" Then she turned back to Hal and asked, "Where's the dickweed?"

Hal wasn't prepared to come right out and say, "the dickweed's in the morgue," so instead he asked, as nonchalantly as a man putting on his pants and shirt in front of a strange woman can ask, "What's it to you?"

"He owes me a buttload of money."

"What are you, like a loan shark?"

"Don't be absurd. I'm his backer. I put up his tournament entry fees and we split the take." She shook her head. "Only now I hear he's blowing our bankroll on Poker Apocalypse satellites. Which I specifically told him not to do."

"Why not?"

"He's dead money in that field."

"Dead money?"

She gave him a sidelong glance. "Are you sure you're his brother? Yeah, dead money. No chance to win. The field's too big, too tough." She strode around the room, her anger waxing. She was tall—almost six feet—taut and muscular, like a volleyball player. "You back someone, you have to be able to trust them not to drag themselves around by their pride. I keep telling Guy there's games you can beat and games you can't beat. You've got to know the difference." She stopped and looked at Hal. "So where the hell is he?" she asked again. "Hiding? Afraid to face my wrath?"

That's when he said the line about the morgue.

She listened quietly while he gave her a truncated version of events: how Guy won the Apocalypse satellite, then feared for his life, then was right. For some reason, he didn't mention the tournament entry chip, still sitting in the pocket of his pants.

She took the news in stride, which surprised Hal. Apart

from her financial stake in Guy, he figured they must
have been at least friends, or how did she have a key to
his place? Knowing Guy, he would certainly have tried
to hit on her, too. Possibly she had joined him in his
candles-and-condoms nights of so-called romance.
With all that, she just stared thoughtfully at the poster
of dogs playing poker over Guy's couch. "This thing always cracks me up," she said. " 'Shut up, bitches.' That's
funny." Then she turned to Hal and said with surprising
directness, "So, dead, huh?" Then, "You sure?"

"What? What do you mean am I sure? I was standing
right there!"

"Uh-huh, yeah. Or either that or the two of you cooked
up this bullshit story so he could skip town and be off in
Reno or somewhere up to his dick in hookers he's paying for out of my money."

"I thought you said you weren't a loan shark. Why
would he have to run?"

Her face clouded over. "No," she said, "you're right.
He wouldn't have to run. He could just as easily have
lied to my face. Guy's great at lying and being forgiven."

"Tell me about it."

"You've got some history in that area?"

Man, thought Hal, *where to begin? How about prom
night when he told me my date had gone home sick but really
she was meeting him at a motel? Or the summer he "borrowed"
my car, drove it all the way to Mexico, wrecked it there, convinced me he'd been carjacked, and yes, had me wire money to
fly him home?* Guy was a great liar—world class—because,
in the manner of all good liars, he felt absolutely no
shame in getting caught. Hal dimly understood that this
was also part of what made Guy a great poker player.
You have to bluff to win sometimes, and you have to not
be afraid of sometimes getting caught.

Hal regarded the staunch redhead standing before

him. He saw in her a kindred spirit, someone who had also fallen victim to Guy's blithe indifference to the feelings and concerns of anyone else. It shook Guy to realize that he'd never experience that indifference again, and he wondered whether this woman felt a similar sting of loss. "Look, uhm . . ." he said, groping for her name. She just gestured to the stitching on her blue satin jacket. "Vinny? Your name is Vinny?"

"What, a woman can't be named Vinny?"

"It's not all that usual."

"It's usual to me."

"Is it short for something?"

"Sure," she said archly. "It's short for 'mind your own business.' "

"Interesting," said Hal, surrendering the point. "Look, Vinny, I don't know how to convince you that Guy is dead—but dead he is. If he lied to you, if he cheated you, I wouldn't be at all surprised. That was his nature. Nor do I imagine I can do much to make it right." At that moment, Hal's stomach rumbled and he swallowed a burp that reminded him of last night's unsatisfactory meal. "But would breakfast be a start?"

They went to an all-night joint she knew, a place called Rudi's Eatateria. As they walked inside, Hal caught a glimpse of their reflection in the restaurant's glass double doors and thought they made rather a Mutt-and-Jeff-looking couple: he slight and wiry, she with her Amazon build. Hal was fussy about his appearance. He knew he was no more than averagely attractive, so he tried to maximize his aesthetics with well-cut clothes and—his one true indulgence—salon-cut hair. Vinny was not that sort at all. She dressed merely functionally, and as for her hair, she had long since surrendered that Medusan mess to the whims of fate. She never wore makeup and would have felt absurd and clownish if she did. This was, she knew, direct fallout from her thirteenth summer, when she took puberty by storm, shooting up eight inches and attaining genuine "towers over boys" status. Now, a dozen years later, she was almost militantly antistyle, a defense mechanism she recognized as rejecting rejection before rejection could reject her first.

A shapeless waitress oozed over and took their orders: scrambled eggs and toast for Hal, a Greek salad for Vinny. Hal thought it was an odd choice for the middle of the night, but Vinny said it was the middle of her day, which made this lunch. He asked how she came to have her day turned around.

"I deal," she said.

"Drugs?" he asked before he could stop himself.

She laughed, for which he was grateful. "No," she said, "cards. Poker. I deal at the Sun King." She swiveled in her seat to show him the back of her jacket, which bore an improbable cartoon caricature of Louis Quatorze sitting on a golden throne throwing fistfuls of coins, chips, and cash into the air.

"Is that how you knew Guy?" Hal asked.

"What makes you say that?"

"Well, I know he won a poker tournament there." Hal's hand strayed to the bruise on the side of his head. "It seemed like a reasonable guess."

"Yeah, no," she said, "that's just coincidence. I met him through his poker coach."

"I didn't know Guy had a coach. I wouldn't think he'd need one. I thought he was a pretty good player."

"Guy? He was fucking gifted. When he was on his game, he had these, like, laser eyes. He could read the strength of your hand, the strength of your will, hell, the numbers on your valet ticket. But when he was off his game, he could tilt—"

"Tilt?"

"Fall apart. Hemorrhage at the wallet. When Guy was in freefall, oh man, it was ugly. That's why he needed a coach. Someone to curb his atavistic urges. Like a batting coach curbs a free swinger."

"I never thought of that. Do all poker players have coaches?"

"No, but everyone has someone they talk game with."

"Aren't they afraid of giving away their secrets?"

"It's not like that. Look, you're an accountant, right? Don't you need someone to check your math?"

"I don't actually do math anymore. I mean, the software does the math." Hal realized he couldn't recall the last time he'd taken pencil and paper to an actual math problem. He found himself suddenly missing the challenge.

"Okay, bad example, but . . . suppose you've got a tricky . . . I don't know . . . audit or whatnot. Don't you need someone to backstop your logic?"

"Yeah, I guess."

"That's why they talk poker. To backstop their logic."

Their food arrived and they ate in silence: one of those awkward silences that happen when people who don't know each other well first share a meal. Hal tried to fill the silence with what he thought was innocuous chat. "So . . . what's Vinny short for? Vincent? Vindaloo?" She didn't answer. Hal kept trying. "Well . . . is it Vinni with an *i* or Vinny with a *y*?"

"Oh, with an *i*," she said, sarcastically. "Definitely an *i*. With a little heart over it instead of a dot." She looked up from her food. "In fact, two *i*'s. V-i-n-n-i-i. Like genii. I'm in the plural." She stabbed an olive with her fork.

"Seriously, do I look like the sort of woman who'd spell her name with an *i*? Give me a fucking break."

Wow, where did that come from? wondered Hal. "Sorry," he said. "I'm not trying to rub you the wrong way. Just making conversation. You know, harmless questions."

"Around here there are no harmless questions."

"How come?"

Vinny burst out with an exasperated laugh. "Man, you just don't take shut up for an answer, do you?" She ate the olive and speared another. "Okay, it's like this. Vegas, see. Most everyone here is from somewhere else. Mostly they came here because it didn't work out back there, wherever there was. Like they couldn't find a job or couldn't hold one, or they just didn't fit in. Used to be they went to California. Now they come here. Vegas is the last refuge of misfits."

"Such as my brother."

"Uh-huh. So when you ask a Las Vegan personal questions about his past and whatnot, you might be turning over a rock. Maybe he was in prison. Maybe divorced. Maybe he's still got a wife somewhere. Maybe two. You never know. Vegas is like this big AA meeting. First names only, please. No outside contact."

"Seems lonely. Isolated."

"It can be. But over time you find out who's got your same disease."

Hal flashed on Guy's many bad habits. "Or cross infect."

"That's one way to put it. Anyway, then you become like foxhole buddies. You make your friends."

"Okay, well, now I understand. 'Don't ask, don't tell.' " They ate on in silence.

Vinny felt bad for being so defensive. She hadn't intended to be. *It's just Vegas,* she thought. *You really do get guarded.* But Hal had neither the cynicism nor shiftiness that marked those who'd lived in Vegas too long. It wasn't fair to treat him according to Vegas rules, since he really didn't know them. Come to think of it, she didn't much like those who did. So, after a moment, she said, "It's Vinton."

"What?"

"Vinny. It's short for Vinton. Family name. Where I come from they're big on family names for first names. Vinton . . . Finnegan . . . Slaughter—"

"Wait, Slaughter?"

"That's right."

"That wouldn't be Slaughter Johnson, would it? The poker author?"

"I don't know if you'd call him an author. He wrote a book, but it doesn't really circulate. Just among his students."

"Was he Guy's coach?"

Vinny nodded, surprised that Hal knew that.

"Is he your coach, too?" asked Hal.

Vinny laughed. "I'm too smart to play poker. No, he's my father."

"Slaughter Johnson is your father?"

"That's right."

"Vinny, I have to meet him."

"Oh, you don't want to meet him. He's an asshole."

"You're calling your own father an asshole?"

"It's not an insult. It's a fact. If he were bald I'd call him bald." She paused, thoughtful. "But he'll want to know about Guy." She pulled out a cell phone. "I'll give him a call."

"What, now? It's the middle of the night."

"You don't know much about poker players, do you? Believe me, that won't be a problem."

4   Slaughter Johnson

"What did you mean you're too smart to play poker?"

They had left the Song Serenade outside Guy's apartment and, having bundled Minty into the back of Vinny's Volvo station wagon, were now heading northeast out of town in the direction of, thought Hal, Kansas. He stared out the window at the passing tracts of houses, slowly coming into view with the lightening sky of dawn. They revealed themselves in a sort of reverse archaeology of Las Vegas, with the oldest subdivisions closest in, and the projects of successive decades claiming subsequent swaths of desert, as the city, like gas, relentlessly expanded to fill the available space. Eventually their drive took them to the booming cusp of development, the osmosis zone where the houses were yet skeletal wood frames or even just concrete pads awaiting a builder's indelicate touch. After that . . . nothing. Just desert. Not even very interesting desert, with cactus or topography to beguile the eye—just flat, endless salt pan extending so far into the distance that one could ultimately start to look at it and think, *You know what? Nuclear testing out here probably wasn't such a bad idea.*

Hal had fretted about bringing Minty along. It didn't seem right to him to impose the company of a dog on an unsuspecting stranger. "Don't worry about it," Vinny had said. "My dad likes dogs better than people." Hal had assumed this was a joke, but something in Vinny's tone suggested otherwise. And so it had occurred to him to ask why the daughter of a poker guru was not herself a player.

When some time went by and Vinny didn't answer, Hal posed the question again. "What did you mean—?"

"I heard you the first time," she snapped. "You've got a lot to learn about patience." Hal felt stung. Another empty mile rolled by. A billboard caught his eye: FUTURE SITE OF RIVERVIEW HOMES. *What river?* thought Hal. *What view?*

Hal often wondered what Guy saw in Las Vegas. Having grown up in Pittsburgh after that city's postindustrial rebirth, they both knew what it was like to live in a place that had—or at least made the effort to have—a quality of life. Vegas, it seemed to Hal, had no authentic culture of its own, just the digested and regurgitated icons of other places and times. New York. Monte Carlo. Rio. Paris. Mandalay Bay, wherever the hell that was. To Hal it seemed like taking virgin lumber and processing it into particle-board, then painting wood grain on top. Granted, the city was spectacular, or at least good at making a spectacle of itself. But, really, what was the point of *bigger, louder, taller* all the time? It didn't take a genius to see that the founding function of Las Vegas was nonstop pursuit of the buzz. But did that not make the city the ultimate pyramid scheme? With no core values or homegrown infrastructure to build upon, it required steady infusions of new cash—and not just money but also raw human energy—to keep expanding and growing. Which, given the *have more, need more* condition of the city, really amounted to just running in place. One day, Hal thought, it would all come crashing down. It had to.

As for Guy, well, he'd always been a buzz junkie, and a city that vibrated at such a high frequency no doubt struck a resonant chord. It occurred to Hal that he really didn't know that much about his brother's day-to-day existence. Had he done anything at all with his time besides play poker? Did he ride a bike? Shop at Sears? See movies? Since moving to Las Vegas, Hal's brother had become a cipher to him; a cipher, Hal realized, that he would now never decode. Perhaps the only way to understand Guy would be to play—

"Poker tests you," said Vinny. "If you know you can't pass a test, you're stupid to keep taking it."

Hal responded warily. He wanted to question her but didn't want to spook her again. "You mean you got . . . that is, one gets tired of losing money?"

"Money's only part of it." Vinny fell silent and Hal wondered if she'd wriggled off the hook again. It occurred to him that his best strategy was maybe just to wait for the water to settle. Eventually she continued. "When you first start out in the game, your learning curve is so steep. Everything's a revelation. You check-raise for the first time, run your first bluff . . . make your first gutsy call. It's all like, wow, this unfolding flower. It's so beautiful. And you win or you lose, but you're, like, in the game, you know? In the moment. You feel so alive. You think, 'I can do this. I can take this all the way to the top.' You know it must be possible because you look around and you see people doing it every day. They're not smarter than you. They're no more self-aware. Lots of them are a complete fucking mess. They've got all leaks—"

"Leaks?" asked Hal, and immediately regretted it, for Vinny clammed up. In that instant he learned what he'd done wrong. He'd snapped her skein of thought and would now have to wait till she tied it together again.

"Leaks," she said at last. "Costly habits. Like maybe they play craps or bet on sports. Pot. Smack. Sex. Booze. I know this one guy. World Series of Poker winner, but an absolute head case. He doesn't feel like a night's complete until he's bought table service in some glam nightclub and run up a five-figure bar tab. If he lives to see forty I'll be amazed. And lose a big over/under, by the way." Guy wondered what a big over/under was but banked the question for later.

Vinny continued: "Thing is, he's a better poker player on his worst day than I could be on my best. He's just got a gift. And that's what happens. Eventually you hit your head against the ceiling of the thing. You realize you don't have the gift. You ain't Mozart. You're barely Salieri. Then you come to a crossroad. You either play small or you quit altogether. And you *can* play small; I mean people do. God knows I see 'em every day. I deal to them. They're not all sad. Some know exactly what they're doing: passing the hours; buying amusement a hand at a time. They won't get rich. They won't get broke. They don't seem to care. Me, I could never do that. It was just frustrating, you know, to not be the best. And to know I never would. You know?"

Hal took his time before answering. He felt like Vinny was making him an offer: if he didn't act like a dork, she'd continue talking to him, explaining things. He could see why that would appeal to her. People love to be the authority. But they don't like talking to dorks. So he chose his words carefully.

"I play clarinet," he said at last.

"Yeah?"

"I'm no Woody Allen." He let a little silence rise and fall before he added, "But it's still fun."

Vinny nodded. "Well, there you go."

Hal seemed to have found the key to Vinny—the light, oblique observation—and from that point forward they danced casually from subject to subject, exchanging personal histories the way normal new acquaintances do. Hal learned that Vinny was in her third year of dealing cards. Before that, she'd lived briefly in Alaska, running a bar with her husband.

"You're married?"

"Was. It was an 'oops' marriage. One where you wake up on the honeymoon and go, 'Oops.' We both knew it. We were a crap couple. I kept his name, though. Barlow. I liked the sound of it. How 'bout you, stud? Any rodeo cowgirl got her lariat around your legs?"

"Not really," said Hal. "I don't seem to inspire passion."

"I don't know," said Vinny. "In my experience you find passion in unlikely places." Hal didn't know what to make of that, so he just let it go.

They left the interstate near Glendale and followed the blacktop for a few miles to a strip of bleached pavement that gave way to crumbly asphalt and hard dirt before ending abruptly at a fenced-in lot that housed an unused horse corral, a massive TV satellite dish, and an ancient Airstream trailer. Vinny parked. Hal got out slowly and stretched. The shock of events and lack of sleep were catching up to him. He felt fatigued. Harsh sunlight reflected off the aluminum skin of the Airstream. Hal wished he had sunglasses. He opened the back hatch for Minty, who bounded out, relieved himself on the first available fence post, then set off happily to explore the surrounding parched scrubland. "Listen, Hal," said Vinny, leaning over the hood of the car to whisper conspiratorially, "when I told you my dad was an asshole?"

"Yeah?"

"I wasn't kidding."

* * *

Slaughter Belvedere Johnson was born in Frankfort, Kentucky, in the waning days of World War II, the son of an army nurse and an amputee soldier whom nothing, it turned out, not even the sweet love of an army nurse, could save from despondency, alcoholism, and an early grave. Raised by a single mother who worked too hard to keep much of an eye on him, young Slaughter fell in with what passed for a bad crowd in those days: Chesterfield sucking young bucks who haunted the pool halls and roadhouses of Frankfort and Lexington, or ventured into Louisville to listen to "Negro music" and chase trim along Fourth Street. A bar fight in 1964 brought him to the attention of local draft officials, who gave him the choice of jail or Vietnam. Rating it a toss-up on the lesser-of-evils scale, he opted to enlist, served two tours, managed to avoid getting killed, and received an honorable discharge.

Johnson returned to Kentucky to begin what he called his straight years, a decade of obeisance to social convention that included a job in sales, marriage to an upright Paducah girl, and regular attendance at the church of her choice. Together they had a son (Belvedere); a daughter (Finnegan); and by Slaughter's count, 1,273 significant fights, the last of which led to an inevitable but in no way amicable divorce. At that point the whole sales/stability/church thing stopped making sense to Slaughter, so he hit the road. He was over thirty, divorced, homeless, rootless, and rudderless. His belief system to that point—don't give a fuck about anything—pretty much shattered under the pressure of his disintegrating life. He drank a lot, smoked a ton of dope, drove his '72 Dodge Dart down to the rims, slept rough, and stared at the stars. It's no wonder he went a little bit nuts.

In the fortuitously named town of Happy, Texas, poker

came to his rescue. Sloping into the local VFW hall for a beer and a break from the sun, he noticed some ol' boys playing cards at a table in the corner. They seemed to be having a good time, and when Slaughter showed some interest, they enthusiastically welcomed him in. He had no way of knowing that this effusive greeting was standard operating procedure in the backroom poker games of west Texas. They even had a name for it, "tickling the trout," but this particular trout put up a surprising fight. For reasons not known to Slaughter or anyone else, he had innate poker skills, dormant and undiscovered. These allowed him to grasp the quick gist of the game they were playing: no-limit Texas hold'em, where each player pits his two hole cards plus five community cards against the other guys' hidden holdings. Slaughter caught on so fast that they figured him for a hustler and, with all due respect, had to credit him for being so smart at playing so dumb. But he wasn't playing dumb. He was just an incredibly swift study, and the thing he got first— the thing that mattered most—was that in a game where you can bet anything you want, anytime you want, up to everything you've got, the big bet is a big club, and if you're not afraid to swing that club, you're much more likely to win. Within two hours he was $500 to the good and had found his place in the world.

For the next few years, Slaughter kicked around Texas and Louisiana, fading the white line between the big games in Shreveport, Houston, Dallas, and Baton Rouge. Everyone thought Slaughter was his fierce nickname, and he didn't disabuse them of the notion because he mastered quite early the concept of image. He learned that he could manipulate players based on how they saw him—could literally train them with his image to fold when they should raise, raise when they should call, and call when they should fold. As a matter of personal preference, he decided he would rather be feared than loved, and so cultivated the reputation of someone who would happily tenderize baby seals for seal Parmesan. Whether he chose this approach because it fit his nature or whether the image ultimately reshaped his personality is a question of chicken-and-egg irreducibility, but one thing was clear: over time, his image and his authentic self merged into one and he became, in fact, a real asshole.

Slaughter moved to Las Vegas and knocked up the first cocktail waitress he met, a tall drink of water named Louise who found her drug habit more compelling than motherhood and soon ran off, leaving him holding the diaper bag, as it were. He didn't much mind. After seeing what his ex-wife had turned his other children into—a couple of soulless yuppies with an inflated sense of entitlement and upwardly mobile aspirations that Slaughter found at once laughable and ineffably sad—he was determined to do a better job by his baby girl. He named her Vinton in honor of some ancestor soldier who may or may not have acquitted himself admirably at Antietam. Raising her with the rigor and discipline he could never impose on himself, he caused within her an immediate and lifelong cognitive dissonance of epic "do as I say, not as I do" proportions. At once autocratic and absent, he regularly fobbed her off on casual babysitters or unsuspecting neighbors while he chased down soft poker games at the Horseshoe, Stardust, or the newly opened Mirage. Eventually he dispensed with the sitters and neighbors, for he took it as read that Vinny could take care of herself and, in the manner of self-fulfilling prophecy, found that she could. Thus, by the age of ten, Vinny was parent to herself and, as children with chaotic parents will do, soon became mother to her father as well.

After a couple of big tournament wins, Slaughter

started making a name for himself in poker. This had an odd effect on him, for while he enjoyed the status of cardroom celebrity, he distrusted praise and saw hidden agendas everywhere. With money and notoriety came paranoia, a toxic addition to an already volatile mix of personality traits including skepticism, stubbornness, arrogance, a mocking disdain for weakness, and an utter inability to suffer fools. Even as he rose in poker circles, he became increasingly alienated and alienating, eventually attaining the status of true eccentric: combative, dismissive, quick to anger, slow to forgive, and burdened by the feeling that he was worthless, yet, paradoxically, worth more than any other poker player in the world. As human interaction came to be more and more problematic to Slaughter, he moved farther and farther out of town, ultimately settling into this Airstream trailer out in the middle of fuck all. He was a bona fide antisocial.

There was one group for whom Slaughter Johnson had uncharacteristic compassion: the young guys coming up in the game. Those who sought his advice humbly and sincerely (and could withstand the demeaning tirades that were part and parcel of his teaching methods) found him an able and insightful poker coach. But he was choosy with his acolytes and published *Swoop and Pummel* in part to keep the wannabes at bay. He would make prospective students read the book, then quiz them on the contents. Those who worked hard and proved adept he kept on; the rest he kicked to the curb.

By the time he met Guy Harris, Slaughter Johnson had already turned the corner on sixty. He could feel himself slowing down, and while he didn't acknowledge it, perhaps was not even aware of it, he felt a growing sense of urgency to create not just capable students but some sort of lasting legacy. He sparked to Guy immediately, no doubt seeing in the young poker renegade the same untamed arrogance that had marked his own early years in the game. In tournament after tournament the two repeatedly butted heads and grew to take perverse pleasure in baiting and testing each other, each busting his ass to carve out the tiniest bit of bragging right against the other. When Slaughter took him on as a student, he sought to wed Guy's youth, guts, and stamina to his own nuanced and subtle approach to the game. He also thought Guy would make a fine match for his daughter, but after a tumultuous attempt at romance—"Me oil, you water; we no mix"—Vinny vetoed that idea. But she was happy to back Guy's play, for she saw that their partnership did both men a lot of good on a lot of levels.

She was not eager, then, to break the news of Guy's death, but she took it on herself rather than leave it to Hal, for fear that her dad might fly into some sort of kill-the-messenger rage. But he didn't explode. He barely reacted at all, just sat back in his leather recliner and stared out the window at some hills in the distance, backlit by the rising sun. Eventually he said, "Well, that was fucking stupid. Why did he fucking do that?"

The contempt in Slaughter's voice instantly raised Hal's hackles, and he found himself responding tartly, "Hey, it's not like he tried to get himself killed."

"Oh, intuitive grasp of the obvious, Brain Boy. Who tries to get themselves killed? I'm talking about the fucking satellite. He was never supposed to play."

"Why not?" Hal looked at Vinny and remembered their earlier conversation. "Oh, that's right. He was dead money, right?"

Johnson snorted a bitter laugh. "He's sure as fuck dead money now."

"Hey, that's my brother you're talking about!"

"And you loved him with all your heart." Johnson

stared out at Hal from under woolly eyebrows. "Even though you only saw him three times a year, and every time you saw him you basically shat on his chosen profession and held him in contempt." Hal felt stung as if struck. "Don't think we didn't talk about you, sunshine. We did. I know who you are."

"Yeah? And who were you? His puppet master?"

"No, his voice of reason. God knows he needed it." Hal could feel his jaw muscles clench. Vinny was right— her father *was* an asshole, and every second in the old man's company made Hal's bile rise higher. Johnson knew this, of course, for he was adept at reading tells, and Hal had no art for hiding his. "Now just relax, buddy boy," said Slaughter, damping Hal's ire. "No one's here to give your brother a hard time. Let's have a beer."

"Beer?" spouted Hal. "It's not even eight a.m."

"True, and while I never drink before the sun's over the mountains, fortunately the sun was over the mountains yesterday. More to the point"—Johnson stretched back in his recliner and was just able to reach and pop open a small fridge—"we need to toast the dead." He pulled out three bottles of beer, opened them, and passed them around. Then he stood and spoke with sudden solemnity. "To Guy Harris," he said with real affection, "a good friend." He offered his bottle to Hal in toast. "And presumably a good brother." Hal was taken aback by the swift shift in Johnson's demeanor. He felt lost at sea. Almost reflexively, he joined Slaughter and Vinny in toast, clinking bottles and drinking in silence.

They made an odd tableau, there in that Airstream: Vinny with her wild red hair, clearly inherited from her father, whose own white hair seemed to be trying hard to break the gravitational field of his head; Slaughter regarding Hal thoughtfully, measuring him in a sense; and Hal, staring down at his feet, trying to get a grip on feelings that were too new, and far too strong, to be swallowed with beer. And yet, in a way that Hal did not expect, nor ever could later adequately explain, he felt in that moment a sense of transition and knew that against all foreseeable odds his brother was being appropriately mourned, and properly sent off, by probably the only three people in the world who held him in their hearts with love.

Outside, Minty McGinty pawed furiously at the desert dirt, kicking up a spray of sand as he tried to reach a kangaroo rat in its burrow. He had no hope of success, for the rat was long gone, off through its network of tunnels to a cool, deep, safe place. Minty, undaunted, pursued his task with a dog's single-mindedness of purpose, so that neither he, nor anyone inside the Airstream, nor certainly the kangaroo rat, noticed the van parked in the distance, and the ratty young man with binoculars checking them out.

5   Skip Loder

Hal wasn't much of a drinker to begin with and was certainly not used to beer for breakfast. But it went down cold and smooth, a tonic against grief, sleep debt, and the rising swelter of the inadequately air-conditioned Airstream. He soon found himself sitting on a bench behind a fold-down yellow Formica table, his head propped on his balled fists, listening to Slaughter tell stories of Guy. "He always thought I sucked," said Slaughter, "but I was just playing down to his level." Hal couldn't tell if he was joking or not.

Slaughter and Vinny explained their working relationship with Guy. It turned out not to be just a straightforward backing deal, where the backed player plays on someone else's dime and keeps a cut of the win. Once Slaughter had grown Guy's skills to a certain point, they became partners, buying into tournaments out of a common bankroll and funneling profits back into the enterprise. Vinny acted as their mutual manager, and though she called her father an asshole, it was clear that she had deep affection for the old man. Hal found himself warming to Johnson as well and thought that the whole irascible rascal thing was at least partly a sham, something cooked up for defensive purposes or like an actor staying in character. Hal wondered what Johnson saw when he looked in the mirror. Did he like and respect himself? Did he feel like his life was worthwhile? These were odd thoughts to be having just then, Hal knew; however, he also knew that Guy had made common cause with this man, and while Guy had made many bad choices in his life, he rarely misjudged a person's real worth. It surprised Hal that these three hadn't been on the same page over something as fundamental as which tournaments Guy would enter.

"Why didn't you want Guy playing in that satellite?" Hal asked. "Clearly he was good enough to win."

"Yeah," said Slaughter bitterly, "after fifteen fucking tries."

"What?"

"Guy was like a dog with a bone," said Vinny. "He was eating up our bankroll. He kept trying and failing, trying and failing. He was going to get us upside down in the thing."

"Upside down?"

"Where you're paying more in satellites than it would cost you just to buy in directly."

"Worse," said Slaughter, "he spooked himself. Became convinced he couldn't win. So of course he couldn't. The more he played, the more he played like crap. That's when he went dead money, and that's when we told him to quit. Shoulda known he wouldn't. Big ego . . . big tournament . . . it made him nuts. You know, your brother had his impulse-control issues." *You got that right,* thought Hal, as he flashed on their mother's last Christmas, when Guy gave grams of coke as stocking stuffers, and then, when no one else thought that was a particularly bright

idea, had a jagged little white Christmas all by himself.
"Still, you could usually talk sense to him. Make him see
his own self-interest." Slaughter shook his head. "But not
with this thing."

"He's in abundant company," added Vinny.

"What do you mean?"

"Apocalypse has the whole town tripping. Just the
satellites alone have broken size and prize-pool records.
Like six times." Hal didn't seem impressed, and Vinny
was at a loss to communicate the magnitude of the event,
its impact on the playing community. It was like someone putting ten grand into a nickel/dime poker game.
It threw the whole thing out of whack. But the Poker
Apocalypse, she knew, was more than just big. It was phe-
nomenal, in the sense of being a phenomenon, with all
sorts of innovations, including RFID chips to keep track
of chip stacks in real time, and an ambitious plan to
turn the whole thing into a prime-time TV show within
forty-eight hours of the last hand. The consummate
showman, Kai Cortland had done such a good job of
positioning and marketing the Apocalypse that though
the event hadn't even been staged yet, it was already
being hailed as a turning point, the new benchmark.
After this, everyone claimed, tournament poker would
never be the same. And the feeding frenzy! Players were
selling their houses, auctioning themselves on eBay,
forming corporations, just to raise the entry fee. "Look,"
she said, "you're a math guy. You do the math. Figure two,
three thousand entrants at a hundred grand apiece—"

"Will they really get that many? At a hundred grand a
throw?"

"At least. This thing is taking on a life of its own. The
wise guys are setting the over/under at twenty-five hundred."

"And betting the over," added Slaughter, from which

Hal was able to gather at least that an over/under was some sort of wagering proposition.

"So the prize pool," said Hal, "will be, like, a quarter of a billion dollars."

"Quite a chunk of change," said Slaughter. "With first prize hauling down something like seventy mil."

"I can't even imagine that kind of money."

"Guy could. It gave him fever dreams."

"And got him killed," said Hal. This launched a long, broad silence inside the Airstream, as each of them mused in their own way about Guy's death.

For Slaughter Johnson, it was an earth tremor undermining the foundation of his faith. He'd known his share of poker scoundrels: liars and cheats, angle shooters of every stripe from garden variety money mooks with their pathetically fabricated tales of woe to hold-out artists so slick they could take you off your bankroll and leave you coming back for more. In his long years in the game he'd been shaken down by crooked cops, held up at gunpoint, Mavericked by elaborate cons, even seen a casino use a phony power outage as a cover for its own orchestrated in-house snatch and grab. With all that, though, he'd always found the poker community to be populated—mostly—by honest and honorable men and women. Where else could you lend thousands on a handshake and get it back the next day? Or leave your cash unattended at the table for hours and have it all be there when you returned? That said, Slaughter had no illusions about fundamental human nature. A hundred grand was major money. A lot of men, he knew, would kill for a lot less.

Vinny, meanwhile, was thinking about the last time she and Guy had made love. He always hated when she called it that, for love, by mutual agreement, was not part of their equation. But she couldn't abide by his name for what they were—fuck buddies—so they settled on shagging as an apt description for the happy mess they could make of a bed. It grieved her to know that she'd never feel his arms around her again, nor inhale the heady perfume of his body, brought home from long hours in the cardroom: what he called "the stench of chipolite," where chipolite was the mythical mineral of which (according to Guy's fabulism) poker chips were made. She knew that Guy Harris had been bad for her in exactly the same way that too much tequila was bad for her, but the buzz was always sweet while it lasted, and for a strong woman like Vinny, too used to men handling her like they were afraid she might break, Guy's casual randiness was a welcome change of pace. She would miss him; in truth, she already did.

As for Hal, he was just lost. All his life, like it or not, he had defined himself in terms of his brother: support of, opposition to, frustration with. Now that definition, Hal's anchor, was gone, and Hal felt suddenly and queasily adrift. What would he do with all his inner conflict? Would it fade, or stay with him, like the scar of some childhood accident growing old on the surface of his skin until all that remained was an itch he would absently scratch long after the memory of the accident that had caused the scar was gone? These thoughts chased each other around his brain until they began to swamp him and drag him down. To find himself in this close, claustrophobic trailer, unexpectedly intoxicated, sweating, overwrought, and imperfectly mourning Guy's death in the company of strangers was suddenly more than Hal could stand. He jumped to his feet and said, "I have to go." Impulsively, he reached into his pocket, pulled out the jeton, and slammed it down on the table. "This is yours. It was Guy's. Now it's yours. I have to go."

He started for the door, but Slaughter stretched out

a long leg to block him. "Hang on there, soldier. How'd you get it? I thought the bad man took it." In fact, Slaughter had known about the chip all along, for in listening to Hal's account of his brother's murder, he had noticed two things: first, that Hal had never actually come out and said the chip had been taken; and second, that Hal had given his pants pocket frequent reassuring pats and glances, a tell if there ever was one. Nor did it surprise him that Hal had elected to keep it secret, for hundred-thousand-dollar secrets are easy to want to keep. What surprised him was the young man's abrupt willingness—need, in fact—to give the chip away. That didn't add up, and Slaughter wouldn't let Hal leave till it did.

So he interrogated Hal, who—intoxicated, overwrought, and in the hands of a master manipulator, easily gave up the truth: how Guy's dying wish was for Hal to win the Apocalypse, and for Slaughter to help him do it. "Which is absurd on the face of it," said Hal. "Your own book says I have no chance."

"Worse than no chance," agreed Slaughter. He picked up the entry chip and studied it. "Might as well melt this bad boy down into earrings."

"Well, you play," said Hal. "You've got a shot at winning. A good one."

"Son, no one has a good shot at winning this tournament. The best I've got is a less long shot than others. Anyway, he gave it to you, not me."

"But he won it with your money. And I don't want it. I just want to go home."

Slaughter shrugged. "All right. Vinny, take him home." He flipped the chip to Hal, who reflexively caught it. "But take this with you."

"What am I going to do with it?"

"Whatever you like. Toss it out in the desert. Sell it

on eBay. Or maybe hold on to it in case whoever came
looking for Guy comes looking for you. Who knows? It
might buy your life."

Vinny dropped Hal and Minty off at Guy's place. She
invited him to stop by the Sun King later if he wanted,
to say goodbye before he left town. But there was diffidence in the offer, as if Vinny had already disconnected
from Hal. This was through no fault of his own; in her
mind, Vinny was the mistress of moving on, and with Guy
dead it was time to do just that. Hal felt a wave of wist-
fulness as he watched her drive away, but if she was the
mistress of moving on, he was the king of letting go. He
climbed the stairs to Guy's apartment, leaving Minty to
amble off and patrol the neighborhood. He didn't know
what he'd do about the dog. Give him to the property
manager, he supposed, or maybe dump him on Vinny if
he went to say goodbye.

Back in Guy's apartment, Hal found his eye drawn to
Slaughter Johnson's book again, and he sat reading it
for quite some time. Having met the man, he could now
detect in the text Slaughter's own mixed sympathy and
disdain for his readers:

> If you didn't know anything about no-limit hold'em
> (and from my perspective you do not) you could
> do far worse than to play what they call the Black-
> jack Attack: Go all in preflop with any hand that
> looks like a great blackjack hand—AA, KK, QQ, JJ,
> TT, AK, AQ, AJ, AT—and fold everything else. This
> would protect you from your own stupid stupidity
> and keep you from getting outplayed by superior
> foes. You'd generally get your money in with the best
> of it and probably win some pots along the way.

But it's no way to win a tournament, for you won't get enough quality hands to sustain you through the rising blinds. What we have here, then, is essentially a strategy for not blowing your own fool head off while you wait to starve to death instead.

Hal had listened to Guy's poker rants enough to know that high cards were to be prized in hold'em, the higher the better, and high pairs best of all. He thought he could see the logic of Johnson's approach. If you had the problem of playing too loose, this would keep your focus on those high cards, the best cards in hold'em. The trick was to stay patient until you—

Hal caught himself. *Dear lord,* he thought, *am I actually thinking about poker?*

He read on, captivated by Johnson's gift for making the game come alive on the page. Guy had always turned Hal off to poker by pitching it as war, a zero-sum paradigm where winning was the main thing, but the *schadenfreude* of having the other guy lose was also a perk. Guy had, in fact, codified his poker philosophy in what he called the Law of Conservation of Happiness: "The happier I am, the more miserable the other sad fucks are." To which he inevitably added, "Good." Seen through Johnson's eyes, though, no-limit hold'em was a thing of beauty, a majestic exercise in problem solving and character building. "To play this game well," he wrote, "is to appreciate its poetry."

The poetry of the flop, the turn, and river. The poetry of two cards in hand, and three on the board, then one, then one, each new card forcing hard new choices—choices that delimit your skill and your guts; choices that illuminate your soul. Bet, raise, reraise, call. Showdown, shuffle, deal. Late position, middle position, early position, big blind, small blind, dealer button, then late position once again, and the wheel goes around and around and around in an endless mandala, a cycle of hold'em not at all unlike the cycle of life itself.

Hal thought about the cycle of life, about Guy's passage from it, and his own place in it. Could there be some underlying link between himself and his brother, not a blood link but a mission link? Could he be destined, in some sense, to finish what Guy had started? Hal sat on the couch, gape mouthed; then he laughed. Clearly, ol' Slaughter's prose packed some punch. That, plus the sleep debt and beer. How else could Hal explain his mental shift from the prosaic and sensible to the mystic and ridiculous? His mission? He knew his mission: wrap up Guy's affairs and get back home as quickly as possible.

First, though, a nap.

He lay down on the couch and closed his eyes. He was, he noted with some surprise, no longer bothered by the smell.

Hal woke to a ringtone rendition of "Friend of the Devil" and opened his eyes to see Guy's Nokia QuikStep dancing across the coffee table, vibrating as it rang. He answered the phone, anticipating what he assumed would be the first in a long line of "I'm sorry to have to tell you . . ." telephone conversations.

Instead, he heard a young man's breathless voice bark, "Get out of there right now."

"What?"

"Pretend you don't live there. *Go!!*"

Spurred by the caller's unvarnished urgency, Hal rose and left the apartment. As he started down the balcony breezeway, he heard heavy footsteps clunking up the outside stairwell. *Pretend you don't live there.* Hal stopped in front of a neighbor's apartment and knocked on the door. Two burly men topped the stairs and strode purposefully toward him. Hal gave his full attention to the apartment door, banging loudly and calling in a plaintive voice, "Priya, honey, open up! Can't we talk?" The men pushed past him to Guy's apartment, bashed open the door, and went inside.

Hal gawked after them. *Did they really just knock down a door?* "What do you want?" said a voice in front of him. Hal turned to face the angry scowl of a wizened little man. "And who the fuck is Priya?"

"Sorry, uh . . ." said Hal, "is this the Sivapathasundarams?"

The man cocked his head toward Guy's apartment. "Next one down."

"Sorry to disturb you." Hal turned toward Guy's apartment, but as soon as he heard the old man's door slam, he reversed his field and scampered for the stairs.

Down in the parking lot, a soft tap on a car horn drew his attention to a rusted-out Chevy van flashing its one good headlight. He approached warily, for between the busted headlight, snapped-off aerial, and faded paint job dappled with primer, the vehicle looked every inch a snatch van. *Hey, kid, you want some candy?* Hal stopped about ten feet away and peered at the windshield trying to get a look at the driver—who eventually leaned out the window and sotto shouted, "Get in, you pussy. I'm not gonna bite."

Hal got in. Behind the wheel sat a young man, not more than eighteen or nineteen, with a mullet of ginger hair spilling out from beneath a ratty baseball cap advertising an online poker site. He wore a dirty T-shirt, threadbare jeans, and sockless Keds, as if, apart from the sleek subminiature cell phone hanging from a copper cord around his tattooed neck, he clothed himself completely from the GapBums catalog. He smoked a cigarette Asian style, holding it between his thumb and first finger, and sucking it down in long, greedy drags, then tapping the ash onto the thigh of his jeans and rubbing it in with the heel of his fist.

He introduced himself curtly. "Josh Loder," he said. "Call me Skip." Hal started to reply, but Skip silenced him with a wave of his hand. "I know who you are," he said. "Quiet, now. Let's watch." Skip peered up at Guy's apartment, and Hal followed his gaze. Every now and then, Hal could see a flicker of movement as one or the other of the men passed before the open door or front window. It was easy enough to conclude that they were ransacking the place, and no great leap to guess what they were looking for. Skip finished off one cigarette and fired up another. "They not gonna find it, are they?" he said.

"Find what?" asked Hal.

"That's right, play dumb. Looks like it comes natural to you." He blew some smoke in Hal's direction and resumed his vigil. After about fifteen minutes, the two intruders left Guy's apartment. Hal was watching them come down the stairs—and then abruptly wasn't, as Skip clamped a hand around his neck and jerked him down flat on the seat. "Relax," he said. "I'm not looking for a hummer. Though after the shit I just saved you from, I might be entitled." Hal lay there for a long moment, regarding the layer of crud—fast-food wrappers, cigarette butts, and empty Red Bull cans—covering the floorboards. "Okay," Skip said at last. "They're gone. Fucking Starsky and Fuckwit. No reason to think they know you, but no reason to give 'em a look, either." Hal sat up to find Loder staring at him coldly. "Before we go any further," he said, "I got to know if you're a queef."

"Queef?"

"Vaginal fart. If you're a queef," he said with great solemnity, "I will have nothing to do with you."

Hal was nonplussed. He'd never been called a queef before, had never even heard the word. But some sort of answer seemed called for, so he managed as best he could. "As far as I know," he said, "I'm not a queef."

"Alrighty, then, let's go."

"Go where?" asked Hal.

"Dude," said Skip, "it's time you played some poker."

6 Frat Boys from Fresno

"Okay," said Skip, "this is gonna be one- and two-dollar blind no limit. Minimum buy-in is fifty dollars, max is two hundred, but only a donk buys in for the min."

"Donk? Min?"

"Idiot. Minimum amount. Geez, don't you speak English? How much cash you got?"

"I don't know," said Hal. "Maybe three hundred and fifty dollars." Skip's idiosyncratic vocabulary reminded him of Guy's. He wondered if pokerspeak was the lingua franca here, or perhaps a sign of club membership.

"All right, well, that's your bankroll. Ideally, you wouldn't put more than a tenth of it in play at a time, but right now you don't have that luxury, so . . ." Skip paused to think of the right thing, the inspirational thing, to say. Finally he settled on, "Fucking try not to lose it."

They were standing outside the Cortland Casino, the Strip's newest, biggest, and most opulent mechanism for picking the pockets of the gaming public. Skip had insisted on valet parking. "You always valet park in this town," he'd said. "Otherwise you look like a putz." That said, the valet, a pert young girl with a visible camel toe in her taut uniform pants, hadn't seemed all that eager to climb behind the wheel of Loder's scuzzy van, especially when she caught a whiff of Minty curled up on a blanket in back.

It had been an invigorating ride over—if by "invigorating" one meant "near fatal." Josh Loder (who looked younger and younger to Hal the more Hal looked) seemed to have no real regard for, or even awareness of, the laws and norms of traffic. He weaved, sped, flipped *everybody* off, and ran red lights while Hal fought the urge to assume the crash position, or possibly hurl, and wondered what the fuck was going on.

"You're probably wondering what the fuck is going on," Skip had said.

"You read my mind," said Hal, searching in vain for a seat belt.

"That ain't mind reading," said Skip. "That's just ghosting."

"Ghosting?"

"Putting yourself in the other guy's shoes. I were you, I'd sure be wondering what the fuck is going on. Ergo, you are. It's a old trick. Poker Tells 101. Okay, short answer: I'm a friend of Guy's." Josh veered savagely to avoid running up the ass of a Mini Cooper. "Was, rather, since he's kacked."

"And you seem to know something about that," said Hal, surmising that kacked equaled dead.

"Yeah, I do, but I can't tell you yet. Gotta hollow a funch first. You trust me?"

The question was ridiculous on its face. Hal didn't trust him or not trust him; he didn't even know him, could barely understand him. Hal marveled at the strong personalities he had met so far: Vinny, Slaughter, now

Skip. Even Minty. This gift of casual intrusion they all had. Was it a Vegas thing? A poker thing? Or just a dog thing?

Finally Hal settled on this: "You were me, would you trust you?"

"Oh, hell yeah," said Skip. "I'm a fucking Boy Scout."

In fact, just eighteen months earlier, Skip Loder had literally been a Boy Scout, right on down to his thrifty, brave, clean, and reverent core. But he had attention-deficit disorder, and when he got caught self-medicating—with marijuana—at scout camp, he was stripped of his merit badges and sent home in disgrace. That's when he discovered online poker, which cured him of his pot habit, his ADD, and the soul-crushing boredom that had chased his 180 IQ straight through his childhood. Six months later, $60,000 to the good, Skip dumped the whole sum onto his NETELLER debit card and ran away from home. Landing in Vegas, he discovered in realworld poker a pace of play so languid by internet standards that everyone around him seemed to be moving in molasses, their every act and stratagem laid bare for his leisurely inspection. A swift thinker to begin with, he quickly and efficiently cleaned up.

It was Guy Harris who saddled him with his dumb pun nickname, the very morning they met as the last two standing at the final table of the Forbidden City's 2 A.M. tournament. Their heads-up confrontation dragged interminably until the dealers were bleary-eyed and the cardroom factotum was raising the blinds by arbitrary sums at arbitrary intervals in an effort to *just get them the fuck out*. In response, and by tacit agreement, the two decided to vex the staff by trading blinds ad infinitum, a whimsical meeting of the minds that instantly cemented their friendship. When the shift boss threatened to call security, they summarily chopped up the prize money, beat a hasty retreat to the nearest cocktail lounge, and drank the morning away.

"Anybody ever call you Skip?" Guy had asked.

"Skip?" Josh slurred. "No. Why?"

"You know, skip loader. Like a . . . whaddyacallit? A backhoe."

"That's a joke?"

Guy had seemed perplexed by the question. "I guess," he said.

"Well, it's pretty fucking funny."

They laughed till they got kicked out of the bar.

Now Skip walked with Guy's befuddled brother through the Cortland toward its poker room. It was Hal's first visit to the Cortland, and the sheer scale of the place floored him, as it was designed to do. The vaulted ceiling soared ten stories overhead, latticed in chrome and steel. A massive dome of stained glass filtered sunshine by day and spotlights by night to give the place a trippy, kaleidoscopic feel. Table games and banks of slot machines rose in tiered rings around the main casino floor, linked by sloping slidewalks that made it easy to move from one pocket of decadence to another. So vast and complex was the casino's interior that shortly after opening, it had had to be retrofitted with interactive "you are here" touch screens, just to cut down on the number of giddy gamblers getting hopelessly (and therefore unprofitably) lost.

When they reached the poker room, Skip drew Hal aside and said, "Here's what: We're gonna sit in a game together just like a couple of frat boys from Fresno. See a few flops, have a few drinks. It'll be fun."

"No thanks," said Hal. "I'd rather just watch."

"Yeah, that's not gonna work," said Skip.

"Why not?"

"Deep cover. You'll see." He steered Hal to a middle-aged woman in a pale green blazer and red bow tie (celadon and crimson specifically, the Cortland's signature colors) standing at a podium just inside the cardroom's entrance arch. Skip asked her to put their names on the sign-up list.

She shot him an askance glance. "I'll have to see your ID," she said.

"Only if I can see yours," teased Skip, earning him a smile from the stern gatekeeper as he pulled out his wallet and flashed the floorwoman a laminated piece of plastic. It seemed to meet with her approval, and she poised her fingers over a keyboard built into the podium's work surface. "Name and game?" she asked.

"One-two no limit," said Skip. "Hal and Joao."

Just then a dealer's voice echoed across the poker room, "I have two on twelve."

"I can seat you now," the floorwoman told Skip. "Get your chips and go to table twelve."

Skip led Hal through the maze of tables toward the busy cashier's cage. "Joao?" asked Hal.

"Portuguese," said Skip, as if that explained everything.

"How old are you, really?"

"Joao is twenty-one," said Skip. "Come on, let's play cards."

They bought their chips—$200 each—and went to the table, where they found two adjacent open seats. Skip insisted on seating Hal to his left. "Believe me," he said, "you'll want me on your right." Hal didn't understand why, so Skip explained. "Information is power in hold'em," he said, "and everyone who acts before you is giving you information you can use. Since play goes clockwise, the player on your left gets to see what you do before he does what he does. A strong player'll kill you with that."

"So you're actually doing me a favor by sitting to my right."

"Sing it, donk."

"Little arrogant, are we?"

"Hey, buddy, arrogance is what confidence wishes it was."

Skip told Hal that they'd wait for the button to pass before joining the game. "We could come in on the blind," said Skip, "but we'll come in after, take our first hand in position." This didn't make much sense to Hal, though he'd seen enough poker to know that the person to the dealer's left had to post a small blind, a dollar in this case, and the person to that player's left had to post a big blind, two bucks here. After each hand, the dealer button moved one place to the left, so that all players took equal turns putting up the forced bet or, alternatively, getting to look at their starting cards for free.

After the button passed, Skip put up his $2 post, and instructed Hal to do the same. Hal watched as several players called the opening bet. When the action got around to Skip, he pushed forward his two stacks of twenty red $5 chips and growled theatrically, "All in. Call if you don't like assignable-value pieces of plastic."

Hal folded; then everyone else folded. Skip leaned over to Hal and whispered, "Grandstand overbet. Sets my tone."

"Did you have good cards?"

"Who the fuck cares? They never call your first all in."

Which flawed piece of poker folk wisdom intersected with Slaughter Johnson's Blackjack Attack on the very next hand, when Hal picked up A♣ J♦. Everyone folded around to him and he pushed all his chips in, just like Skip. Unlike Skip, he issued no truculent challenge, for his mouth had suddenly turned too dry to speak. The button and small blind folded—but the big blind called. At the dealer's instruction, both players turned over their hands.

The big blind had A♦A♠.

Panic swept over Hal. He broke out in a sweat, oddly, on the soles of his feet. "I thought you said they never called!" he croaked.

"Well, they do when they got aces," said Skip. "Never fear, you got outs."

"Outs?"

"As in 'out of the shit.' Cards you can win with." Skip read the dealer's name tag and said, "Rosemary, my donk here really needs a couple of jacks, m'kay?" The dealer said nothing as she slipped the top card off the deck face down, then turned the next three cards—the flop—face up. A ten, a six, and . . .

"A jack! I got a jack!"

"Yeah, now all you gotta do is find another one."

The dealer burned another card and placed a king adjacent to the other cards. Hal's face fell. "No jack."

"Hang on," said Skip, as Rosemary burned and turned the final card. A queen. Skip smiled with satisfaction. "Yeah," he said, "you split the pot."

"No, I don't. He has aces."

"You both have a straight, numb nuts."

Hal studied the community cards, the ones that all players use to complete their best five-card holding, and it slowly sank in that he'd been saved. With a final board of J-T-6-K-Q, each player used an ace from his hand to complete the straight. "He doesn't have to play both his cards?" asked Hal.

"Nope. Just the ace." Rosemary split the pot in two and passed Hal his half. Within thirty seconds, Hal had gone from panic to despair to elation . . . and ended up right back where he started from. Skip glanced at him

and seemed once again to read his mind. "That," said
Skip, "is what we call freerushing. Cool, huh?"

It was cool. Hal had to admit it. As Rosemary pitched
him his cards, he felt an odd tingle of anticipation, wondering what the next hand would bring. Then, as if
looking over his own shoulder, he caught himself and
realized where he was and what he was doing. Playing
poker! Guy would freak a little if he saw this. In truth,
Hal was freaking a little as he did it. And then an odd
thing happened. Hal fell into the moment so completely that he lost track of everything else. He discovered, as so many had discovered before him, the true
enchantment of poker: its capacity to make the rest of
the world disappear. The past ceased to exist. The future extended no further than the next two cards.
Christmas cards, thought Hal, in the sense that every
hand was a gift box waiting to be opened. Most of the
time, the box was empty—junk cards—and he had to
fold his hand. He found he didn't care. Even when he
wasn't in the hand, there was just so much to watch.

*That guy scratching his nose, does that mean something? Is
it a tell? Or does his nose just itch? No, there's something on
his mind. Look how he looks at his chips. He wants to bet. He
can't wait to bet! Man, if I was in a hand against him, I'd
fold in a heartbeat. But what if he doesn't look at his chips?
Does that mean he's weak? Can you just take the pot away
then? My God, that's how you bluff!*

Hal admired the way Skip worked the table, engaging some opponents, alienating others, telling jokes,
pontificating . . . selling himself as the intended frat boy
from Fresno. Seemingly clueless, a home-game hero up
his own ego, yet he remained detached and analytical,
dissecting the game with the precision of a surgeon. He
played a lot of hands, and the cards he showed surprised
Hal. On one hand, he raised preflop with 6♣9♣ from

under the gun (first to act after the blinds), got called, hit two pair, and won a monster pot. *But 6-9 is a stiff in blackjack,* thought Hal, who now got it that there was more than one approach to this game than the Blackjack Attack. In short order, Skip became the focus of everyone's attention and energy. Skip invited the focus, encouraged it, and used it as a filter through which he poured his own actions and compelled others to pour theirs. There was, Hal realized, a difference between playing this game and *playing* this game.

And while it was all Hal could do to keep up with posting his blinds, protecting his cards, and betting or folding in turn, he noticed that Skip spent quite a lot of time looking away from the table. At first he thought Skip was just bored, though how one could get *bored* sitting in a poker game was suddenly beyond Hal's comprehension. Soon he realized that Skip's gaze kept returning to the cardroom's several entrances, and also to a glass-enclosed private room in the back, where, judging from the tuxedoed casino muscle guarding the door, the high rollers hung out.

"What are you looking for?" Hal whispered.

"Just play cards. I'll let you know."

So Hal just played cards. He played a pair of tens into a $200 win, and an A-5 into a $100 loss. The latter taught him a lesson, for he lost to someone holding an ace with a higher card. *That second card,* mused Hal, *what did Guy used to call that? A smacker? A stomper? Kicker, that's it! A kicker. Note to self: Don't play aces with bad kickers. . . .*

Skip tapped him on the shoulder. With a barely perceptible nod, he directed Hal's attention to the far side of the cardroom, where two burly men had just walked in. Hal would probably have come straight up out of his chair, but Skip, anticipating this, kept a firm hand clamped on his shoulder. "Just chill," he said. "Just watch."

The men crossed the cardroom floor to the private room in back, where they exchanged words with the tuxedoed muscle, and were waved inside. "That's the high-limit poker room," Skip told him. "They call it the Aquarium. That's kind of a joke."

"I don't get it."

"Bad poker players are called fish. Fish don't last long in there. The stakes are too high."

"How much do they play for? House payments?"

"Houses."

"Wow."

"Yeah, wow." Skip looked down at his stacks of chips, a perfectly respectable win of over $500. "Makes you wonder what we're doing here. Still, money is money. I guess if you can afford to play in that game it doesn't feel much different from this." He sighed, in a way that made Hal wonder how someone so young got so old. "Rack your chips, We're cashing out."

Following Skip's lead, Hal placed his chips—a modest profit of less than a hundred dollars—into a plastic chip rack and got up from the table. They headed back toward the cashier's cage, past the etched-glass picture windows that offered the punters a view of the rarefied action within the Aquarium. There were three tables inside. Two had short-handed games going on, with just five players at one table and four at the other. The high rollers sat in richly upholstered swivel chairs, with waiters and cocktail servers hovering close at hand. Hal couldn't tell what stakes they were playing, but he noticed—gawked at, really—the bricks of hundred-dollar bills that the players casually threw into pots already thick with chips and cash.

A fireplug of a man sat at the third table, eating a meal off a linen-covered catering cart. He had a stubbly brown and gray crew cut, and narrow eyes squished into a permanent squint by his overhanging eyebrow ridge and the broad, flat, triangular expanse of his nose. His big hands and muscular forearms made the utensil in his hand look like a shrimp fork, but he worked it like a forklift, shoveling food into his mouth with the focus and determination of a man scarfing down his first meal of the week.

The two burly men bent low in huddled conversation with the diner, who listened, then scowled, then threw down his fork in disgust. Hal was no lip-reader, but it was easy to see the fricative *fuck!* blasting from the man's mouth. Ropy veins bulged in his thick neck, and his hammy fists clenched. Hal didn't have time to take in much more, for Skip pushed him past the Aquarium and on to the cashier's cage. They cashed out, and Hal felt a genuine thrill—a rush, nothing less—as he pocketed his profit. *Money for nothing!* he thought.

Skip led Hal out of the cardroom at speed. "Where are we—" But Skip just shushed him and walked on. They walked the length of the casino and didn't stop until they reached the sports book—*a* sports book, rather, for the Cortland had three. There, Skip plopped down into a heavy leather chair in front of a laminated desk with high sidewalls and a built-in TV screen showing a horse race from some faraway track. He nodded Hal into the adjacent chair. Hal glanced at the screen. At a track called Howland Meadows, a horse named Amelia E was running away from the field.

Skip leafed through an abandoned, heavily marked and multiply folded *Racing Form* for a few moments, preoccupied. Then he tossed it aside and said, "Well, this is a pickle. A great big kosher fucking dill of a pickle, swimming in brine, no bout adoubt it. You know who that guy was, back there in the Aquarium? That Pete Rose–looking motherfucker?" Hal shook his head. "No, you wouldn't. His name is Marko Dragic," said Skip, pronouncing the surname with a soft ch. "They call him Dark Mark. He was a top tournament player twenty years ago. Since then he's been languishing."

"Languishing as in not winning?"

"Languishing as in in prison. He just got out last year."

"What was he in for?"

"Nothing much," said Skip. "Just murder."

7 Ligara

When Marko Dragic was a child, everyone beat the crap out of him: his father; a succession of stepfathers; the odd drunken uncle; and almost every kid at school bigger than him, which was almost every kid at school. Adolescence, though, transformed his tiny, scrawny frame into a compact, muscular ball of rage. He took up boxing, punched himself raw in sweaty gyms, and called himself a boxer. Really, though, he was just a thug, someone who delighted in pushing other people around simply because he could. He got kicked out of school for fighting, but he didn't much mind; apart from the pretty French teacher he fucked for a while, school never held his interest anyhow.

Dragic discovered poker in the rakja-soaked *Srpska kafanas*, the Serbian taverns of his Akron, Ohio, home. He found poker to be an oddly satisfying outlet for his incipient savagery and took fierce pleasure not just in felting his foes, but in humiliating them and breaking their will. As water finds its level, he gravitated to Las Vegas, where loan-sharking, extortion, and opportunistic stabs at blackmail funded his poker habit. Soon that habit became self-funding, for the unrelenting Darwinism of the green felt jungle served Dark Mark's merciless brand of poker terror in excellent stead.

No fan of the fair fight, Marko quickly developed a taste for angles, and in his time he worked them all: corrupting or coercing dealers into dealing him seconds, collusion, signaling, chip dumping. In one famous incident he was caught with a pocketful of contraband chips at the main event of a big buy-in tournament. It was never clear whether these were counterfeit or merely bootlegged from a smaller event into the big one, but in any case, the tournament director gave Dragic the thumb. By way of retaliation he (allegedly) lay in wait outside the TD's home and broke his legs.

Such a setback did not much retard the upward spiral of his career, for the fact of his fearlessness made him a dominant force at any poker table. More often than not, he accompanied his moves with blistering verbal assaults that crossed (or, more appropriately, obliterated) the lines of propriety. He didn't care. He didn't give a rat's ass about acceptable behavior, etiquette, common decency, anything. All he wanted was to win—to subjugate and humiliate—by which action he hoped to fill the bottomless hole of his own self-loathing. This was, of course, impossible. No matter how much he triumphed at the poker table, or successfully bullied other players, he never seemed to feel any better about himself. In fact, he just felt worse.

Things came to a head at the main event of the 1985 Pro Bowl of Poker. Camera crews were on hand to record the action, and Marko discovered in limelight a new narcotic of powerful palliative capacity. At that time there was no such thing as a real poker celebrity, though

Amarillo Slim Preston, Doyle Brunson, and a few others had made modest public names for themselves. With a flash of visionary insight that anticipated the poker boom by a good fifteen years, Dragic dreamed of remaking himself as a full-blown poker superstar. All he had to do was win.

He made it to the final table with a commanding lead, a 10-to-1 chip advantage that should have ensured an easy victory. However, as he hammed it up for the TV cameras, he momentarily lost the plot, made a loose call, and let his opponent, Tall Paul Rogers, double up. On the very next deal, perhaps in an effort to salve his psychic pain, he forced a confrontation with an inferior hand, and Tall Paul doubled through again. After that, Dragic went completely off the rails, and six hands later he had become architect of the most spectacular meltdown in modern poker history.

But he was only half done.

Most poker players, when they self-destruct like that, go off somewhere private to lick their wounds. Others try to rise above their fall, graciously congratulating their foe. Some do rage, it's true, against the awful unfair unfairness of it all, not seeing or acknowledging that the only real bad luck they had was waking up inside their own skin that day. Marko Dragic took this projective blame game to an uncharacteristic new height: he killed Paul Rogers.

Right there on the tournament floor. Right there in front of the cameras and everything. Patiently unclipping the velvet ropes from a nearby brass stanchion, Dragic walked over to where Rogers was giving a television interview, swung the stanchion like a baseball bat, and clouted Tall Paul into oblivion. Had he stopped at that, he might have gotten off with manslaughter, but the fact that he continued to kick and stomp Rogers's body (and the fact that the cameras caught it all) predisposed Dragic's eventual jury to see his actions in the grimmest possible light. They gave him thirty years.

Prison didn't break his spirit. Quite the opposite. A closed community that prizes bully behavior merely served to accrete his megalomania and inflate his feelings of frustrated entitlement. Then the turn of the century arrived and poker became a pop epidemic, minting new celebrities every damn day. It riled Dragic to think of all of these lesser lights cashing in while he was trapped behind bars. So he worked on his game, his demeanor, and his parole board pitch. When they finally turned him loose, he emerged determined to take his place among poker's known elite—to shove them all aside, in fact, and be recognized as the biggest poker star of all.

It hadn't worked out that way. While he was able to amass sufficient skill and bankroll to play in the biggest cash games in town, that one necessary big-ticket tournament win yet eluded him. He remained unknown and uncelebrated, and the gnawing, aching fact of this metastasized within him. Those close to him learned to gird themselves for explosive bouts of violence at any time. Those not close happily gave him a wide berth.

". . . Anyway, that's the street rumor version," concluded Skip, "all or none of which might be true."

"And how does Guy fit in?" asked Hal.

"Not sure, exactly. Except that he and Marko had this weird moment at an Apocalypse satellite."

"The one Guy won?"

"No, an earlier one. Couple of weeks ago. They're down to six at the final table, Marko, Guy, and these other four pumpkins." Skip and Hal had left the sports book and were making their way back to valet parking to collect Skip's van. "Dragic's pushing hard for a chop, a split of the prize money. Except he's all Ligara about the money."

"Ligara?"

" 'Like I give a rat's ass.' He just wants the tournament entry chip, and the mooks are happy to take the fat cash overlay he's offering. But not Guy. You know, he wants that chip, too, and he's not shy about saying so."

"And not particularly polite, I'm guessing."

"No, yeah, you got that right. Anyway, here's Dark Mark going ballistic for a deal, and here's Guy saying, 'Blow me,' six ways from Sunday. Finally the floorman's all, 'Fuck this, let's play cards.' " Hal and Skip reached the casino exit and walked out into the twilight. *Twilight?* thought Hal. *Where did today go?*

Skip continued, "So they start to play again, but Marko's got this gleam in his eye—"

"You were there?"

"Yeah, I was. You can learn a lot by sweating a player like Guy. Dark Mark, too. He's a mean son of a bitch, but he knows how to push people around. It's interesting to watch." Skip handed his ticket to the valet. "Only now he's gone as soft and squishy as a used Trojan. He's calling and folding, calling and folding. It makes no sense to me. Then suddenly I realize that he's calling and folding to *everyone but Guy.* The motherfucker is dumping his chips."

"Dumping his . . . what? I don't . . ."

"That's right; I forgot. You're a fawn. Dumping your chips is where you lose pots on purpose to let another player build up their stack."

"Who would do that?"

"Someone playing partners."

It took a moment for Hal to sort this out. He framed a dim picture of two or more tournament players agreeing in advance to split up any prize money they won, and further agreeing to help each other out by, essentially, pooling their resources at critical moments. "So Dragic was in cahoots with the other players?"

"I didn't think so at first," said Skip. "I thought he was just pissed at your brother and was dumping his chips out of pure fucking spite."

"That seems kind of self-defeating, doesn't it? Couldn't he have won the tournament?"

"Sure, I guess. At that stage the blinds and antes are so high that anything's possible. But it turns out the fix was in."

"What do you mean?"

"I saw him later in a casino bar. With the mirplo who won the tournament."

"Mirplo?"

"Brain fart. Numb nuts. Dragic was buying his TEC. And looking like the cat who ate the fucking canary."

Hal tried to integrate this new information into his thinking. "Somehow he arranged to make a deal with the others without Guy even knowing?" asked Hal. Skip nodded. "So he already has a tournament chip. So why would he send his goons after Guy's?" Another thought crossed his mind. "Come to think of it, how did you know they were his goons?" And yet another thought chased that one through. "For that matter, why were you watching Guy's apartment in the first place?"

"Man, that's a buttload of questions. Okay, first, I think he's chasing Guy's chip for the same reason everyone else is. It's worth a hundred grand, and a shot at millions. He'll use it to back some other horse, increase his chances of a payday, like. Second, I wasn't sure they were his goons until they circled back to the Cortland, which is why we frat boyed over there, duh. Third, I wasn't watching Guy's apartment. I was watching you."

"Why?"

"Guy asked me to."

"What, from the grave?"

Skip snorted a laugh. "Nah, I saw him yesterday before you two hooked up. He said he was in some shit, and if anything happened I should look out for his big brother."

"I don't need looking out for."

"In this town you do. Expecially when you got a hundred-thousand-dollar bomb in your pants."

"How did he even know I was coming?"

"Didn't you say you were?"

"No, I said I wasn't."

"Guess he figured you'd flip."

"Yeah," mused Hal, "I guess he did." *Am I really that predictable?* he wondered. *And weak?*

A valet drove up in Skip's van and handed over the keys. Skip and Hal climbed in. Hal braced himself for the expected McGinty assault—but it didn't come. He turned around and looked in back. "Skip, where's Minty?"

At that moment, the van doors flew open and a swarm of cops grabbed them both and dragged them out. Next thing Hal knew, he was kissing pavement, with his hands clamped tight behind him and some policeman's knee in his back. A pair of scuffed brown brogans loomed into view. Their owner crouched down, and Hal found himself staring once again into the beady black eyes of LVPD Detective Danny Ding. "Hello, chipmunk." Ding glanced back at the casino. "Any luck in there?" He gestured to the cop holding Hal to let him go. The cop stood up and dusted his hands as if they were dirty. Hal rolled over, sat up, and watched Ding cross to where Skip lay spread-eagled on the ground. "Joshua Loder," Ding intoned with all the emotional intensity of someone reading a phone book, "you're under arrest."

"What for?"

"What do you think, you mayonnaise motherfucker? For the murder of Guy Harris."

8 Wishful Drinking

The cops bundled Skip into a squad car. Hal stood up and started to protest, but Ding cut him off. "Easy there, sport. He's in the system now." Hal's eyes met Ding's, and he read the threat in them. It was clear to Hal—in exactly the manner of picking off a tell, he realized—that if he tried to force the issue, he'd be arrested, too. For what, he couldn't imagine. Obstruction? Or just being a mayonnaise motherfucker? He took a step back, hands raised, palms out, a gesture of surrender to authority.

"Hal!" yelled Skip, "Watch my van!" Then he was gone, off down the Cortland's long, sweeping driveway toward the Strip. Ding shot Hal a beady wink, got in his own car, and took off, leaving Hal standing alone in the valet port of the Cortland Casino, feeling, yet again, completely lost at sea.

Could Skip really have killed Guy? It made no sense. Apart from the fact that he seemed genuinely to have been Guy's friend, who kills a man and then pals up to his brother? *Someone who wants that entry chip, you mirplo.*

Still, it didn't square. Guy had always talked about going with your gut in poker. "There's no point in putting a man on a hand," he'd say, "if you won't follow through on your read." Hal had never understood those words, but now he thought he did. Ding had arrested Skip, but so what? Hal's gut said the kid was kosher. But so what? He was gone now, into the jaws of authority. Hal wondered if he'd ever see him again.

He went looking for Minty, but an hour of cruising up and down the aisles of the Cortland's cavernous garage and whistling flatted first bars of Beethoven's Fifth yielded nothing more than odd looks from the young and athletic valet staff as they trotted past to or from parked cars. Eventually he had no choice but to call off the search and commend Minty to the care of the gods of dogs.

It must have been his imagination, but it seemed that Skip's van actually balked at the touch of a rational hand at the helm. *She handles like an auditorium,* thought Hal as he left the Cortland and navigated south toward the Sun King Casino with a plan to tell Vinny about Minty, turn over Skip's van, cab it to the airport, and vanish from this weird weirdness for good.

The Sun King had been designed to out-Europe all the other European-themed casinos in town: the Paris, the Venetian, etc. A miniature Palace of Versailles (if a hundred acres of ormolu gaudiness can be said to be miniature), it catered lavishly to those who think that the more you pay the more it's worth. However, in a textbook example of mixing apples and ducks, the property's developers had also chosen to locate it five miles south of the Strip, so as to be the first casino seen by weary drivers up from LA. The result was an unappetizing appleduck sauce, a casino too far from the center of Vegas action for all the high rollers, yet too expensive to be an appealingly cheapo depot for inbound road warriors. Now the Sun King stood poised to be the first of the twenty-first century megasinos to sink beneath the weight of its own debt service and failed expectations.

Still, it had its charm: a certain quirkiness that transcended the lame marketing stance ("Louis XIV, the *Fun* King!"), the lost location, and the ridiculously overblown physical plant. Those who liked it loved it, and especially loved its poker room, where dealers like Vinny Barlow, recruited and trained by hip, young management, contributed to a clubby, home-game atmosphere.

Hal walked into the cardroom and found Vinny dealing a $1–$2 blind no-limit hold'em game. He watched as she pitched the cards with bionic precision and ran her game with a firm hand and a quiet but authoritative mien. Even Hal, with his limited poker experience, could see that this was how the game was meant to be dealt.

Vinny smiled when she saw him and said, "I'm on a break in twenty. Can you wait?"

Hal nodded. He could wait. He knew exactly where.

In a seat in her game.

Hal couldn't explain his choice. Of course it made no sense to just plonk down and play poker in the midst of all the weird weirdness. Then again, what better way to kill twenty minutes than to see a few flops? With that, Hal Harris crossed a certain line of seduction and became, though he certainly wouldn't have called himself such, a poker player. Like so many millions before him who'd rather see a few flops than read a book, do a sudoku, go for a hike, watch TV, study philosophy, or make love, Hal was hooked—yet another emphatic reply in the negative to the ongoing rhetorical question, "Do you know anyone who started playing poker who's *stopped* playing poker?"

He didn't know it, but Hal was making the classic and time-worn mistake of jumping into a short session.

Vinny knew, but as a dealer, plus impartial, plus somewhat amazed to see him playing in the first place, she
could hardly caution him against it. But quality poker,
successful poker, she knew, relied on solving the riddle
of one's foes, and this took time—time spent "breathing into" a poker game, acquiring its rhythms, figuring
out where the undefended treasure lies. By playing hit-
and-run poker, Hal ran the risk of playing too many
hands too quickly with too little information. It would
have been best for him to catch no playable hands at
all, and so not get pilloried by his own impatience. But
the trouble with impatience is how it colors one's perception, and turns unplayable hands into playable ones.

At the start of his second orbit, Hal picked up 6♥5♥.
He knew this hand didn't fit Slaughter Johnson's Blackjack Attack profile, but he also knew he hadn't played a
hand yet. *Maybe they'll think I'm tight,* he thought, only
vaguely aware of what he thought that meant in strategic
terms. Mostly, he just thought his cards looked pretty—
so identical in suit, so adjacent in rank—so he played
them. Thus did Hal join the long parade of poker players ensorcelled by suited connectors. He called a small
opening raise, watched the small and the big blind both
call . . . and then . . . well . . . flopped huge.

His eyes grew wide and his nostrils flared as he stared
down a flop of J♥7♥2♥. Vinny knew Hal had a big hand.
Everyone did, for he waved his tells like a flag. He glanced
down at his chips. Shifted in his chair. Acted out of turn.
Placed his bets with shaking hands. He was like a training video for what not to do at the poker table. The betting was checked to Hal. His primal understanding of the
game warned him not to scare off the customers, so he
made a minimum bet. Vinny recognized this as a mistake, for he was giving anyone with a high heart favorable odds to call and draw to a higher flush, and her

keen read on the other players at the table suggested
that there were at least two big singleton hearts out
against him. Professional that she was, though, she kept
quiet as she briskly burned and turned. She laid out an
offsuit four: a brick; a card that changed nothing in the
hand. Once again the action was checked around to
Hal. Once again he underbet the pot, and once again
got called. Vinny grieved for Hal's missteps yet hoped
that the odds of a heart coming on the river—better
than 4 to 1 against if other players held hearts—would
run true, and that his hand would hold up.

The river card was the T♥, a train wreck for Hal, and
one he never saw coming, of course. The small blind
checked. The big blind checked. The original raiser
hesitated, then checked. *There's the ace,* thought Vinny,
recognizing the false stall. She hoped Hal would check,
out of either prudence or timidity, but now, at last, Hal
made a decent bet, fifty bucks. The small blind folded.
The big blind folded. The preflop raiser sighed theatrically, then reraised all in, another false tell that only the
most unschooled poker player would ever fall for. Hal,
being that unschooled, called without much thought. A
second later, he looked genuinely shocked to see Vinny
pushing the pot in the direction of the ace of hearts.

"Urk," said Hal. And so added another lesson to his
poker education. Later, he would sort it out and realize
what he had done wrong. He would internalize the experience and, to his credit, never give proper drawing
odds to an opponent again. Interestingly, though he
lost his whole buy-in, and stumbled away from the table
in a terrible state of shock, he wasn't thinking, *Never
play poker again,* but rather, *Do better next time.*

"That was some stinky bad poker." Hal turned at the
gravelly sound of Slaughter Johnson's voice. "In fact,
worse than bad. That gave bad a bad name."

"Thanks," said Hal ruefully. "I enjoyed it, too. What are you doing here?"

"Came to see you, sunshine."

Just then, Vinny walked up. "I only have a few minutes," she said. "Let's get started."

Started? wondered Hal.

Vinny led them back through the casino to a dealers' break room. There they sat around a wobbly plastic table drinking weak coffee out of Styrofoam cups that bore the goofy cartoon likeness of the Sun King. Hal quickly brought them up to date on the day's tumultuous developments and found himself not all that surprised when they were not all that surprised. He'd already figured out that the poker community had some sort of jungle radio working for it.

"Okay," said Slaughter, "this puts his phone call in context."

"Whose?" asked Hal.

"Marko Dragic. He called me about an hour ago. Said he knew I ran with Guy and wondered if I had Guy's Apocalypse chip. I told him no. He said if I knew who did, he'd like to meet that person."

"Did you tell him it was me?"

"I think he already knew."

"How?"

"Prancing around the Cortland with Skip Loder? What, did you think you were undercover? I'm guessing Dragic saw you, made you, and dropped a dime on Loder just to muddy the waters."

"Then Skip didn't kill Guy?"

"That pup? You think he could take down your brother?"

"Well, no."

"Then start using your head, will you?"

Hal felt a hot flush of embarrassment. Didn't they

know he was doing the best he could under very trying circumstances? He was supposed to have gone home today, but he'd already missed one flight, and it didn't look like he was going to be catching the next. Not, he noticed, that the prospect seemed to bother him much. As infuriating as Vinny's and Slaughter's company was, he found he really enjoyed it. These were lively people— *alive* people—much more stimulating than the drones and proles who peopled his world. "What did Dragic want?" he asked.

"Not sure," said Slaughter. "He seems to be recruiting TEC holders and working out backing plays with them. Offering an overlay, they say." Once again, Hal felt lost in the lingo, so Vinny and Slaughter walked him through it. They explained that a backed player in a tournament usually keeps just a fraction of his potential earn—"thirty percent is typical"—in exchange for someone else fronting his buy-in. Word had Dragic making splits up to 50/50.

"I don't see how he can make money," said Vinny. "It seems like the more players he recruits, the more he stands to lose. Especially dead—" She caught herself, but Hal read her intent.

"You can say it," said Hal. "Dead money like me."

"Sorry," said Vinny. "No offense."

"And none taken. You'd be dead money at a tax audit." Hal studied the problem for a long moment, at last offering, "Maybe he's trying to corner the market. If he owns most of the whole field, he probably wins no matter what."

"No edge in that," said Slaughter. "Poker's too iffy, the field's too large, and even if he had a one hundred percent corner, he'd still lose to the juice."

"Juice?"

"The Cortland's taking three percent off the top for

expenses and another three for dealer tips. If he owned every player in the room, all he'd do is go extravagantly broke."

"Maybe it's a marketing angle," mused Vinny. "Team Dragic, like. With hats and T-shirts and a big cash infusion from some online site sponsor."

"Dragic doesn't strike me as the hats and T-shirts type," said Slaughter. "He's all about publicity, but for himself, not some team."

"So then what?" asked Hal.

"That's the question, isn't it?" said Slaughter, and the gaze that he now fixed on Hal suddenly made his intention clear.

"Which you want me to get the answer to," said Hal.

"I'd go see him myself," said Slaughter, "but I don't have what he wants."

"Suppose I gave it to you."

"Suppose you did."

This gave Hal pause. "This morning you didn't want it."

"I still don't want it. I want to know who killed Guy."

"So do I."

"Then there we are." Slaughter sighed, and for the first time Hal caught a resonance of empathy in the weathered old man. "Hal, this is your call. You can go see Dragic or I can. I have a hunch you'd get more out of him than I would; he'd be more on guard around me. But it's no secret he's a bad guy. He tossed Guy's flat, maybe more. Whatever you do, have a good long think about it first.

"I'm saying it's one egg you can't unbreak."

So it was that Hal Harris found himself nursing a beer in a bar down on Paradise Road, not far from the Cortland: a randomly chosen little dive called Foxxy's where he could sort his thoughts with no distractions apart from the barmaid's cleavage and an early season baseball game on TV. By this process—what Guy used to call wishful drinking—he tried to parse the pros and cons of the situation.

Pro: I have a ticket to "the biggest poker tournament in the history of ever."

Con: Bad guys want it.

There were other issues, such as his responsibilities back home. The weekend gave him grace, he knew, but if he wasn't back at his desk on Monday morning, he'd piss off a lot of people: clients who counted on him and colleagues who'd have to cover his ass. Oddly, this thought did not disturb him.

Pro: Poker . . .

After all these years, Hal finally got what got Guy off about poker. It was, at bottom, a puzzle to be solved, and though he'd beaten his head against the puzzle for less than a day, he already got that it was endlessly fascinating, something he could work at forever and never completely command.

Hal chided himself, though. Poker? *Poker?!* Poker was so secondary—tertiary—was there such a word as quadriary?—to all this. Then again . . .

Pro: If I play in the tournament, I might win it.

Con: Fucking ha.

Hal remembered something Guy used to say: "The trouble with too far is you never know you're going till you've gone." Hal was a sensible person. He never went too far. Yet here he was, it seemed, staring *too far* right smack in the face. He knew what Guy would have done: just say fuck it and plow ahead. Hal was much more circumspect . . . cautious. At that moment he felt that his caution had cost him, that he had paid with unfulfilled days and years for his unwillingness to go too far.

"You live like a lawn," Guy had often said. "Manicured, you know? Landscaped within an inch of its life. Me, I walk down a beach. I pick up everything I find and turn it into a party hat. That's what you need, Hal. More party hats. Or even any."

Hal knew he didn't really owe it to Guy to fulfill some melodramatic deathbed promise. Maybe, though . . . maybe he owed it to the dead to have a life.

A real life, not a lawn.

"Fuck it," he said at last. "This is my party hat. Let's at least see how it fits." He paid for his drink and walked outside to Skip's van.

Where Minty McGinty came flying out of nowhere and knocked him flat on his ass.

9 Asian Dye Job

Where had Minty been? Hal wondered as he drove back to the Cortland. Why had he gone walkabout? What sort of bizarre homing mechanism brought the dog back to him? And why did he have to be so painfully projectile all the time? Hal had no answer to these questions but was starting to see Minty as a myth almost, more than an actual animal, moving through the space of Las Vegas on a dimensional plane all his own. He could certainly see why Guy had loved this dog, for they were very much two of a kind: independent, peripatetic, each a force of nature in his way.

Which was all well and good, but this time Hal was determined to corral the beast. He had found a roll of moldy duct tape under the passenger seat of Skip's van and now moved methodically from door to door covering the door-lock buttons with wads of tape. He locked the van from the outside and looked in at Minty through the rear window. Minty just lay on his blanket and eyed Hal reprovingly. Hal promised the dog he wouldn't be long, but Minty's expression said "ligara" so clearly that

Hal wondered if he was starting to read minds, or at least dogs' minds. *Deny a dog his freedom?* Minty seemed to say. *What kind of monster are you?*

Leaving the van in the cool depths of the Cortland's self-park garage, Hal returned to the casino and found it a much different place near midnight than it had been in the sleepy afternoon. Gamblers packed the craps and blackjack tables three or four deep, slapping down bets, and cheering or mourning each outcome in turn. Slot jockeys worked their machines at a frantic pace, mainlining adrenaline with each spin of the reel. Outside Flesh, the Cortland's signature nightclub, self-consciously gorgeous young women stood on line, smoking cigarettes, talking on cell phones, or adjusting their boobs inside their tiny black cocktail dresses. *What were they thinking when they bought those dresses?* Hal wondered. *"Can't wait to show off these tits in Vegas"?* As for the guys standing by, admiring the women and hoping to be deemed cool enough for admittance to the club, it was just easy to read their minds, for each wore his thought like a cartoon balloon over his head: *Sure hope I get laid tonight.*

Sure hope I get laid.

Hal made his way through the casino to the cardroom and soon stood outside the Aquarium once again. Though he knew of nowhere else to look for Dark Mark, he doubted that Dragic would still be there, for many hours had passed and Hal assumed that the man had better things to do than spend all day inside a poker room. But this just betrayed the depth of his ignorance about high rollers like Dragic, for whom the idea of leaving a poker room on any errand less pressing than open-heart surgery was risible and strange.

Nor is this a characteristic of just high rollers. A slender young man who had been playing all day, albeit at much lower limits, was toying with the tiny jade Buddha he used as a card protector when he noticed Hal walk in. His steeply arched eyebrows arched even more, and though he continued to play his hands, he kept an eye on Hal and the Aquarium.

Peering through the etched-glass windows of the Aquarium, Hal discovered Dragic sitting at the one table just then in action. Hal didn't know what kind of stakes they were playing for, but judging by the huge mounds of chips and cash at the other players' places and the single forlorn stack in front of Dragic, he could guess that things weren't going well for Dark Mark. That guess was almost immediately confirmed when Dragic called a river bet and, on seeing his foe's holding, furiously shot his cards into the muck. He stood and strode away from the table, his beefy hands on his thick hips, and his face twisted into an expression of pure disgust.

That's when he saw Hal.

Locked him in a pit-viper gaze.

And smiled.

With a beckoning finger, he gestured Hal into the room. Hal felt his stomach churn as he crossed the threshold. With sudden clarity he could read his own mind, and his mind was saying, *This is not a good idea.* But Dragic's bodyguards stepped aside to let him through, then closed ranks behind him, like a pair of three-card monte shills locking the sucker in place. Dragic crossed to Hal and extended a thick calloused hand adorned with a prison tattoo of the ace of spades. Hal surrendered to a bone-crushing shake and allowed himself to be led to an empty table.

The craggy Serb looked him up and down, sighed, and said, "So you're that asshole's brother?" Hal didn't know how to respond, so he waited in silence for Dragic to go on. Dragic continued to hold Hal in his gaze, which Hal found completely unnerving. He felt as though he was being X-rayed. Or maybe microwaved, for he seemed to be heating up. It struck him as rude for Dragic to eye him so frankly belligerently. What had he ever done to this guy? He couldn't know it, but this was how Dark Mark treated everyone; the world was his enemy, bar none. Hal's own reaction was also typical. As a matter of course and a matter of tactic, Dragic pissed people off.

"Your brother owed me money," he said at last. "Did you know that?" Hal shook his head. "No, you wouldn't. Why would you?" Hal didn't process the thought consciously, but he knew Dragic was lying. Maybe it was Hal's nascent poker sense kicking into gear. Maybe he just couldn't fathom Guy borrowing money from so patently dangerous a source, not with ATM Hal always on call. Or maybe just the realization that in this realm people lied all the time. "Yep," continued Dragic, "Guy owed me money. I was supposed to collect this week."

"And how is that my problem?" Hal said suddenly, surprising himself with the edge in his own response. *Where did that come from?* "Do you think I inherit his debt?"

Dragic thought for a moment, then said somewhat randomly, "If I wanted your money I'd turn you upside down and shake you like a piggy bank." He seemed quite pleased with the allusion, and Hal detected the streak of self-satisfied egoism that ran through him. Dragic continued, "No, the money's chump change. I can write that shit off. I just want you to know what was going on. Guy told me he left the money in his apartment for me, and I sent some friends around to get it, so that was that with that." This take on events was so obviously false that Hal couldn't actually believe he was hearing it. What kind of mirplo did Dragic think he was? Hal's irritation ratcheted a notch higher, but Dark Mark just pushed on with, "Okay, that's old business.

Now, new. You have his tournament entry chip, right? I want to buy it."

"Why?"

"Why? Oh, why? What do you care why? I'll give you fifty grand."

"It's worth a hundred."

"To who? You? You gonna play in the tournament?"

"I might."

At this Dragic laughed, a hawking, honking sound so discordant that Hal had to stifle the urge to reach out and clamp a hand over Dragic's mouth, a move he sensed would not be all that enthusiastically received. Marko's laugh sputtered to a stop and his lips settled into a dismissive grin. "So, you're gonna play in the Poker Apocalypse, huh? Hundred-thousand-dollar buy-in tournament, and you think you have a chance? How is that? Do you even know how to play poker?"

"I've got a month to learn."

Hal braced himself for another abrasive laugh, but it didn't come. Instead, Dragic leaned back in his chair, arms crossed over his chest. "Do you know where you are?"

"In the presence of greatness?" asked Hal with undisguised sarcasm.

Dragic's goons involuntarily lurched forward, but Dragic stopped them with his upraised palm. "Let's be honest," said Dragic in a soft, cold voice. "You can't win the Apocalypse. You couldn't win a one-table shootout against a mixed field of nuns and corpses. So why don't you be a good boy, cough up your tournament entry chip, take your damn found money, and go back to wherever the fuck you came from. This is Vegas and this is real. You've got no fucking business here."

"You know what?" said Hal, unconsciously revisiting Guy's own response to Dark Mark. "Blow me." He stood up and tried to push past the goons, but they blocked his exit. "What?" said Hal truculently. They looked at Dragic, then responded to his nod by moving aside to let Hal pass. Hal started away but couldn't resist firing off the last word. "Guy didn't owe you money," he told Dragic. "He wouldn't borrow money from a . . . a . . . queef like you."

"Queef?" asked Dragic. But Hal was already gone.

The young man with the jade Buddha watched him go. He placed the icon atop his chip stack, rose from the table, and followed Hal out.

Irate and confused, Hal pinballed all around the casino past the ranks of table games and down the endless banks of slot machines, pausing occasionally to bash the flat of his hand against the side of one in anger. He couldn't understand where the anger came from, nor how his meeting with Dragic had gone so south so fast. He had planned to be so cool, a spy in the house of risk, the novice no one would suspect of having a clue. Instead he had . . . what was that expression? . . . gone on tilt. Tilted so hard so fast. Hal didn't really know what he'd hoped to accomplish, but pissing off Marko Dragic and spiking his own blood pressure to dangerous levels had not topped the list. He felt a certain sense of despair, for if he couldn't even hold a conversation with a poker player without freaking out, how could he hope to hold his own against thousands in a tournament? Hal caught a glimpse of himself in the reflection of some bar's back glass. His hair was a mess. His clothes hung wrinkled and loose. The feral look about him was utterly foreign to his experience, except . . . *I remind me of Guy,* he thought.

He walked on: past the snack bar selling five-dollar apples; past the keno lounge, where nearly comatose oldsters played what Guy called the world's second dumbest game after Russian roulette; past the cashier's cage, where everyone seemed unhappy, because no matter how much they won, it was never enough. Weaving through a particularly large and loud crowd of drunken bachelorettes, Hal suddenly realized that he was lost. He wasn't progressing toward the parking garage—had, in fact, no idea where the parking garage might be. His breath shortened. Sweat broke out. An odd combination of vertigo and claustrophobia washed over him as the interior space of the Cortland, at once vast and densely packed, now overwhelmed him. He began to walk faster, looking for any clue or sign or landmark that might help him orient. It wasn't his first time lost inside a casino, but it seemed to reflect a certain loss of inner control, and that's what scared him. *Where am I? How did I get here? What happened to the stable platform of my life? Has it all been built on sand? Quicksand?! Help!!!* Hal was jogging, then running. His breath became ragged and rushed. Just when he feared he might hyperventilate, he found himself . . . right back where he started, at the poker room.

He looked inside the room, at the dozens of tables and the sea of faces. *All those players,* he thought. *All those games. Where do you start? How do you begin?* He had the urge to walk back inside, take a seat at a table, and just . . . start . . . playing. But . . . *Later,* he thought. *I'm in no shape for that now.* He didn't know it, but with this choice he was making one of poker's best decisions: the decision not to play at all when you know you can't play well. He started away, determined to leave the casino— if he could only find the exit.

As if echoing the thoughts in his head, a watery voice nearby asked, "Man, you even know whe' you goin'?" Hal pivoted toward the voice and found himself facing a slightly built young man with strong Asian features:

skin the color of flax, smooth chin and cheeks, cobalt eyes beneath razor eyebrows. But what caught Hal's attention—what rang a certain bell—was the young man's hair. Black beneath and blond on top, it presented a stark two-tone look, like something out of *Vogue for Men* by way of Tokyo Pop. *Asian dye job,* thought Hal. The young man introduced himself. "Name Lanh," he said. "Lanh Tran. You li' coffee?" he asked in an oddly composited accent: part Southeast Asia, part South California. "The coffee he'e te'ible." He wrinkled his nose, then smiled engagingly. "Le's ge' sone." He grabbed Hal by the arm and steered him quickly away from the Cortland poker room—shooting, Hal noticed, a furtive glance over his shoulder as they left.

Hal allowed himself to be led. There was information to be had here, and this time he was determined to get it.

They went to a coffee shop, the kind that serves $3.99 steak-and-egg breakfasts at three in the morning. A server poured their coffee into cheap brown plastic mugs intended by design to mimic ceramic or china but missing by a fairly wide mark. Lanh tinked the mug with a long fingernail. "Belie' this shi'?" he said, clipping the final consonants of his words in a way, it struck Hal, that seemed studied or forced, not the pronunciation of an immigrant trying to speak proper English but, really, the other way around.

This was, in fact, exactly the case, for Lanh's experience told him that white guys had a preternatural fear of Vietnamese poker players. When they heard the accent, he knew, they assumed he was cut from the same world-class cloth as Men "the Master" Nguyen or David "the Dragon" Pham. It gave him an edge at the table. So Lanh cultivated what he called his Saigon twang and worked hard to sell the notion that he was another Vietnamese lion of poker, fresh off the boat and much to be feared.

As it happened, his name wasn't even Lanh. It was Larry, Larry Harwood, of Tustin, California, the adopted son of born-again Christians Lenny and Penny Harwood. Through a boyhood steeped in spirituality—a rondelet of Bible schools, Teens for Jesus summer camps, youth ministries, and campus crusades—Larry'd had it pounded into his head that he came from a heathen people and owed thanks to the divine Christ and the sainted Harwoods for his rescue from depravity, darkness, and the certain promise of hell.

Neither the divine Christ nor the sainted Harwoods were enough to meet the needs of Larry's restless mind, but whenever he took up a new pursuit, be it chess, Dungeons & Dragons, or Magic: the Gathering, his parents condemned it as secular and sinful and sent him back to the Bible. Larry tried hard to let the book ignite his holy spirit, but in the end it was just a book to him; it ignited nothing. So he passed his childhood in an understimulated, guilt-ridden, conflicted state, as his parents never failed to remind him that if it weren't for them, he'd still be living in squalor and godless ignorance. He owed them, and he owed God.

Determined to be a dutiful son, he went to Biola University in La Mirada, California, to study theology and follow a pastor's path. But a wrong turn on a rainy night led Larry past the nearby Hawaiian Gardens Casino, where something called out to his blood. Maybe Guy was right; maybe the Vietnamese people just had the gamble in them. Or maybe Larry's timorous nature sought one last act of rebellion before surrendering to the will of the Harwoods and Christ. For whatever reason, he went inside. There, to his shock and delight, he found wall-to-wall Asians—Chinese, Japanese, Koreans,

Filipinos, and of course Vietnamese—all gambling, laughing, competing, having fun, *and all without guilt!*

He was home.

The Harwoods disowned him without much thought, which suited Larry just fine. At the age of twenty-one, a born again Buddhist, he embraced his lost heritage with a vengeance. He chose Lanh as his *nom de jeu,* for it meant quick minded or street smart, and certainly Lanh considered himself to be these things. The fact that he was usually transparent in his motives and rash in his actions was more or less completely lost on him. This is called a leak, and Lanh had plenty, the biggest of which was his inability to fully purge the Bible thumping of his formative years. Though he taught himself to play poker with a fiery abandon equal to any Tuan, Duc, or Harry, the sense that he was sinning never quite left him alone.

So his big wins were rare, and his move to Las Vegas only modestly successful. He had good luck with the tourists and weak-minded locals who bought his boat person persona and what they assumed to be his birthright mastery of the game. But to more sophisticated players he was an easy read, a sort of cultural transvestite who never seemed altogether comfortable in his chosen role. They couldn't quite figure out where he was coming from, but they usually knew where he was going. On his best days, when he had his Lanh Tran thing going on, he could temporarily forget himself and play excellent poker. On his worst days, he wished he was in church.

Guilt wracked Lanh when he heard that Guy Harris was dead, for he thought his own ill-conceived attempt to hijack Guy's tournament entry chip had done the man in. So he was grateful—and then guilty for his gratitude—to learn that Guy had died by knife. And beneath all this lay a deeper emotion, a bedrock attempt at end-justifies-means rationalization, for Lanh had learned what most poker players did not know: that entry into the Poker Apocalypse in the right circumstance and under the right aegis was a virtual lock to deliver a life-changing payday. Devout in the belief that enough money would make his guilt go away, Lanh would do anything to get rich. Even try to bluff the purchase of Guy's tournament entry chip in hopes of rolling him and running away.

Even run him off a road.

Even run the ol' Hanoi hustle past Guy's dim bulb brother, who he remembered having seen with Guy a few months earlier, and whom he assumed, based on Hal's recent meeting with Dark Mark, now held Guy's tournament entry chip. Lanh figured it would be easy to hoodwink this guileless straight; after all, the man couldn't even find his way out of a casino.

But Hal Harris was starting to learn the art of the bluff, too, and he was about to run one on Lanh.

10 The Flying McGinty

Hal sipped his coffee and waited. He didn't know much about poker yet, but one thing he'd already learned was the value of position, how you had the edge when the other guy went first. He figured if he just kept shtum, Lanh would have to go first, perhaps tipping some clue to his real intent. Because another thing he'd already learned was they always had a real intent. So he sipped his coffee and waited. Lanh found this vexing. He had expected Hal's curiosity to get the best of him pretty quick. After all, how often does a stranger just walk up to you, start talking, and invite you to coffee? Clearly this chump was too dumb to wonder, so Lanh made an ad hoc adjustment to his approach, pitching it even lower on the cluelessness scale. In this sense you could say that Lanh misread the strength of Hal's hand, interpreting him as weak.

"You play poker?" asked Lanh.

He waited for Hal to answer, but Hal just stirred some sugar into his coffee. Another silence formed and held until Lanh was obliged to break it. "Poker good game," he said. "Ve'y popular now." Hal still didn't rise to the bait, and Lanh was further vexed. "TV show all time." This was a very difficult person to have a conversation with. "Poker tour'men'." Lanh thought that Hal must be not just ignorant but actually slow-witted, so he recalibrated his pitch again, dumbing it down even more. "You hea' abou' Poker Apo'lyp?" How could he not? Among other things, it was wall-to-wall advertised all over town and especially here at the host casino.

But Hal just sipped his coffee, peering over the top of his nonchina mug like the last float on the clueless parade.

Lanh charged forward, getting out ahead of his hand in the sense of giving away more information more quickly than he'd planned. "Bi' tour'men'! Everyone wan' play. But too e'spensive. Hunna gran' to enter." Nothing. What was the guy, deaf? "So people ma' kum-kum, yeah?" Hal stared at him blankly, though in this case he really did not know the meaning of the phrase. "Pa'ne'shi', li'. One skill guy. One money guy." At this point Lanh expected Hal to mention Guy's tournament chip. It would be the natural response. But Hal was not in a natural mode. For the first time in his life he was deep into the devious. Moreover, he could read Lanh well. He knew that Lanh wanted an organic entrée into the subject, much in the manner of a bar hustler who has a lock proposition bet if only he can make the mark bring it up.

Hal decided to give him a little rope. "How would that work, exactly?"

Lanh quickly sketched out the logic and logistics of tournament backing plays. If a player was light on funds, he could sell percentages of his action to other players, and in this way piece together his tournament buy-in.

Said Hal, "That doesn't seem like such a good deal."

"Good deal both way," said Lanh. "I go' skill, no hunna gran'. You go' entry chi'—"

Hal pounced. "How do you know about that?" The question threw Lanh, like an unexpected check-raise from a previously passive opponent. How could he account for such knowledge without revealing the link between himself and Guy?

But inspiration came to Lanh's rescue, for he remembered that this was Hal's second visit to the Cortland today. "Ski' Loder tell me," he ad-libbed. "You know Ski', yeah? I see you ea'lier. You here together."

"Ah. Skip Loder told you I had a tournament entry chip. And where did he say I got it?"

"No say," said Lanh curtly. He was starting to lose patience. This should have been an easy play, a matter of convincing a lesser mind to let the Vietnamese lion bring him a massive payday. "Look, man," he said, "I worl'-class player. You ha' chip. We make kum-kum, both win." Well, that was the pitch. He hadn't intended to make it this way, had certainly envisioned a defter approach, but somehow he'd been flanked, outplayed in the hand.

Hal, for his part, was really getting annoyed with Lanh's mock accent. It seemed offensive somehow, even coming from the mouth of a Vietnamese. But he seemed to be learning that strategy, not emotion, should rule his play, whether at the table or away from it. When you yielded to emotion, you yielded edge, as he'd done with Dragic. So Hal swallowed his irritation and pressed his edge. Pushing his coffee cup aside, he said, "To be honest, Lanh, right now I'm leaning toward playing in the tournament myself." He could see Lanh fighting hard to hide his flinch. "But, you know, give me your phone number. I'll call you if I change my mind." It was like a quick raise designed to inspire a rash reraise, and in this case it had the desired effect.

"No!" said Lanh, panic in his voice. "No call! Act now! Big danger fo' you wi' chip. Eve'bod' want!"

"Is that right?"

"Bad men! Dar' Mar'!"

"What do you know about Dark Mark?"

"Eve'bod' know Dar' Mar'. He big plan for Apo'lyp. Buy in all player, ma' big team."

"How would that help?" asked Hal. "Apart from amortizing the risk?"

Lanh shrugged. "Who know? But two side: Dar' Mar' side, no Dar' Mar' side. No Dar' Mar' side dangerous."

Lanh did his best to sell real apprehension for Hal's safety, but the play backfired when Hal asked, "And you're willing to go against him? Be not on his side?"

Lanh stumbled, recovered. "Vietnam people no' scare."

"I'm not afraid, either," said Hal. "Thanks for the coffee." Hal stood up. He thought of one more card he might play. "You're not ugly, are you?" The completely non sequitur nature of the question silenced Lanh. "Do you know anybody ugly? A big, ugly guy? Friend of yours, maybe?"

"What you tal' abou' now?" Hal gauged Lanh's reaction. He didn't know for sure, but he believed that the blunt suddenness of the question had elicited an honest response. He was learning to trust his reads.

And feeling pretty good about himself. Through this short exchange he had confirmed that Dark Mark had some sort of scheme in play, and while Lanh attempted to project fear of Dragic, Hal suspected that Lanh actually wanted to be involved in that scheme, which apparently required a tournament entry chip. He now knew why Lanh had tried to romance the chip away from Guy: Lanh was a low roller, fundamentally a loser. He had no legitimate way into the Poker Apocalypse and so, clearly, was pursuing other avenues. Yep, Hal was feeling pretty good about his deductive skills, and his whole general play of this hand.

Which may be why he now overplayed it.

"By the way," he said, "what kind of car do you drive?"

"Huh?"

"I'm guessing Lexus."

"How you know tha'?"

Now it was Hal's turn to cover a blunder. "I . . . I'm good at guessing what cars people drive, that's all. It's a gift." The line sounded lame and Hal knew it. He felt himself growing hot with embarrassment—the embarrassment of a busted bluff. He strode away quickly, but already the damage was done. Lanh watched him go with narrowed, knowing eyes.

There's a lesson in that, thought Hal as he crossed the casino floor carefully following the signs to the parking garage. *When you bluff a guy off his hand, don't show him your fucking cards!* Hal tried to track the exact emotion or motivation that had caused him to talk about the Lexus. It seemed to be a need to show how smart he was, how badly he'd fooled Lanh. In fact, he had made a common poker player's mistake. Slaughter Johnson would have told him—hell, any competent player would tell him—if you have a tell on a guy, the last thing you do is let him know. They don't need to know how smart you are. They just need to give you their money.

Hal put it behind him. He had at least extracted the valuable information that Dark Mark was running a team of players and, if Lanh could be believed, had some sort of plan to tip the odds of winning in his team's favor. Was there really a threat in going against Dragic, or was that just Lanh blowing smoke? With that, Hal realized that he really didn't know so much more than he knew before, because all of this new data came from a suspect source. Clearly, Lanh had been trying to gull him, so how could he believe a word Lanh said? To doubt another person's word was new for Hal. In his old life—was he really already starting to think of three days ago as his old life?—he could pretty much take everyone at face value. Out here in Pokerville, it seemed, nothing was quite as it seemed.

Hal made his way out of the casino and into the parking garage. When he got back to the van he found—to his surprise, but not really—that Minty was gone again. The passenger door was open, and the wad of duct tape covering the lock had been gnawed clean off. Hal shut the passenger door, not quite knowing what to do. Should he whistle for Minty or look for him, or trust that the independent-minded canine would continue to take care of himself?

At that point the point became moot, for a sharp shot to the kidneys sent Hal hard against the side of the van, then sprawling to the ground. He looked up and saw Lanh standing over him with a tire iron in his hand and a feral look in his eye. It occurred to Hal that he had badly misread this opponent. He never imagined Lanh capable of violence—but he should have, for didn't Lanh run Guy off the road in his car? Wasn't that a precedent of desperation? Good poker players remember their foes' histories, and Hal should have done the same. Now he lay flat on his back, about to be teed up like a golf ball. So he did the only thing he could think to do.

He whistled.

The opening bars of Beethoven's Fifth.

As loud and as flat as he could.

"Wha' you doin'?" shouted Lanh. "No whistle! Gi' me chip!"

But Hal kept whistling. It was the only play he had. Like sometimes when you bet yourself into trouble and the only solution is to bet yourself right back out.

Lanh raised the tire iron over his head. Hal braced himself for the blow—but it never came, as a hundred pounds of flying McGinty slammed into Lanh broadside, knocking him to the ground. The tire iron skittered away and Hal scrambled for it, but he really didn't need to, for just then Minty did something amazing: he pinned Lanh beneath his massive body and, gently but with authority, clamped his giant jaw on the slender man's windpipe. Lanh went limp and Minty settled in, sprawled out on top of him as if Lanh were a throw rug and his neck were Minty's favorite chew toy. Hal had no idea how Minty had learned this trick, or how the dog knew to use it here, but clearly Guy had been right in describing him as one smart fucking dog.

It was with these words that Hal began to run his bluff. "This is one smart fucking dog," he told Lanh as he got up and dusted himself off. "All I have to do is say the word and he'll snap your neck like a chicken bone." In fact, Hal didn't know what command would make Minty strike. He hoped he didn't utter it by accident. "Now tell me," he said, "what the fuck is going on."

"I jus' wan'—"

"And drop the phony baloney accent, will you? That's really getting on my nerves."

Lanh looked up at Hal with real surprise in his eyes. He thought he had his dialect dialed in. No one had ever called him on it before. "I just wanted the chip," he said, letting his perfectly inflected Orange County English show through, like the black roots of his dyed blond hair. "I want to win the Apocalypse."

"No, there's more to it than that," said Hal. He toed the tire iron with his foot. "This is some fucked-up shit. If I understand the way these tournaments work, even if you enter you're likely to lose." Hal struggled to remember what he'd read in Slaughter's book. "What is it? Something like one in ten in a tournament makes the money. I don't see you going off on me with a tire iron for a ten percent shot. What's the angle?"

"No angle, man. I just wanted in."

"Minty . . ." said Hal in a low voice he hoped would convey the command, *Raise the stakes.* Minty, proving again that he was one smart fucking dog, responded with a guttural growl.

"All right, all right!" shouted Lanh. "I'll tell you the play!"

In the world of tournament poker during the first years of the twenty-first century, poker teams were all the rage. Mostly they fronted online poker outfits: Full Tilt, UltimateBet, PokerStars. . . . Each of these sites and many others did everything they could to attract big-name players to their brand. Incentives included publicity, promotion, career management, and of course, large, large wads of cash. The tightest teams actually pooled their resources, paying tournament fees out of a common bankroll, and recycling their individual tournament winnings back into that bankroll for the benefit of all, much as Guy and Slaughter had done, though on a vastly grander scale. Even the loosely knit teams—more like associations or affinity groups than actual partnerships—discovered a certain strong benefit to the team concept: moral support. When one of their number made the final table at a tournament, the others would gather to root him home. They gave him strategic advice. Shared their insights about his foes. Kept him focused on his game. Helped him close that crucial gap between a final table appearance and an actual tournament win. This combination of mutual psychological, tactical, and financial aid proved deadly effective. By the time the Poker

Apocalypse rolled around, team players were tearing up the tournament fields. It was becoming harder and harder for free agents to book tournament wins. Either you were on the bus or off the bus, and those off the bus were finding it increasingly difficult to catch.

So the big tournaments became oceans of matching T-shirts, hats, hockey jerseys, vests, hoodies, and anything else you could think to slap a logo on. This created an impression to the casual eye that the players might be in collaboration, for so many were clearly playing for the same teams. And if they were sharing strategic insights or working from a common bankroll, what would prevent them from taking the next step and actively helping one another win?

The top players would tell you that collusion didn't happen. Even players who owned pieces of one another, like shares of complementary mutual funds, insisted that they played as hard against their horses as against anybody else. They knew that the popularity of poker rested on its integrity; that if the public thought the fix was in they would reject the game and turn their fickle attention elsewhere. For this reason, if not for moral high ground, the teams and their players all strove to come off like Caesar's wife: above suspicion. To hear the players tell it, they succeeded in this.

But poker players have been known to lie.

It was easy enough, for example, for two cooperating players to have a tacit agreement to help each other out. If they happened to find themselves at the same tournament table, they'd just make sure not to play big pots against each other. Each thus faced only eight active foes at the table instead of nine, and in a tough tournament field, that 11 percent reduction in real competition could make a significant difference. And although in a large tournament, the chance of allied players sitting at the same table was relatively small, that likelihood increased with the size of the team's roster. Further, with tables being broken and recombined throughout the course of a tournament, colluders could at least occasionally find themselves in a position to do each other some good.

They could do even more good by establishing who had the strongest hand and having the weaker holding step aside. Their advantage would be like that of two golfers playing best ball while each of their opponents would have to go it alone—except that here the victims would never even see the extra ball in play. Again, this was a relatively small edge in the real world of tournament poker . . . but any good poker player will tell you that the game is won through the accumulation of small edges. Even illicit ones.

Chip dumping, chip passing, whipsawing—the ol' bingo bango bongo, where an unsuspecting victim got caught between two cooperatively aggressive bettors— all of these covert strategies were available to players who chose to use them. Yes, there was a price to pay for getting caught, but it was small: you could be bounced from a tournament or banned from tournament play. It's not like you'd get arrested, or even taken to a back room and roughed up. Moreover, cheating of this sort was relatively hard to detect, as cooperative aggression bore a strong resemblance to garden-variety competitive play, where battles between raisers break out all the time. So if you were colluding, and your collusion netted even one big tournament win, the risk-versus-benefit calculus was greatly to the good for you. At the end of the day it was only a sense of fair play that put the rein to tactics such as these. Not every poker player had this sort of moral compass.

Certainly Dragic didn't. Or if he did, it was obliterated by his bitter regret at having missed out on the dizzying spike in poker's popularity, and by the feeling that he was somehow owed. Team Dragic, then, had no T-shirts, no hats, no website. It had been cautiously and secretly assembled from among those Poker Apocalypse qualifiers who shared Dragic's belief that rules were for fools. Lanh Tran desperately wanted to join that team— and hated himself for wanting it so.

"So my chip . . ." mused Hal, "would have gotten you on Dragic's crew?" Lanh nodded as best he could with Minty's mouth on his neck. "But not me?"

"You're a straight," said Lanh. "Plus dead money. So why don't you just give me the chip, let me hook up with Dragic, and we'll split the take?"

Hal ignored him. "How does Guy's death figure in? Was he blowing the whistle or something?"

"I don't know anything about that," said Lanh.

"No, no, of course not," said Hal contemptuously. "Why would you? You only know what you know. In fact, how do you even know any of this?"

"I just know," said Lanh. "You listen, you hear."

"Oh, so it's true because it's true. Is that what you're saying?"

"Look, believe me or don't believe me. Just get this fucking dog off me, will you?"

"What, so you can whack me with a tire iron again?"

"I'm sorry about that. That was a mistake."

"Oh, you think?" Hal wondered what could drive a man to a mistake like that: attacking another man, or even killing. As an accountant, Hal had such a familiar relationship with money that it really didn't mean that much to him, but he knew the deep, almost mystical link in most people's minds between money and survival. It seemed hardwired into their psyches, how if you lose some money you lose some fundamental grip on life. He had often seen the panic in clients' eyes when he told them that the IRS wanted this or that significant sum. He had heard them wail, "How will I *survive?*" It struck him that most of them could actually afford to take the hit. Survival wasn't really an issue. Except in their psyches. Except in their souls.

Guy, Hal knew, had also always been immune to lucre's lure. Where other poker players drew a connection between chips and money, then money and survival, to Guy those chips had always been just "assignable-value pieces of plastic," no more emotionally meaningful than bottle caps or tiddlywinks. "To win," Guy once told him, "you can't be afraid to lose."

Hal looked down at Lanh. How had Lanh's journey through life made him so desperate about something ultimately so insignificant? What were they talking about, after all? A poker tournament? A tournament win? A great big pile of cash? How did it make your life rise? Then it came to him. *It just did; that's all.* If fear of losing was the benchmark currency of human emotion, then the will to risk was the other side of that coin. It had to be. Were it not, man would still be living in trees wondering where his next banana was coming from. People had to try. Try to win whatever game they chose to play. Whether it was the "find love and raise a family game," or the "get so rich it makes you sick" game, or even the Poker Apocalypse.

Lanh was pathetic . . . but understandably so. His inner compulsions drove him as, Hal realized, they drive everyone. "Minty," Hal said, not knowing whether this would really work or not. "Up, boy." Minty cocked his huge head and looked at Hal. Hal suddenly understood where Minty got his smarts. He was a poker player; he'd learned to read minds. So Hal just smiled and nodded, and let his mind speak. Minty hefted himself to his feet, ambled away a few strides, and lay down again.

Lanh stood up. "Now what?" he asked. "You gonna call the police?"

"You gonna attack me again?"

"No."

"Then, no. Go on, get out of here."

Lanh started away. He turned back and said, "I'm still gonna try to get into the Apocalypse."

Said Hal, "I imagine you are."

Lanh walked away, looking back over his shoulder to make sure that Hal didn't change his mind and sic Minty on him. Hal watched him go, hoping that his read was right, and that Lanh wouldn't be a problem again. Then he dug deep into his pocket and pulled out his tournament entry chip. He studied its shimmering silver surface and thought of all the promise stored inside: all the hopes and dreams. Not of money, but of triumph—pure and unadulterated success, possibly the strongest narcotic of them all.

Hal had an actuarial frame of mind. He could calculate probabilities like his brother could calculate pot odds. Even without that ability, he was canny enough to analyze a situation and know pretty much where he stood. If Dark Mark was running a secret team through the Poker Apocalypse, then the game was gaffed in ways that neither Hal nor anyone else might ever know. For a tyro like Hal to think he could win was madness and Hal knew it. But he didn't care. He held in his hand a chance to try, a shot at success. And that, he felt, was really all that mattered.

He was going to enter the Poker Apocalypse.

And damn it, he was going to win.

PART TWO

The Education of a Poker Player

You're born broke, you die broke.
Everything else is just fluctuation.

11 The Isness of It All

"Raise," said Hal. He hadn't looked at his cards. He didn't need to. He knew that the chimps in the chairs all around him wouldn't call. They couldn't. They were crippled by fear, short-stacked and desperate. Having played in this particular no-limit hold'em tournament—the $500 buy-in daily event at the Emerald Isle—for the better part of five hours, they couldn't stand the thought of seeing all their effort squandered so near the money bubble. Slaughter Johnson had impressed upon Hal how ass backward this thinking was. "You've got to be in it to win it," said Slaughter. "You can go broke with low-money finishes." Hal saw the seductive logic of it, though; he saw how a player's commitment of money, time, and effort could make him tighten up when the money got close. To have come so far and worked so hard, and then have nothing to show for it, not even your buy-in back, was an emotional burden greater than some players could bear. So they clenched. Played in fear. And then they were, as Slaughter described it and Hal had come to see it, meat.

So Hal raised, everyone folded, and he collected the blinds and antes, adding them to the massive ziggurat of chips he had built in the tournament so far. He was well on his way to winning it, and Slaughter and Vinny, watching from the rail, had every confidence that he would, for Hal had already revealed a terrier's tenacity in poker: instinctively, he knew how to close. Sure enough, he bulled his way to the final table and won the event going away.

Hal's learning curve had been dizzyingly steep. It didn't hurt that he had a latent knack for the game—what Slaughter called Hal's poker gene—the same knack that Guy had demonstrated, but one unsullied by Guy's big ego and bad habits. Nor did the ticking clock hurt. Knowing that he had just a month to bootstrap himself up to championship-caliber play, Hal devoted every minute of his days, and every fragment of his mind, to solving the particular problem of tournament no-limit hold'em. Deeply analytical by nature, he instantly absorbed and internalized all the information Slaughter fed him, and fed it back out as flawless, gutty game. He thrived in the hothouse environment, with barely time enough to learn everything he needed to know, and therefore no time at all to second-guess or to doubt. It didn't hurt that he didn't fear. Per Bob Dylan, "When you got nothin', you got nothin' to lose"; no expectations hindered Hal's progress.

Slaughter, too, was stepping up his game, struggling to process all he'd ever learned about poker, and communicate these concepts to Hal in concise, precise, meaningful ways. He had, for example, boiled down successful tournament poker to three simple criteria: hand selection, aggressiveness, reads. With proper hand selection, Slaughter explained, any chimp in a chair could make it halfway through a poker tournament. All you have to do is fold bad hands and push good ones.

But that's a recipe for mediocrity. Absent an incredible run of great cards (and opponents who will pay you off) eventually the rising blinds will grind you down to the felt.

To hand selection, then, add aggressiveness: the willingness to bet with or without good cards, and the ability to steal pots that aren't rightfully yours. Using this tool in concert with hand selection, any given tournament player could win on any given day. Get on a good run, find some hands and some unsuspecting victims, and you've got your ticket stamped to the final table, where the blinds get high, luck kicks in, and anything can happen. The trouble with aggressiveness, though, is how it defines you as an aggressive player. You can run the table, but only up to a point—the point where your enemies wake up with a hand. Raise often enough, steal recklessly enough, and eventually someone will trap your ass for all your chips. No one's that scary to someone holding pocket aces. Aggressiveness, then, can win from time to time, but blind aggression is riding for a fall.

Therefore, *abre los ojos:* open your eyes. Study your foes and make judgments about their hands. Put reads on them, in other words. Put them on a range of hands, and then narrow that range based on available information (such as betting patterns, physical tells, and history) until it becomes clear, by deduction, what few hands they might actually have. With accurate reads, you can push when you're ahead, retreat when you're beat, run programs, bust bluffs, avoid catastrophic confrontations, and dominate almost any tournament field. Perhaps because Hal was so new to poker, his reading ability was pure and clear, uncluttered by the cynical doublethink that clogs the cogs of some veteran players' minds. And Slaughter Johnson, in all his years in the game, had never seen anyone as good at this as Hal. Not Guy. Not

Slaughter himself. It was clear to Slaughter that Hal was some sort of poker savant, a world-class talent who'd just been waiting to discover the game.

Of course, tournament poker is filled with world-class talents who lose. So to Hal's package of traits, Slaughter added the fourth and most critical one: heart. He taught Hal to never give up, no matter how grim the situation. "As long as they're still dealing you cards," Slaughter said, "you've still got a chance." But the temptation to capitulate is strong. Hope departs, and with it goes discipline. Then even a strong player can go weak, throwing in the towel by throwing in his last chips on some ridiculous cheese like T-7 offsuit. To Slaughter, that was simply unacceptable, a humiliating surrender to the whims of fate. He didn't tolerate it in himself and wouldn't put up with it in Hal. Surrender once, he warned Hal, and it was over between them.

Not that Slaughter had much hope for their partnership, even after he discovered Hal's abundant natural gifts. There was just too much ground to cover, and much of his best advice conflicted with other parts of his strategy package. For instance, Slaughter favored waiting for premium opportunities during a tournament's early rounds. "Patience is precious when chips are cheap," he told Hal. At the same time, though, a starting tournament field featured lots of dead money, and you really had to get your share of those poorly defended chips before they found their way into more capable hands. How could one square these opposing ideas? How could one be patient and aggressive at the same time? The answer lay in something deeper than definable tournament tactics. It lay in *nuance*—but how do you teach nuance? You can teach the logic of making a standard raise of three times the big blind, but how do you teach tuning that raise to get desired results? How do you teach verbal backspin, where the right word at the right time can induce a call or fold? How do you teach the shoulder stall, a false tell where the bettor conveys inner conflict with the muscles of his upper arm, such that an unwary foe will actually raise into a made hand? These were just some of the countless tricks of tournament play that Slaughter had accrued over the years. So many tricks, so many approaches . . . How to choose the crucial ones, given that he couldn't possibly teach them all?

Go off in all directions at once, decided Slaughter. *You're bound to get somewhere eventually.*

Slaughter knew that Hal's quest was absurd on its face, but Hal was determined—so determined that he had quit his job to try. Slaughter honored Hal's determination, and matched it. With long experience as a poker mentor, he knew the difference among a bad coach, a good one, and a great one. A bad coach could tell you what you were doing wrong. A good coach could tell you how to fix it. A great coach could tell you one thing that would fix five things. That's what Slaughter tried to do: fix five things at once. It helped that Hal was naturally gifted, but they still had a ridiculously long way to go.

They made Vinny's Summerlin town house their headquarters, and there they talked and studied poker, and played marathon heads-up sessions, or sometimes three-way matches with Vinny sitting in. At first, Slaughter found plenty to critique in Hal's play, for Hal made a whole range of rookie mistakes, like handling his cards carelessly, telegraphing his bluffs, or chasing draws when the pot odds didn't warrant. But Hal learned fast and adapted fully, his actuarial mind bootstrapping him up to dizzying heights of discipline and clarity.

Hal's adjustments were sophisticated and showed a deeper understanding of poker than Slaughter would have thought possible for someone so young in the game. Learning, for example, that "draws are death in no limit," a typical poker newbie might simply stop calling with draws unless the pot was laying the right price. This would have been the correct, tight thing to do, but it was an unimaginative and uninspired approach, and Hal quickly moved beyond it. He started leading at pots with under-bets, small wagers that if called by his opponents would actually give him the right odds to draw to straights or flushes. Slaughter knew that smart players would recognize such weak leads and punish them with monster reraises. But the first time Slaughter tried this on Hal, he was surprised to find himself staring down the barrel of a flopped set, for Hal was already a step ahead, disguising his bets on the draw with identical bets behind made hands. Hal quickly evinced a flexible, creative approach that morphed and moved and changed gears so seamlessly that even Slaughter couldn't keep up. It soon became clear that Hal was playing poker on a whole other level.

"How are you doing it, son?" Slaughter asked late one afternoon as they sat on Vinny's rooftop patio, watching the crimson sun set in the west. Hal was hitting on all cylinders, basically shredding just about every game or local tournament he played.

"I don't know," said Hal. "I'm just thinking about the isness of it all."

"The isness of it all?"

"Poker taken as a whole. The gestalt. If I think about any aspect of the game, I just get confused, but if I think about everything at once—the big picture—it all fits together."

"You realize that makes no sense."

"None of this makes sense, Slaughter." Hal ran his fingers through his hair. "Me playing poker, trying for this tournament. Why? I probably won't win, and even if I do, so what? It won't bring Guy back." But Slaughter was thinking that it would bring Guy back: a different, better version of Guy, a poker player who fulfilled Guy's promise without the burden of Guy's flaws.

" 'The isness of it all.' " Slaughter rolled the phrase over in his mind. "How does that work exactly?"

"I don't know, you know. When a hand starts, there are all these paths through it. Most of the time, every path is a dead end; you just fold. But when you don't fold, other paths open up: raise now, raise later, check-call, check-raise, trap, whatever. I guess you'd say with every hand I just look for the right path."

"A decision tree."

"If you say so," allowed Hal. "But it doesn't feel like I'm even making decisions. Honestly, Slaughter, sometimes I just *see* the path, like it's glowing neon green and all the other paths are dark."

"That must make it easy."

"Easy? No. But . . . 'There's no fucking point in making a plan for the hand if you're not going to trust your plan and act on it.' "

"You're quoting me to me?"

"Far as I'm concerned, I'm quoting scripture."

"Don't lay that shit on me," said Slaughter with sudden earnest defensiveness. "I'm no guru. I'm just a guy who knows stuff."

"I know that," said Hal. "Still . . ."—he cocked his head to one side and half smiled—"I know it's crazy, Slaughter, but I actually believe we have a chance in this. If nothing else, it'll be great to see the look on Marko Dragic's face when he sees what game I've got."

Slaughter was silent for a long time. When he finally spoke, his voice was soft and subdued. "We have history, you know. Me and Dragic."

"Really?"

Slaughter nodded. "Shared a lot of tables back in the early eighties. At that time you couldn't find much in the way of big games around town. They played high at the Stardust, Caesar's . . . at Binion's when the Series was in town. That's about it. Mostly it was a grind, and when the grind didn't go your way it could really get on your nerves."

"Especially if you're Dark Mark."

"Yeah." Slaughter drifted back on the wave of a memory. "One night we're playing stud at the Maxim—"

"Maxim?"

"Oh, man, it's not even there anymore, is it? It was just off the Strip on Flamingo Road. I think it's a Westin now. Anyway, we're playing thirty- to sixty-dollar limit, which was a big game then. There's one fish in the game and he's going off. I mean *off.* Hemorrhaging at the wallet like you've never seen. Everyone's getting well. Except Dragic. For some reason, the guy just seems to have his number. He's eating up all of Dragic's chips and crapping them out to the rest of the table. Eventually the tourist decides he's had enough and goes off upstairs to bed. The game breaks instantly, of course, because there goes the guppy. Stuck like he was, I figure Dragic'll squawk, but he doesn't. Doesn't say a word. Just melts into the night.

"I don't see him again till the next day, when he rolls in all fat and sassy. Says he looked up the tourist, played him heads up, and picked him clean. That story's absurd on its face. We broke that fish; he had no money left. Nor is Dragic flashing bankroll. He's back down at the five- to ten-dollar game, trying to rebuild. But he's happy. Happy as a hot dog at a vegetarian barbecue.

"We all waited for that tourist to come back around,

but he never did. We missed him. He was good for the game.

"Years later I'm friends with a house dick at the Tropicana. We're talking about all the crazy shit we've seen, like guys do when they talk. He says nothing holds a candle to this one thing back at the Maxim, where he used to work. He says in this one guest room some guy just painted the walls with another guy's blood. I lined up the dates. It was Dragic."

"What did you do?"

"Do? Nothing. Dragic was already in jail for whacking Paul Rogers. When he got out, well, let's just say I didn't go to his homecoming."

"Do you think he had Guy killed?"

"I'd take the bet. He holds grudges like a sponge holds water."

"And Skip said Guy pissed him off."

"Right. So don't you do the same."

"But if he's trying to fix the Apocalypse . . ."

"Let him. Here's the thing you need to know about poker cheats, Hal. They're most of them notoriously bad poker players. If they weren't, they wouldn't need to cheat in the first place. Usually they can't even get out of their own way. You just play your game. Let the rest of it take care of itself."

Hal nodded in agreement, but Slaughter saw the lie in his eye. Maybe Hal was some sort of poker savant, but away from the table he was still an easy read, at least to Slaughter. "I'm not shitting you," said Slaughter. "He's not your problem. What do you think you're going to do? Crack his scam?"

"I might."

"No. All you're going to do is fuck yourself up. If you spend all your psychic energy trying to guess who's play-

ing cozy, you'll just end up missing something important, something *real*. Hal, look . . ." Slaughter turned toward Hal, and the setting sun threw muted ruby shadows
across the lee side of his face. "You're already a good
poker player. You're on your way to being a great one. I
have to admit I've never seen anything like you, and I'd
back your play in half a heartbeat. But the Poker Apocalypse will be far tougher than these dailies and week-
lies you've been playing. One mistake—one loose call
or busted bluff or reckless adventure—and you'll be
riding the rail so fast it'll make your eyeballs bleed.
Don't think about Dragic. The only one who can beat
you is you. You know that, right?"

"Right," said Hal. He nodded again. This time Slaughter allowed himself to believe he'd gotten through. And
in a sense he had, for in that moment Hal had a firm
commitment to focus on his game and let the problem
of Team Dragic take care of itself.

Which commitment lasted right up until the moment
Skip Loder mentioned G-String.

12 The Ears Have Walls

"Reraise," said Hal.

Sitting on his right, Skip cast Hal a sidelong glance. "Man," he said, "you're starting to sound like a broken record." They were seated together in a $5 and $10 blind no-limit hold'em game at Kittens, an off-Strip property whose pneumatic waitresses in booty shorts and "Love the Pussy" wife beaters attracted a disproportionate crowd of testosterone-fueled young men out for a night on the ogle. This made the Kittens poker room one of the loosest and wildest in town, especially late on a weekend evening when the vodka Red Bulls kicked in.

The original raiser folded, as did Skip. "I'd have played this crap, too," he said, ruefully. "It's my favorite crap of all."

The dealer pushed Hal the pot. "DPCH," said Hal.

"Don't play crap hands, my ass," said Skip. "Like you're in there with pocket fifteens all the time."

Skip had been out of jail for several weeks, and in the time since his release, he and Hal had fallen into an

easy routine of study with Slaughter during the morning and afternoon hours, followed by tournaments or
cash play throughout the evening and well into the night.
They made good companions. Hal provided the sort of
anchor that a potential shipwreck like Skip needed, and
Skip reintroduced Hal to the tame/wild symbiosis he'd
enjoyed with Guy; created a new one, rather, one without the lifelong baggage of sibling rivalry.

Skip hadn't particularly minded being in jail, apart
from the fact that he was (a) not guilty and (b) lost for
days in a maze of bureaucracy, a limbo in which he lin-
gered while the highly diffident Detective Ding got
around to clearing his alibi. Of course it stood up, for
Skip had spent the entire timeline of Guy's murder—
where else?—playing poker. And if logging in and out
with his player's club card wasn't enough, didn't they
have cameras? Didn't they have film?

But Danny Ding had been busy annihilating another
week of his life with scut work and bad coffee, so it took
some time to check out Skip's story and then find him
in the system and pry him loose. In the meantime, Skip
had bonded with the boys in lockup, broadly believing
their lies and validating their self-image. A go-along,
get-along sort in any situation, he had codified his survival strategy as "jokes, smokes, and tokes."

"It's simple," he'd told Hal. "All you gotta do is make
everyone feel good and bribe who needs bribing. The
rest takes care of itself. Seriously, I could write a book."

The dealer pitched the next set of cards around the
table. Someone in early position made it $30 to go. Skip
called. "Reraise," said Hal again. "Make it two hundred."
He put in a stack of $10 chips and coolly regarded the
original raiser, who wilted under the strength of the
reraise and released his hand. "What is with you?" whis-

pered Skip as he folded and Hal claimed another pot. "Got ants in your pants?"

"I just figure if I raise behind a raise and a call, then there's that much more money in the pot to win."

"Yeah? You think?" Skip shook his head. "Tell you one thing," he said, "I'm not giving you position anymore. From now on, I'm sitting on your left." To tell the truth, Skip was somewhat in awe of Hal, and of the transformation he had undergone, for Hal had become the sort of player Skip admired most and tried his best to be: icy under fire, creatively aggressive, unafraid to act, capable of bold and unexpected moves, and utterly untiltable. Skip was aware that his new friend had almost instantly lapped him in terms of poker expertise, but he kept this opinion to himself. While Skip knew that "arrogance is what confidence wishes it was," he figured it wouldn't help Hal to get cocky, not with the Poker Apocalypse now just days away. The guy had a big enough hill to climb. No sense weighting him down with his own ego.

The night wore on. Hal and Skip feasted on a rota of drunken youngsters playing above both their bankroll and their skill set. Most of them were tragically loose, calling off their stacks with middle pair, bottom pair, ace high, whatever. Most, therefore, could not be bluffed, but that didn't seem to be a problem, for all Hal and Skip had to do was wait for semistrong hands, bet the shit out of them, and get paid off. Hal realized that this circumstance was actually ideal, for beating this table required no tricky play whatsoever. A thought formed in his mind and he shared it with Skip. "You know you're in the wrong game," said Hal, "when bluffing works."

"Now you're speaking in aphorisms?" asked Skip.

"He's been doing that for some time," said a familiar

voice. "He doesn't even know he does it." They looked left and saw Vinny slip into the empty seat beside them.

"I thought you didn't play anymore," said Hal. "Especially . . ." He looked around at the tawdry décor and let the thought die unspoken.

"Especially here?" asked Vinny sweetly. "Where they drop their cleavage in the drinks?" Hal just reddened. "I know, I know," continued Vinny. "You're only here for the game." She halfway turned in her chair and looked at them both. "I won't lie to you," she said. "Dad sent me out to make sure you're not getting into too much trouble."

"How much is too much?" asked Skip.

"I don't know," said Vinny, with a wolfish grin. "Let's find out."

They killed the game. Absolutely murdered it. Throughout the long night they strip-mined every bankroll anyone put in play. It was inevitable, really, for they were three very skilled players chowing down on drunk, passive, weak opponents. Nor were they fighting each other. It wasn't collusion, exactly, just mutual respect and a shared awareness that they were all playing from the same playbook—Slaughter Johnson's—such that there was no reason to try to hit hard targets when easier ones would inevitably present themselves. It made a difference, though, that they each had only seven players to worry about per deal, while the rest of the table faced a full nine foes, including three who were savvy, disciplined (sober), and unlikely to make rash mistakes. Eventually they broke the game completely and, rather than pass one another's money back and forth, decided to call it a night.

Dawn found them at breakfast at Rudi's Eatateria, the same all-night hash joint where Hal and Vinny had gone the morning after Guy's murder. It seemed like a lifetime ago to Hal. He remembered asking Vinny what tilt was. *Could I ever have been so naïve?* He knew tilt now; had experienced it firsthand. But Hal Harris had a gift. He never made the same mistake twice. So, having gone through the emotional roller coaster (and subsequent crap poker play) of tilt, he had recognized that state of mind, identified and isolated it, inoculated himself, and made himself more or less immune.

Over pigs in blankets and waffles sticky with syrup, Skip regaled Hal and Vinny with stories of his "hard time in the joint," most of which, by Skip's nature, painted him in a stoic, heroic, political prisoner sort of light. The tales made amusing enough breakfast entertainment.

Then came this one.

"There was a crankhead," said Skip. "A bouncer at some skanky strip club. Night Moves, I think it was. Typical meth paranoid. Walked around the common room all day saying, 'The ears have walls, the ears have walls.' Yet he couldn't shut up. We called him G-String."

"G-String?" asked Vinny.

"For his pending charges. Seems he went postal one night, yanked off some stripper's G-string with his teeth. They got him for attempted rape, assault with a deadly weapon—"

"His teeth?"

"Well, you tell me. Anyway, he had this wild-ass fantasy about how the fix was in on the Poker Apocalypse." Hal and Vinny exchanged looks. "What?" asked Skip.

"Nothing," said Hal. "Go on."

"What on? That's the story. Crankhead bouncer claims some big-deal poker player is running a team of horses into the Apocalypse, but with tools."

"Tools?"

"Chip dumps and counterfeits. Whipsaws. Hand signals. Says they've got this whole complex code so that everyone in on the hack knows exactly what cards everyone else has got. Windtalker shit."

"Did he say who the player was?" asked Hal. "Did he show you the code?"

"Were you not paying attention? I said, 'crankhead bouncer.' He doesn't know who the player was 'cause there is no player. He doesn't know the code 'cause there is no code. The whole thing's a figment of his tweaked imagination."

"No," said Vinny. "You don't make something like that up. It's got to be rooted in something."

"Well, in this case the 'something' is supposedly a stripper at Night Moves who claims the deal got blabbed to her during a particularly vigorous lap dance. But it's all bullshit. Don't you know that jail is a gold mine of misinformation? People are constantly telling you things that are just not fucking true." Skip essayed a chuckle. "Just like a poker game." But when he looked at his friends' furrowed brows, he asked, "What is with you two?"

"Where's G-String now?" asked Vinny. "Still inside?"

"Nope. Made bail. Hocked his mother's house to do it. Hope she likes living in her car."

"Could you get in touch with him?" asked Hal.

"Sure. I've got his number in my cell phone." Hal and Vinny laughed at Skip's joke—then gawked when they realized he was serious. "What? He's a crankhead bouncer. You never know when you're gonna need some muscle. Don't forget, someone dropped a dime on me."

"And we think we know who," said Vinny.

"Yeah? That's a guy I'd like to have a chat with. I'm telling you this much, jail food did nothing for my girlish figure. Too damn starchy."

"Later with that," said Hal. "We need to see G-String."

"Later with *that*," said Skip. "Right now I need about ten hours of sleep and fornication with a tall redhead." He leered at Vinny in a sort of joking-but-not-really kind of way. "Know where I can find one?"

She responded nonverbally.

By pouring maple syrup in his lap.

Hal wasn't used to sleeping in the day. Even with the curtains drawn tight in the guest bedroom of Vinny's town house, even with Minty McGinty's soothing snores at the foot of his bed, even using every trick of deep relaxation he knew, Hal could manage nothing better than a fitful doze. He tossed. He turned. He ran odds in his head. *Odds against getting dealt a pair: 16 to 1; against flopping a flush: 118 to 1. Odds against getting pocket aces: 220 to 1. Odds against ever falling asleep: fucking infinite.* Eventually he muttered, "Screw this," and got out of bed. Throwing on a T-shirt and gym shorts, he padded out to the kitchen.

Where he found Vinny with her head down on the kitchen table quietly crying.

Hal had little experience with female energy. The girls he knew, the girls he dated, were tightly wound types who wore their hair in congenital buns, talked about their feelings from a dispassionate distance, undressed in the dark, and made love—girls Hal knew never fucked—with the detached precision of the CPAs they almost inevitably were. To see Vinny weeping—to see her raw emotion on display—made Hal instantly uncomfortable. He tried to back out of the room, but Minty had followed him in and now lay like a great, hairy speed bump in his path, causing Hal to stumble backward over him and hit the floor with a thud. Vinny looked up and smiled through tears at the sight of Minty painting Hal's face with earnest licks of apology.

"Are you okay?" she asked.

Hal stood up rubbing his ass. "Bruised dignity," he said. "I'll live." He looked her up and down. "What about you?"

Vinny walked to the sink and splashed cold water on her face. "I'm fine," she said, flashing him a bravado smile.

"So, fine for you is sitting alone in the kitchen crying?"

"It passes the time," she said. Hal waited. "You don't want to hear about it." He waited some more. Hal had no natural gift for intimacy, but patience was now a strength of his game. Eventually, Vinny said, "I miss your brother. More than I thought I would."

With that, she was back in her mind to her last night with Guy. She had wanted to turn off the lights, but, *"Leave 'em on,* Guy had said. *"I like to see the equipment."*

"Equipment?" Vinny had put her hands on her naked hips in mock pique. *"That's what this is to you? Equipment?"*

"Oh, yeah," said Guy. He stroked her freckled breasts in a gesture at once awestruck and urgent. *"Equipment, tools, utensils, gadgets, gear."* He ran a finger down the length of her belly. *"You're a whole fucking hardware store, honey."* He reached between her legs. *"I could shop in here all night."* And then he had taken her, making love to her with the same sense of awe and raw urge. He lit her up. He always did. Even the memory did.

"He made me feel good about myself," she said, with a sigh. "Not too many men can do that."

"You deserve it," said Hal.

"What does that mean?"

Hal shrugged. "You're a good person," he said. "You deserve to feel good about yourself."

Vinny generally didn't, though. She saw herself as guarded, mistrustful, ungainly, oddly proportioned, too tall, and not particularly lovable nor capable of love. She dwelt in a prison of her own suspicion, years of failed relationships having warped her into a defensive stance that held the world at arm's length and self-consciously scorned it from that safe remove. A good person? Honestly, she didn't think so. But validation is powerful stuff, and Hal was offering his. It made her want to offer some in return—in her guarded, arm's length kind of way. "How about you?" she asked. "Are you a good person?"

"I don't know," he said. "It's a shaky concept. I have yet to see any version of morality that doesn't add up to self-interest in the end." At that moment, Hal was thinking about where he'd found himself: on a quixotic mission to avenge his brother's murder by . . . what? Playing a game? It made no sense. And it had cost him the stable foundation of his life. "Then again, who knows why anyone does anything?" *For instance,* he thought, *I don't know why I'm doing this.* And he leaned in and kissed her.

And she kissed him back.

Who knows why anyone does anything? As two lonely people cast adrift on a certain sea, they suddenly clung to each other like mutual driftwood. As two lonely, guarded people deeply in need of feeling okay about themselves, they extended to each other the mightiest aphrodisiac there is, really: approval. And they clung to the approval even more desperately than they clung to each other, for with approval, anything is possible; and for approval anyone will do anything. Not that they were reckless. They measured the moment with care, both of them. In the nature of poker players, they weighed the risk against the gain. They came to the same conclusion: that the pot odds justified the call. But it was a hunch at best, a hunch of the heart. As such, their quickly blooming passion was not something they could substantiate with any better rationale than, well, it seemed like a good idea at the time.

And it was. It was a good idea right there on the kitchen floor, with Minty showing more interest in a dust bunny comprising largely his own stray hair. It was a good idea later in the shower, where the frankness of their mutual discoveries—*"I like to see the equipment"*—made them feel like schoolkids playing truth or dare. And it was a good idea yet later again in Vinny's bedroom, after the fact of which Vinny no longer felt like crying and Hal needed no relaxation techniques to drift off to sleep.

Sometimes sleeping with someone can be more intimate than making love. Being that vulnerable—naked and unconscious—in someone's company for the first time can forge a bond beyond the mere insertion of tab A into slot B. Sometimes it just feels right. The way you lie up against each other; the way your bodies fit, like you've been meant to fit together that way since forever. The way you can wake up and roll over and think, *Oh, you're here?* and have that be okay. Not just okay, but *right*, deeply and profoundly right, with a rightness that stretches so far in all directions you suddenly can't remember having slept any other way, ever.

It's like flopping the nuts. You don't have to calculate the odds. You know your hand is good.

When Hal and Vinny woke together in the dark, they felt content and whole, the Adam and Eve of Vinny's town house, so in love and unashamed that they didn't even mind the jarring intrusion of Skip Loder's voice as he stood in the doorway of the bedroom and tsked and mocked.

"Well, well, look at these randy raccoons over here," he said. "I leave you kids alone for five minutes and what happens?" He shook his head. "Fucking prom night." He hit the wall switch, flooding the room with light. "Come on, get dressed," he said. "We've got us a date with G-String."

But G-String had a date of his own just then.

A date, as it happened, with death.

13 Draw Run

Washroom attendant Miguel Herredia was a proud man: proud to have made his way to America from his native Nicaragua at an early age and against steep odds; proud to have built a family and found a way to support it; proud to pay taxes and watch cable TV in his adopted homeland; and very proud to have been named Employee of the Month at Night Moves more times than anyone except pole dancer Violet Frenzy, who, it had to be acknowledged, possessed attributes and techniques with which Miguel could not compete. Mostly Miguel Herredia was proud of his washroom, which he strove nightly to keep spotless—no mean feat in a strip club, where bodily fluids fly. Always ready with a fresh towel, a candy, or a condom, Miguel was friendly but firm. He tolerated no nonsense or lewd acts and asked patrons who insisted on doing lines in the stalls to at least flush before they sniffed so that Miguel, staunchly *contra las drogas,* could maintain a veneer of plausible deniability. In his fantasies (and who could work in a washroom night after night for seventeen years without an active and fulsome fantasy life?), Miguel was a military leader, and the men's room was his command bunker. He liked to keep it in fighting trim.

So it was with some irritation that Miguel walked into his washroom that evening and found the floor slick with blood. Miguel, of course, had seen plenty of blood in the bathroom, from cokers' nosebleeds, from the fallout from fistfights, and from working girls hiding the fact of the rag. Blood did not bother Miguel. Blood was part of the cost of doing business. But the *amount* . . . It was going to take quick work with a mop to get this shit cleaned up before somebody stepped in it or, worse, *slipped* in it. This was Miguel's sanctum; it was not meant to be treated so rudely.

Miguel traced the blood to its source: stall number three—the ever-troublesome handicapped stall. Why the state of Nevada saw fit to require such a nuisance in a strip club was beyond him. Spacious and private, it was nothing but an open invitation to trouble: fornicators—threesomes, *foursomes*. . . . He'd once even found an entire craps game going on in there, and he'd be damned if he'd tolerate *gambling* in his washroom. Now he pushed open the door and found a first: a corpse. He recognized the man instantly as a bouncer, one of the club's few *jergadores* who had never given Miguel any trouble, apart from his shoddy aim around the urinal and a blatant disregard for all the prominently placed EMPLOYEES MUST WASH HANDS signs. Miguel's first thought was suicide, for the man on the can sat in an almost normal state of repose, apart from the matte black knife handle protruding from his sternum and the really obscene amount of blood running down his legs and out across Miguel's nice, clean floor. But then Miguel de-

cided that it was highly unlikely for someone to punctu-
ate a suicide by slicing out his own tongue and stuffing
it in his left ear. So, probably, murder.

Much as it pained him to allow outsiders into his
sanctum (never mind letting anyone *see* it in such a
state), Miguel felt constrained to call the police. Though
he knew this was in no way his fault, he suspected that
the event would give Violet a big leg up for this month's
Employee of the Month.

Which leg she would no doubt wrap around some
middle-aged conventioneer's face to seal the deal.

"Well," said Skip, "we'll just have to talk to the stripper." He sat on a red vinyl banquette sipping overpriced
beer from a plastic bottle. "If I can only remember her
name." Skip gravely eyed the nearest pole dancer, not at
all put out, it seemed, at being in a topless joint so lately
the scene of a major violent crime. No sense in letting
all that skin go to waste.

"How 'bout we *don't* talk to her instead?" said Vinny,
neither looking nor not looking at that stripper or any
stripper. "And how did G-String get his job back here in
the first place?"

"Tough union," said Skip. "Apparently if you assault
someone in your workplace, you still get to earn while
you're out on bail." Hal, meanwhile, sat between them
feeling queasy and self-conscious. Strip clubs didn't thrill
him to begin with—he always felt so naked in his need—
but to be here now, with Vinny, in the first throes of
whatever it was they were in the first throes of, well, it
just seemed wrong. "It's on the tip of my mind," continued Skip, his brain grinding in frustration. "I know it
was something made up."

"A stripper using a fake name," remarked Vinny. "What are the chances of that?"

"Patty Cake . . . Pearl Necklace? Something like that."

"Look, let me ask you," said Vinny, "don't you think a tongue in an ear is a pretty obvious *keep out* sign?"

"Oh, we don't even know that's true," said Skip. "Rumors just fucking fly in a dive like this."

"Well, it's no rumor that G-String's dead. And no coincidence, either. Someone doesn't want anyone chasing this shit down."

"What, you're gonna fold your hand every time someone puts in a little bitty raise?" Skip beckoned the dancer with a dollar and tucked it into her panties. "That's not how we play poker."

"Skip, this isn't poker. This is real—"

"Poker!" shouted Skip suddenly. "Penny Poker! That's the chick's name!"

"Yeah, that's great," said Vinny. "Listen—"

But there was no listen in Skip just then.

And half an hour later, they were in a private room getting a private dance and a full debrief from one Penny Poker, who, for the right price, had no difficulty baring her breasts and spilling her guts at the same time.

To hear Penny tell it, most guys she dances for want nothing more than to sit there silently, nostrils flaring and eyes open wide, while she bars them up. She knows what they're doing. They're imprinting: storing up the sight of her for later, for the first convenient moment when they can beat off to the tune of her tits and ass and crotch. That's fine with Penny. She likes being the object of their quiet desire. It turns the tables on the whole man/woman power thing, makes her feel like the boss for a change.

Every now and then, though, says Penny, you get you a talker, and these come broadly in two types: your boasters and your confessors. Boasters have image problems, and you can leverage your tips by just admiring whatever they want admired. Confessors have guilt problems, and a liberal application of "It's all right, honey" is all they need for their good time.

Whether this Edouard character was a boaster or a confessor Penny couldn't for sure say. He seemed to split the difference: cacklingly pleased by his role in the conspiracy, but fearful that "they" would find out, and then his ass would be grass. Penny gathered that there was a wife in the picture somewhere who at once hated the poker Edouard wasted his time playing (when he wasn't wasting his time barring up at Night Moves) yet loved the proverbial cheese he brought home. It was in the name of bringing home said cheese that Edouard decided to join what he described as some mysterioso "Project X." Penny wasn't particularly into any Project X, but in her experience, the more they talk the more they toke, so she gave Edouard his rein. All it took, really, was a noncommittal "Isn't that interesting, honey?" to open his file and start the data dump. Of course, you couldn't be sure that a word of it was true, for strip clubs, like pokeys and poker tables, were rife with self-aggrandizers, shameless liars, and the genially misguided who could literally not distinguish what was real from what existed only in their minds.

This much at least was clear, or anyway claimed: that Edouard had won a seat in the Poker Apocalypse, and that that got him an offer to join Team Dragic. According to Penny, Edouard couldn't stop talking about the "lock edge," something he said would nut him a huge payday whether he won the tournament or not. He didn't, in fact, expect to finish in the money at all, but it didn't matter, because the fix was in and everyone on Team Dragic was gonna get so well it was sick.

"So what is it?" asked Hal. "Stake deal? Percentage? Common bankroll? Buyout?" These words meant nothing to Penny, so she responded by touching her breasts. Vinny, though, noticed the gleam in Hal's eye. It spooked her, for she'd often seen a similar gleam in Guy's eye and recognized it as his "trouble with too far" look. She wondered just how deep recklessness ran in the Harris blood.

Penny wracked her brain, eager to keep the meter running as long as possible. Plus also, this was fun. Usually her job was just *stroke*. Stroke the ego or stroke the winkie, one way or another, it was all about the stroke. But this was cool. This was spy shit. She remembered one other thing. "He said something about a draw run."

"Draw run?" asked Skip. "What the hell's a draw run?"

"Could he have meant dry run?" asked Vinny, despite herself. Maybe there was a little "too far" in her, too.

"That's it," said Penny. "Dry run. At Grossinger's. That's that Jew joint, right?"

"It's a Catskill-themed casino," said Skip. "Not sure you'd call it a Jew joint."

"Well, you should see if they have a poker game there or something, because he said they were gonna do a dry run at the Jew joint."

They asked her a few more questions, but it quickly became clear that Penny had given them everything of value she had "except, you know, the usual." But the boys weren't interested in "the usual," and though Penny cocked a speculative eyebrow in Vinny's direction, Vinny just patted the girl's knee and said, "Have a good night."

* * *

Slaughter Johnson's three young protégés debriefed him the next morning in the cozy confines of his Airstream. He was not amused. He thought he'd made it clear to Hal that winning the Poker Apocalypse rested more in Hal's state of mind than in the gamesmanship going on around him.

"But if the fix is in—" protested Hal.

"Fuck the fix," said Slaughter. "I told you before, Hal, you can't get caught up in that shit." He paced up and down in the Airstream. With all four of them crammed into the aluminum shell, there wasn't all that much room to pace.

"So what am I supposed to do, just let 'em do what they want? Pass hand information? Dump chips? I can beat anyone, Slaughter, but I can't beat everyone."

"And he can't go in there blind," added Skip. "That's just stupid."

Slaughter cast a sidelong glance at Skip Loder and said, "Josh, I've got a feeling that this whole big stack of stupid has your name on it."

"Now come on now, man. That's just not nice."

"Dad," said Vinny, "it's done. Let's let it go and move on." Something in her voice made Slaughter's eyebrows arch. She was, he noticed, sitting thigh to thigh with Hal, more densely packed than even the narrow dimensions of the Airstream required.

Skip, meanwhile, had pulled out his cell phone and hit a number on speed dial.

"Who are you calling?" asked Hal.

"Grossinger's, duh."

"You've got Grossinger's on speed dial?" asked Vinny.

"Honey, I got 'em all on speed dial. A poker player checks games like a surfer checks waves. And as I recall . . ." Just then someone answered on the other end. Skip asked a couple of quick questions, then closed his phone with a satisfied snap. "Yep," he said, "that's what I thought. Guess what Grossinger's has on this week: the Mini Apocalypse. Same starting chips. Same blind structure. Only a hundred times less buy-in."

"So, a grand," said Hal. He turned to Slaughter. "What do you think?"

Johnson just shook his head. "It should be abundantly clear by now that I am not the boss of you. You'll play where you want to play"—he looked at his daughter from beneath his white caterpillar eyebrows—"and sleep where you want to sleep."

"Daddy!"

"You think I don't know?" Again he shook his head. "The two of you practically oozing for each other." He continued, "What I'm afraid of, Hal, is that you've lost your focus. Are you in this to vex Dragic? Find out who killed Guy? Or just ride the fucking isness of it all? I don't know what your motivation is, and I don't think you do, either. But let's not kid ourselves: you start turning over rocks, pretty soon you're gonna find you a scorpion." He sighed—sighing up the accumulated years of his life, his profession, his impaired parenthood. "I don't care if you get yourself stung, but if you get Vinny—"

"Daddy, you're not the—"

"When they put me in the ground, honey. That's when I won't be the boss of you." He turned back to Hal. "Hal, you're the most naturally gifted poker player I've ever met." Hal reddened under Slaughter's praise. "Trouble is, for you this isn't about poker—but while you're playing, you'd better *make* it about poker, or you won't last ten minutes no matter how gifted you are. As for the rest of it, Project X"—he snorted a laugh—"fine. Keep your eyes open. Try not to let it make you crazy."

"What do I do if I find something hinky?" asked Hal.

"I don't know," said Slaughter. "We'll drive off that bridge when we come to it."

"*We?*" asked Hal.

"Awful lot of rocks out there, son. You can't turn 'em all over by yourself."

14 Herding Cats

Grossinger's Casino owed its theme to the Thimk Tank, a market research firm that specialized in what it called "imagitising," a synthesis of polling data, focus group input, and statistical analysis used to formulate product branding that was at once high concept, eye-catching, and almost completely wrongheaded. In tapping Borscht Belt nostalgia, the Thimk Tank set out to wed to casino gaming the thinnest cultural vein this side of "friends of the autoharp." Were it not for Grossinger's choice location—literally in the shadow of the Cortland Casino, and thereby blessed with its spillover traffic—the joint would have long since joined on the scrap heap of bonehead marketing such other Thimk Tank missteps as Ford's (Dinner!) Theater and the Ritalin Kids® Action Figure series.

But the Mini Apocalypse, though, that was a good idea. Piggybacking on the frenzy of greed created by the upcoming Big One next door, the Mini stood poised to be the largest, most successful poker tournament Grossinger's had ever hosted. By the time Hal, Vinny, Skip, and Slaughter rolled in, the registration line stretched all the way from the Adirondack Ballroom back past the Dirty Dancing Disco and the Woodstock Arcade, damn near to Shecky's Deli. The four waited until the last minute to register, and so got seats at the final tournament tables to be filled. Since these would be the first to break as the tournament went along, they hoped each to get looks at a couple of different table lineups at least, assuming they played well enough to stay alive as the field thinned. Even at that it was a daunting task, for, short of obvious whipsaws or clumsily marked cards, cheating was notoriously hard to spot at the poker table.

"If they're signaling, it'll be subtle," said Slaughter. "Maybe the way they make their bets, or maybe something they say."

"What, like, 'I've got pocket aces'?" asked Skip.

Slaughter glowered. "You taking this seriously, Josh?"

"Oh, absolutely. It's just . . . how will I know if 'Damn it's cold in here' means 'Damn it's cold' or 'I'm sitting on a monster'?"

"Something just won't smell right," said Slaughter. "You won't even know what it is. You'll just know." Hal remembered Guy's line about a rift in the fabric of space. "But either way it's distracting," continued Slaughter. "That's the problem with gaffed games. You don't know for sure if they're gaffed, but you spend so much time fretting and sweating it, you forget to play your game."

"Why do I suddenly feel like I'm herding cats?" asked Skip.

"Do the best you can," said Hal. "Remember, it's information we're after here, but information flows both ways. Whatever you see, whatever you discover, keep it to yourself."

"Gotta make adjustments," said Skip.

"No! If you adjust, you'll tip your hand."

"So I'm supposed to lose on purpose?"

"Play your game, Skip," said Hal. "Yours, not theirs."

"Whatever. I still bet I last longer than you."

"Just keep your eyes open and see what you see, okay?"

"A big-ass herd of cats."

Like the Apocalypse, the Mini was structured to give participants lots of play, with long levels and gradually rising blinds. Normally in a tournament such as this, a strong, thoughtful player's first order of business would be to identify and attack the dead money in the field. For some, this meant establishing a superaggressive image and attempting to steamroll the table. Others would adopt a more measured approach, teasing chips out of the loose and weak through value bets and takeaway bluffs. Hal had quickly developed a taste for the former approach, but the downside of this strategy was the risk of an early bustout, for weak and loose players are gamblers by nature, and you never knew when one would call you down—and run you over—with an inferior, or even vastly inferior, holding.

Slaughter had taught Hal not to fear the prospect of an early bustout. By Slaughter's logic, if your plan was to come out fast, you had to have faith in that plan, and execute it fearlessly, regardless of the outcome. Sometimes it wouldn't work out, but it was better to have a plan, any plan, than to lurch through the tournament from hand to hand meekly reacting to whatever your foes shoved in your face. Of course, no smart player gets so stuck on his template that he ignores his table's reality, its hazards and opportunities. But a game plan gives you a point of reference: a script to work from and improvise off of. In this case, their game plan would be more conservative than usual, for their fact-finding mission required that they go deep into the tournament and get as many looks at as many players as possible, as they set out to discover that which was hidden, deeply disguised . . . or maybe not even there at all.

Hal was assigned to table 123, not even in the Adirondack Ballroom, but in a spillover room, the adjacent, much smaller Oneonta. As play began, there were only three other people seated at his table—typical for the opening moments of a large field tournament, with some players stuck in traffic, some kibitzing with friends, some off grabbing a last smoke, some yet lingering in lucrative cash games (or trying to get unstuck before they disengaged), and some just letting the damn tournament start without them because why the hell not?

Of course, players not yet seated still had to pay their blinds, the mechanics of which were handled by the dealer at each table, who plucked one (small blind) or two (big blind) green $25 chips off each absent player's stack in turn. The players already seated could be counted on to go after that dead money, for this was poker, and in poker you don't leave free money lying on the table, even only $75 in blinds in a tournament with a starting sum of ten grand in tournament chips. While Hal understood the impetus to attack undefended blinds, he also knew that picking up 75 chips, or 750, or even 7,500 during the opening moments was no guarantee, or even a reliable predictor, of success. After all, it wasn't like you could get a little ahead and cash out. You were in the tournament till you won it or busted. That's the way it was, and that's what prompted Slaughter to say, "You can't win a tournament at the first level, but you sure as shit can lose one."

So when, on the third hand of the tournament, Hal got 7♦6♦ in the small blind, with the big blind's seat vacant to his left and the player on his right raising to

$100 on the button, his first inclination was to fold. But then, as is routine for good players, he did the math. With $175 already in the pot (the big blind, his small blind, and the raiser's bet), his $75 call would give him pot odds of 175 to 75, or 2.3 to 1. Against a hand like A-A, he'd be crushed—a 3-to-1 underdog—but in a steal situation like this the raiser was much more likely to have half a hand like K-J, or even nothing but pure cheese, in which case Hal was probably no worse than 3 to 2 against, so he was getting the right price to call. He thought about reraising but felt that that move would be too transparently a resteal; he'd likely get called and have to play the rest of the hand out of position, so he decided to just call and see a flop.

5♣4♥3♦. *Oh, my.*

Hal thought about the hand he hit. He knew that flopping a straight to a starting hand like 7-6 was about a one-in-a-hundred shot. . . . Rare, but not supernova rare. Now the question was how to exploit the windfall. The typical play would be to telegraph weakness by checking and letting his opponent make the expected continuation bet in position. But, "Typical plays are for typical players," Guy used to say. Hal paused to think things through, and to check out the foe he was facing.

The bettor was a man of middle years wearing an oversized golf cap with the legend "Nickel City Dodge" in dumb gold brocade, and a yellowed white polo shirt with the name "Bud" stitched on the breast pocket. Hal recognized Nickel City as the nickname for Buffalo, New York, and so provisionally assigned the value of "tourist" to his foe. Of course, you can't tell where a person's from just by his clothes; for all Hal knew, these could be thrift-store finds, or the last remnants of what the ex-wife chucked on the lawn the day she threw him out for good. So Hal hunted for more information and was rewarded with . . . the time. The man's watch, he noticed, was set three hours ahead. *In from back east, then. Either fresh off the plane or on so short a turnaround that he can't be bothered to reset his watch. Probably eager,* thought Hal. *Maybe too eager.*

Quickly sorting through all the available information, Hal concluded that if the guy had any piece of the flop—A-5, say—he'd definitely call along, possibly even overplay his hand. So Hal bet $150, a little less than two-thirds the size of the pot, trying to make it look like a stop-and-go steal, and hoping that Buffalo Bud had either a real hand or the will to get frisky. After thinking for a long moment, Bud called. Bud's chest, Hal noticed, rose and fell steeply beneath his polo shirt. *He's sitting on a monster,* mused Hal. *Two pair or a set. He wants me to do his betting for him.* Some players, Hal knew, were capable of faking strength with the deep-breathing act, but Hal didn't take Bud for that level of actor. Part of this was just how Bud presented himself: as a straightforward player. Part was Hal's bedrock assumption of everyone he played against: kosher until proven tricky, according to the received wisdom of *Swoop and Pummel.* More to the point, as this was only the third hand of the tournament, Bud couldn't yet know whether Hal was the sort of player to buy a fake-breathing tell. So Hal took it at face value, and while he was currently ahead in the hand, if the board paired on the turn or the river, he was prepared to shut down. *You can't win a tournament at the first level, but you sure as shit can lose one.*

But the turn was a perfect brick, the K♠. Now there was no flush draw, and if Bud was drawing to a full house or quads, he had either four ways to improve his two pair or ten ways to improve his set. Hal measured the pot: $550. If Bud had the set, he'd certainly pay off another bet, for though he was badly trailing in the hand, he had every reason to believe he was ahead. Then again, Hal didn't want Bud reraising all in, for his mission in this tournament was to go deep and gather information, not to bust out on the third hand, no matter how big a favorite he was. He realized that he was working at cross purposes to himself and wondered how such inner conflict would be interpreted by his foe. He bet $500, a little less than the size of the pot.

Bud delayed a long time before calling, and Hal read the delay as a theatrical stall, not legitimate doubt. *He still thinks he has the best hand. He thinks he's milking me.* The river card was the 2♥, giving Hal the nuts. Hal didn't figure that this changed the dynamic: if Bud could call the turn, he could call again on the river. So Hal bet $1,500 and waited for Buffalo Bud to act. Once again, the man went into an extended stall.

Finally, he said, "I'm all in."

Really?

Hal double-checked the board, making sure he hadn't misread it, then pushed his chips forward, saying, "I call."

Bud's face fell. "That damn deuce caught you up, didn't it?" he said, turning over an ace and a deuce. "Guess we split the pot."

Guess we don't, thought Hal. He flipped over his hand. Bud's eyes grew wide. "You . . . what? You called my raise with that? How could you call my raise with that?"

Hal didn't answer, for Slaughter had taught him early on, "When you lose, don't whine, and when you win, don't gloat." He was aware, though, that Bud had made a couple of mistakes in the play of the hand: preflop, he had priced Hal in with a minimum raise; also, he had completely failed to consider the possibility of the higher straight. Still, Hal knew that anything he said would be needling, and what's the point of giving the needle to

someone who's just busted out? Nor did he have the opportunity, for Buffalo Bud had already stumbled away
from the table, shocked to have squandered his $1,000
buy-in in just three hands—though, of course, if he'd
lasted all day and failed to make the money, his financial return would have been exactly the same.

Well, mused Hal as he stacked his chips, *that's that
with that. Too bad I'm not in it to win it.* But with an early
double-up of his starting stack, he was now much better
situated to build steady control over his table and go
deep into the tournament.

Beyond that, he'd just have to see.

Five hours and many broken tables and seat changes
later, Hal was starting to get frustrated. His quest for evidence of collusion was, so far, a dry well. He'd seen
some curious and questionable moves, but nothing he
couldn't chalk up to flawed logic, misguided optimism,
or just plain bad poker. Two players had tangled in a
raising war, trapping a third between them in a classic
whipsaw, but both players had real hands, pocket aces
versus pocket kings, and the poor guy in the middle was
on A-K, so no collusion there. As for verbal cues, all the
chat he'd overheard seemed to be nothing more than
the usual mix of banter, blather, and cliché. A boister-
ous big man sitting at Hal's latest table, for example,
carried on several conversations at once, seemingly giving the tournament only a fraction of his attention. Introducing himself as "Big Mo," he asked everyone their
names and peppered them with questions about their
background, philosophy of poker, taste in music, opinion on world affairs. Though Hal found Mo's constant
yack a little irritating, it could hardly be called suspicious.

Hal had no idea how Vinny and the others were doing. He had caught a glimpse of Slaughter moving between tables on the far side of the Adirondack Ballroom, but that was a while ago, before the last break. He wondered if any of them had had any more luck than he, or were they all herding cats as well? There was nothing going on here. People playing poker, that's all; he was wasting his time.

A player to Hal's right busted out, and the seat stayed vacant for a few minutes until a tiny dapper man approached the table, big rack of chips in one hand and a clutch of seat cushions in the other. He stood barely three feet tall, but piled the cushions carefully on his chair, then clambered atop, attaining a perch like a lifeguard overlooking a swimming pool. Big Mo greeted him effusively. "Hey, Mouse!" boomed Mo. "Mouse Skowron, everyone. He's kind of a big deal."

"Give me a break, Mo," said Mouse. "How can I experience ego death if you keep telling everyone how wonderful I am?" And while Mouse's response seemed good-natured enough, Hal thought he caught a whiff of something behind it, like maybe Mouse didn't want that much attention drawn to him. Many players prefer to sneak in unnoticed, especially if they're going to try to sell themselves as less schooled or skilled than they are. Hal figured that Mouse was just annoyed at having his cover blown or some intended image play taken away.

At least that's what he thought at first.

Mouse set an iPod on the table, plugged in, adjusted some settings, then sat waiting for a hand, drumming his fingers on the felt in time to the music he heard.

Hal didn't get the whole iPod thing. Poker, as he had come to understand it, was about gathering and sorting available information, and he knew from his own experience that there were often tells you could hear but not see. Voice cracks. Unguarded sighs. The uncharacteristically loud pronouncement of a bet size. Why deny yourself access to that data stream? Just to stave off boredom with the rockin' sounds of Flash Cadillac and the Continental Kids? It didn't make sense. Of course, if there was a loudmouth like Big Mo at your table, or someone intentionally trying to rattle you, you might want to tune him out, but for most players, it just seemed like the buzz of poker alone wasn't enough. They needed yet more stimulation, and found it in music. Hal wondered if the day would come when he'd become that jaded.

Hands came and went. Mouse Skowron proved to be a moderately aggressive player, adept at adopting orphan pots while staying out of dicey situations. He gave an appropriately wide berth to the other aggressive players at the table: Big Mo; a cadaverous bald man who called everyone "Sport," and so was called Sport in return; one or two others; and Hal himself. Curiously, to Hal's eyes, a couple of the players showed Mouse similar respect—more respect, in fact, than his play initially seemed to warrant. It must be as Mo had said, that Mouse was "kind of a big deal." Some people didn't seem to want to mess with him at all.

Sport, for example, raised in early position to three times the big blind, with Mouse calling along behind and everyone else folding. Though the flop wasn't particularly threatening, 9-4-2 rainbow, Sport took his sweet time deciding what to do. Mouse waited patiently, tapping his fingers idly on the padded table rail. Finally, Sport checked, then folded to Mouse's bet. It was no big deal, just another hand of poker, but when it happened a couple more times, it struck Hal as strange. This sort of play—preflop strong, postflop weak—was not characteristic of Sport's approach. Nor was *raise, then fold* in any sense sound tournament strategy. Sport, Hal decided, must know something about the strength of Mouse's game that Hal didn't know. Hal dialed into the tiny man's play and watched him attentively.

Once, back in high school, Hal and Guy had tried to form a band. Hal played a fair guitar, but Guy's drumming was abysmal, an active offense to Hal's immaculate sense of cadence. "Keep the fucking beat!" he yelled so many times that one day Guy just got fed up. He dropped his drumsticks, called Hal a "rhythm Nazi," and walked away. So ended Narcolepsy's bid to be the next big thing out of Pittsburgh.

Hal no longer played guitar, but he could keep a beat in his sleep, and the more he watched Mouse's fingers tapping on the table, the odder the action seemed to be, for his tempo was all over the place. What could Mouse be listening to that had such a shifting time signature? Zappa? Some sort of jazz/samba/polka fusion?

Or maybe . . .

Maybe nothing at all.

Hal felt a rush wash over him. Was this it? Evidence of the dry run? He looked around the tournament area. iPods were ubiquitous. Grooving to unheard music, Hal realized, would give perfect, innocuous cover to someone tapping out a code. And such an easy hack! Different fingers could represent different suits, and the number of taps could equal card rank. Or the data could be buried deeper than that, much deeper. Maybe the fingers just tell you to look at the eyes, or the elbows, or how the chips are stacked. Maybe . . . Who knows?

Hal continued to watch his adversary, but he felt suddenly self-conscious, unnecessarily overt, as if the mere act of observing would spook Mouse and shut him down. Moreover, as Slaughter had predicted, focusing on the suspected hacker drew his attention away from the game. A couple of careless loose calls later, Hal was at risk of short stacking himself. That wasn't the game plan—not now that he had his quarry in sight.

So Hal got back to business, giving first priority to his playing decisions. He knew he couldn't crack the code right now anyhow, not unless it was trivially simple—unlikely—and not unless he got a look at some revealed hands to measure against. With that, his understanding of the situation took a quantum, but dismaying, leap forward. It would do him no good to know that the fix was in, not unless he could discover how, exactly, the fix was being applied.

It could be anywhere, *everywhere*. Here's Mouse drumming his fingers in time to his iPod—or not. There's Big Mo talking about his vacation home. It's right off Route 99—or is he conveying pocket nines? The woman beside him adjusts the straps of her sundress. Is she transmitting hand values, or just getting comfy? At the next table over, someone makes a huge all-in bet and another player calls, then mucks without showing. Was that a bad call . . . or a chip dump? Hal felt paranoia creeping in and chided himself for it. Nevertheless, the feeling remained.

Once you become convinced there are monsters under your bed, monsters are pretty much all you see.

15 Hello, Queef

Hal held pocket jacks under the gun, a problematic hand in problematic position. Had he been further around back, he'd be inclined to raise with this notorious "little big pair," but here he just called, hoping to start a limpfest and generate the right kind of odds to draw to a set. Big Mo called, as did Sport. The small blind completed. Mouse tapped the table with his index finger, indicating "check"—and then continued to tap in his now customary, oddly cadenced way.

The flop came Q♣J♦7♣. The small blind and Mouse both checked quickly, putting the action on Hal. With flush and straight draws out there against him, he knew he needed to bet to protect his trip jacks, but unless he hugely overbet the pot, it might be difficult to close out the draws. A call from any one of them could give the right price to either or both of the others. Moreover, he had become certain that Sport was more than casually interested in Mouse's finger tapping. It was a long shot, Hal knew, but perhaps the play of this hand could give him the link he was looking for. Hal hated giving his foes correct calling odds—considered it one of poker's cardinal sins—but he reminded himself that today, in this tournament, he had a different agenda. Without losing control of the betting, then, he decided to try to get to a showdown as cheaply as possible, so he led at the flop with a half-pot-size bet.

Hal was, he realized, already lost in the hand. He had flopped huge but was giving draws easy calls. This sort of play was uncharacteristically meek for him, and once again he felt he was working at cross purposes to himself. He was also aware of the danger of Heisenberging the action: skewing others' play of the hand by his own deviation from optimal. Oh, well. The bet was out there now. He'd just have to wait and see what happened.

Sport called. The small blind folded. Mouse called. Hal hadn't learned much with his bet. He had, in fact, muddied the waters quite substantially, for the small size of his bet might have encouraged not only draws to call, but also hands like queen-little or even pocket tens. Inwardly, Hal had to laugh. He was certainly making a hash of the hand.

The turn was the T♣, putting a third club on board and completing a straight for anyone holding A-K, K-9, or 9-8. Hal knew that one of his jacks was a club. Unlike many other players at his level of experience, he didn't need to check, for early in his training he had mastered what Slaughter called good card hygiene, where you look at your cards once, memorize them, cap them with a chip or some other kind of card protector, and then never lift them off the felt again for the duration of the hand.

Mouse checked. Hal figured it unlikely that Mouse would check a made hand here (except possibly 9-8, the idiot end of the straight), for while Hal believed Mouse was tricky enough to go for the check-raise, he didn't think Mouse could rate Hal as frisky enough to bet into so scary a board. No, Mouse would be content to take a free card here.

Hal looked left and saw Sport's hand straying to his chips. *Okay*, thought Hal, *there's a bettor.* He tapped the felt to indicate a check. As predicted, Sport bet out, two-thirds of the pot. Mouse called quickly, which put the action back on Hal. He suspected he was facing at least one made hand, possibly two, but he still had outs, since any queen, nine, or three on the river would give him a full house; the case jack would give him quads. Even if he wasn't leading at that moment, his redraws were getting the right price to call. Hal called.

The river was intriguing: the 6♣. Hal noticed Sport flinching as the card hit the felt. *He just got beat,* thought Hal.

Mouse checked. This was to be expected, for if he'd been on a bad straight or a weak flush on the turn, he had to figure himself for trailing here. Hal wondered if he could take this pot with a big bet. Mouse certainly looked weak (though looks can be deceiving), and Sport . . . well, Sport looked ready to cry. *He must really think his hand's no good.* Of course, Hal realized, there was always a chance that Sport was selling a fake-weak tell, which Hal would know soon enough if he checked and Sport bet. But his real motivation for checking lay in his original plan for the hand: to get to the river as cheaply as possible and see what everybody had.

But there was a problem with that plan. If Hal checked and Sport checked behind, protocol would call for each of them to reveal their hand in turn, first Mouse, then Hal, then Sport. Theoretically, any player at the table could ask to see all remaining hands at this point—a rule designed to protect against collusion, interestingly enough—but in practice, usually someone turned over the winning hand and everyone mucked without show-ing. Hal could thus get a look at one of the hands, but not both—not unless he asked to see all hands, which would betray him as . . . uhm . . . someone on the look-out for collusion. He wondered if he could sell ordi-nary curiosity: *Dealer, this is just so darn interesting, I'd like to see what everyone's got.* He decided he'd have to try. He would check, and then if Sport checked behind, he'd ask to see all hands. Slaughter had warned him not to call attention to himself, but he didn't believe it would blow his cover too badly—people asked to see hands all the time. Still, if he had stumbled into part of Dragic's dry run, this was bound to sound the alarm. Well, that's poker: *You don't bet, you don't get.* "I check," he said, planning to ask to see all hands if Sport checked behind.

But Sport didn't check . . . exactly. With a shrug and a mumbled, "I can't win," Sport spun his cards toward the muck.

And Big Mo stopped them!

His big, fleshy hand smacked down on the cards, halting their progress toward the discard pile. "Dealer," said Mo, "I want to see all hands."

"You can't see my hand," barked Sport. "I folded."

"You didn't fold," said Mo. "You're last to act and you didn't bet, so that's a check. Three players checked on the end. Dealer, I want to see all hands."

"Give me those fucking cards!" said Sport, suddenly frantically angry.

But Mo just kept his beefy hand on Sport's discards. "Careful, you're gonna get yourself F-bombed," he said, alluding to the common tournament practice of penal-izing players who say "fuck" by sending them away from the table for twenty minutes, during which time their antes and blinds continue to be drawn from their stack.

Early in a tournament, this is merely annoying; late, it can be fatal.

"Fuck you!" shouted Sport. "Dealer, I want my hand mucked. Call the floorman."

The dealer called for a tournament director. Hal glanced to his right and saw Mouse trying with undisguised urgency to catch Sport's eye. But Sport was in full rant mode now, and there was nothing for it but to wait for the tournament director's decision. In due time, a floorman came over and of course ruled that the hand had to be shown, but not before he admonished Big Mo to keep his beefy mitts off other players' cards.

"Sorry," said Mo with not the slightest hint of remorse. "My bad."

The TD then instructed the dealer to show the hands. The dealer turned over Mouse's first. He held the 7♣8♣; the river had given him a straight flush. Hal turned over his pocket jacks, then turned his attention to Sport's holding.

Mo lifted his hand off Sport's cards. Sport made a desperate grab for them. Hal couldn't imagine what he planned to do—snatch them and run away? Tear them to unrecognizable shreds?— But the point was moot, because Mo slapped his big hand back down on the cards before Sport could get them. "Back off," Mo growled. He looked up at the tournament director. The TD nodded, and Mo flipped over the cards.

A♣K♠.

"Nut straight on the turn, nut flush on the river," said Big Mo dryly. "Good laydown."

"Fuck you," said Sport again. Which, with the floorman standing right there, got him his penalty. He stormed away from the table, furious and hot with embarrassment. The dealer pushed the pot to Mouse, who seemed to be working very hard to keep his face a mask.

Hal looked at Big Mo, who shot him a smile and a quick wink.

"How do you fold that hand?" asked Skip. "No way in hell do you fold that hand."

They were sitting in Shecky's Deli, not far from the tournament floor, killing the final few minutes of the dinner break. Hal was toying with the last of his club sandwich. Vinny sat next to him, casually close. Slaughter and Skip occupied the other side of the booth. "You do if you know you're beat," said Slaughter quietly. "Which, apparently, he did."

"But there wasn't even a bet!"

"And I think that was a mistake," Slaughter continued. "If I understand the situation correctly..." He turned and looked at Hal.

"You know what I know," Hal said, with a shrug.

"Then Mouse should have bet to protect Sport. Given him a chance to fold."

"Maybe he expected Hal to bet," said Vinny. She had busted out early in the tournament, her aces cracked by runner-runner two pair, and had seen nothing suspicious in her short time in play.

"Evidently he did," said Slaughter. "But he shouldn't have counted on that. The problem is position. A classic whipsaw has the victim caught between two aggressive bettors, but if Mouse doesn't lead at the pot, and Hal doesn't rise to the bait, then it's on Sport to lead out. If he does, though, Mouse can't raise, for fear of losing Hal in the whipsaw. So he'd have to just call and hope that Hal calls behind. Like I said, I think he made a mistake."

"As did Sport by check-mucking," said Hal. "If he bets a little and Mouse raises, he can get away from a hand he knows to be a loser, and nobody's the wiser. If he bets and Mouse just calls in order to get a call out of me, then Sport just looks way unlucky with his nut flush." Hal paused for a moment, then continued. "Know what I think? I think Sport lost the plot. I think he was so freaked out by Mouse making a straight flush that he forgot to play his role."

"And so left himself open to exposure," added Vinny.

"Fucking mirplo," said Skip. Like Vinny, Skip had had a very short tournament trip, though he was the instrument of his own demise when he pushed top pair, top kicker into an overpair and lost his whole stack on nothing less than a reckless adventure. It was a move at odds with every goal they had set for this tournament, and one that Slaughter would have labeled pure bonehead. As he'd written in *Swoop and Pummel*, "When all the money goes in the middle, top/top shouldn't be good. If it is, someone made a mistake."

So Skip had mirploed himself right out of the tournament, but in the nature of poker players, he had been vague about his bustout and blamed bad luck, not bad play, for his early exit. Skip had a strong poker game—when he brought it—but he had too much faith in the power of the big bet. Until he learned that you can't blow better hands off a pot (and it was an open question as to how many iterations of this lesson he would need), he would never be better than an occasional tournament winner; greatness would elude him.

Slaughter was still alive in the tournament, having survived an early card drought and built his stack back to an average position. He'd seen almost nothing of note during his hours of play. But one incident did come back to mind, triggered by Hal's tale of Mouse and the iPod. At the time Slaughter hadn't thought anything of it, but now, in the context . . .

"There was a guy at my first table before it broke," said Slaughter. "I think he was working the iPod hack, too, only with a Blackberry. Never stopped banging away on it."

"Which only makes him like everybody else in the world these days," offered Skip.

"Yes," said Slaughter, "except for two things. First, he had his Blackberry up on the felt, by his chips."

"Mostly they do that below the table, out of sight," said Vinny, with a laugh. "The new courtesy."

"Mostly they do," agreed Slaughter. "Plus, this guy was no good. Slow . . . deliberate . . . almost clumsy."

"Did he use his thumbs?" asked Vinny.

"Not exclusively."

"So then . . ." she thought it through. "Different fingers for the suits, and you just count the keystrokes for rank."

"I don't know," said Skip. "It sounds a little obvious, doesn't it?"

"Purloined Letter," said Hal. "Hide in plain sight."

"It's the dry run, right?" said Vinny. "Maybe they're testing what works and what doesn't."

"Or maybe it's a false lead," said Skip.

"Or maybe it's nothing," said Hal.

"I don't suppose," said Skip, "that he was kind enough to tap seven times with his left pinkie and then turn over the seven of clubs."

"Sadly, no." Slaughter sighed. "That's the proximate difficulty, kids. Everywhere we look, we don't know if we're looking at something or nothing." The more he thought about Sport's gaffe, the more he realized how extraordinarily lucky Hal had been to witness it. "Well," he said at last, "at least we got one gift."

Hal looked at his watch. The dinner break was over. "Yeah, we did," he said. "Let's go find another."

Slaughter and Hal made their way back to their respective tables. Vinny departed, off to free Minty from solitary confinement in the town house and give him a run at some squirrels. Skip stayed behind to sweat Slaughter and Hal.

When play resumed, Hal picked up where he left off, playing the sort of selective-aggressive poker appropriate to the middle stages of a large-field no-limit hold'em tournament. As the blinds and antes rose, he increased the frequency of his steal attempts to something on the order of twice per orbit. This put him in some dicey situations, such as raising under the gun with 9-8 suited, but as long as no one seemed interested in playing back at him—and so far no one did—he'd continue to grab what pots he could. Such steals gave him the luxury of folding his own crap-hand blinds without losing ground against the rising price of play.

Hal had noticed before, and at this moment found the notion reinforced, that players who made it this deep into a tournament routinely and conveniently triaged themselves into two groups: those content with an any-money finish, and those committed to going all the way. The former group—Scaredy Scaredersons, Skip called them—could be counted on to screw down their starting requirements, avoid confrontations, and generally fold like origami cranes in the face of betting pressure. The latter group was scarce at Hal's table, so he was able to build his stack by winning without a fight. On the downside, these players were so kosher, so straightforward, that Hal could barely imagine any of them participating in a giant conspiracy to fix the tournament's outcome. They just didn't seem up to it.

Still . . . confirmation bias . . . if you stare long enough, that bare tree branch scraping against your bedroom window will start to look like a witch's hand. Did the player in seat six really have a cold, or was her incessant sniffing and snuffing laden with hidden meaning? *Cough once for hearts, twice for spades. . . .* Did the fat cowboy in the big blind really misread the board, or was his busted flush merely a means of shipping his chips to other stacks? Were the dealers in on it? Hal knew it wasn't *that* unlikely for a foe to get pocket aces, queens, and kings on successive hands, but still . . . *Come on, tree branch, be a tree branch! Stop driving me fucking nuts!*

After a flurry of bustouts, Hal's table broke, and he racked his chips and walked across the tournament floor looking for his new seat assignment. There were now fewer than fifteen tables left; sometime in the past hour, the bubble had burst, and Hal, along with all the remaining players, had made the money. He'd been so wrapped up in hack hunting that he hadn't even noticed. *Maybe the way to win,* thought Hal, *is just don't play to win.* The notion brought a wry smile to his lips as he found his new table and planted himself in seat three, out on the dealer's port wing. But his smile died when he looked down the length of the table and found Marko Dragic staring him down.

"Hello, queef," said Dragic. "Welcome to the game."

16 Aces Over

Baseball signs are a great example of codes that work. You look at the other team's third-base coach and you have no idea what he's communicating to the batter or runner as he touches his crotch, licks his fingers, lifts the bill of his cap. What does it all mean? You don't know . . . you *can't* know . . . unless you have the key to the code. *The next sign after I touch my nose is the one that counts. Everything else is just noise. And if I wipe my chest at the end, that means the opposite. Got it, rook?*

Codes in poker are a much trickier proposition, in that you have to hide not just the meaning of the code but the fact of its transmission. Start flashing signs like a third-base coach and you're bound to get some askance looks or possibly a boot in the butt. So if you're designing codes to convey hand holdings at a poker table, you have to nest them in the conventions of poker table behavior, and there really aren't that many things that are normally done at a poker table. Not things that convey meaning.

People do talk at a poker table, so that gives voice

codes a certain utility: You can couch a lot of information in the spoken word. Start a sentence with the letter *s*, say, and you're transmitting spades. Throw a number in there somewhere, that's the hand rank. *Steelers are favored by seven, I hear.* But code talking can seem so random. *Have you heard there are twelve signs in the zodiac?* Seriously, who talks like that? And most poker players aren't talkers to begin with. Instruct them to voice code their hand values, and they'll just come across as stilted and strange. Call attention to themselves. That's the last thing you want.

So maybe you arm your gang with iPod or Blackberry tap codes. Or train them to position their card protectors or chip stacks just so. Or you carve out some nonverbal signals from among a range of innocuous actions. *Look at cards, shuffle chips, scratch chin, rub eyes. . . . The sign after the eye rub is the one that counts.* Maybe you put it all out there—the voice hacks, the tap codes, the body signs—figuring that the more different methods you use, the less you'll make plain to prying eyes. Now, though, you're piling layers of complexity onto an already complex situation. They all still have to play poker, remember, and thinking about code on top of thinking about poker . . . it may be more than some members of your crew can handle. Which is why you dry run your hacks: to find out which ones are easy and clear, and which are more trouble than they're worth.

At that, codes alone might not be enough. They'd be plenty in a cash game, where you can seed the lineup with confederates and then take all night to exploit your edge. But what will you do in a big tournament where tables break, players get moved, and just the sheer breadth and depth of the event serves to dilute the efforts of you and your merry band? You could expand the crew, of course. Put enough secret colluders into the same event, they're bound to have an impact. Will the money be there to pay them, though? Say you owned 90 percent of the tournament field (a ridiculous proposition, granted, but let's pretend). Even if that got you 100 percent of the prize pool (it wouldn't), you'd still have all those mouths to feed. Can you earn everybody out and still have enough left over to have made the whole fucking charade worth your time, sweat, and risk? Probably not.

So, then, don't increase the size of your conspiracy; improve its efficiency. Load in every tool you can think of—whipsaws, chip dumps, bent dealers, marked cards, the works—recognizing, of course, that the more effective any of these strategies are, the more likely they are to give themselves away. Marked cards get noticed and taken out of play. Chip dumping smells fishy. And the ol' whipsaw? It'd better work the first time, because by the second or third time it'll be waving red flags you can see from space.

Plus, can you trust your crew? They're no angels—you couldn't recruit them if they were. How do you know they aren't forming rogue cliques behind your back, planning to ride your gaff all the way to the final table, and then step out on their own? What recourse would you have? Legal? Ha! So you'd better hope they're naturally loyal or easily scared. Here's a tip: scared works better than loyal.

Then there's luck. You might have all your beautiful ducks in a row but still hit a land mine en route to the pond. Say you've got two players working the whipsaw, and they've got it dialed in to perfection. One's on A-K, the other has Q-Q, and the poor monkey in the middle is drawing deliciously slim with A-Q. Not so slim, of course, that he can't river a straight, say. Bad beats gut good players every day; there's no law that says they can't kill conspiracies, too. So the best laid plans of blah-blah-blah, and the next thing you know you've got a handful of low money finishes to split among a crew expecting a fat payday. You tell 'em better luck next time. They tell you go fuck yourself. Or maybe they tell the cops, oh well.

Of poker it is often said, "It's a hard way to make an easy living." For most players, they'd show more profit in the long run doing almost anything else. (For many—lifelong losers—they'd show more profit just doing nothing at all.) Likewise with cheaters. Considering how tough it is to work a good poker gaff, and considering how the difficulty increases geometrically with the size of the tournament field, you'd be much better off investing your effort in just getting good. In fact, if you think about it, you'd have to be a real fucking megalomaniac to think you could put in the fix in the first place.

Marko Dragic was a real fucking megalomaniac.

But he was playing with an overlay, of a sort: he didn't care about the money. The cronies and flunkies could keep the money. All he wanted was the status and stardom that went with winning the biggest poker tournament in the history of ever. In fact, *fuck* the money—he'd probably make it all back, and then some, in endorsements and TV deals the first year.

So Dragic had put together a crew. He'd recruited like a big-program university football coach, hunting up the right mix of talents for his team: card mechanics, dirty dealers, anyone who proved able to learn Dragic's codes and use them effectively. Plus poker skill, of course; they had to know how to play the game brutally well, at minimum, and he tested them by playing them heads up for their own cash. He was hard to beat, and therefore happy to lose. Then there was the moral-fiber factor. Some poker players simply could not be bent—but not so many as you might think. In Dragic's experience, rectitude was inversely proportional to payout; a big enough pile of cash could make the sternest ethics melt.

As the satellite season for the Poker Apocalypse wore on, Dragic had refined his pitch so that everyone who won a satellite (bar the obviously luck struck or hopelessly twee) got at least the opportunity to join Team Dragic or, failing that, to sell Marko his or her entry chip at a very attractive price. In this way, Dragic had put together a field of some one hundred runners: pirates of poker callously capable of winning by legitimate and illegitimate means alike. Their plan was to work the Apocalypse like a giant funnel, pouring chips to Dark Mark, who would then storm and board the TV table with a massive chip lead, there to claim the glory that (in his megalomaniacal mind) he so richly deserved.

And if legitimate and illegitimate means didn't work, Dragic had still other hacks in mind.

Now, looking down the table at Hal Harris, Dragic wondered how much of this, if any, Hal had figured out. Was it just coincidence that he had entered the Mini? Was he trying to win this thing, or just be a thorn in Dragic's side?

"Yeah, that's quite a thing you called me. Queef. I had to Google it to find out what it meant." Dragic shook a finger at Hal. "It's not a nice word. I should be queefing insulted." Dragic looked around the table. "Anyone know that word? Queef?" Nobody answered. Several players shook their heads. The dealer, a strawberry blonde named Tacoma, just blushed as she began the deal. Dragic hooked a thumb toward Hal. "This queefing guy. Thinks he can play poker. His queefing brother could play. Guy Harris? Anybody know that queef?"

"The guy that got killed?" offered one of the other players.

"The queef that got killed, exactly," said Dragic. He allowed himself a faraway look, as if wallowing in Guy's memory. "Now there was a motherqueefing queef. Me personally? I'm glad he's dead." Dragic eyed Hal, checking to see if he'd rise to the bait. Hal's face stayed blank, but he could feel himself clenching inside. Dragic was a needler, and in the way of needlers, he made you feel inferior, small and exposed. The textbook defense is to ignore them, but this isn't always easy, and it always has the effect of diverting at least some of a victim's concentration from the play of his cards. That's the power of the needle: it demands a response, and even a nonresponse is a response. Hal suddenly got it about iPods; in that moment he devoutly wished he had headphones to block out Dragic's disruptive noise.

In any case, Hal had no interest in an early big confrontation with Dragic. The Gods of Table Change had given him a chance to study at close quarters the player who mattered most. He was aware that Dragic might have no hidden allies at this table, but if he did, this was Hal's golden opportunity to pick off their signs, maybe even break the whole code.

But . . . wouldn't you just know it. On his first hand at the new table, Hal picked up pocket aces. And Dragic, in early position, opened the pot for a big raise, five times the big blind. This was standard operating procedure for a needler. First you piss 'em off; then you put 'em to a test. Everyone folded around to Hal, who paused to think things through.

Should he make a big reraise? He suspected that Dragic would read such a move as a knee-jerk peeved response to his verbal assault, or his image, or just their queefing history. If Dragic had pocket kings or queens,

he might come back over the top, figuring either to get
Hal to surrender (and thus be broken in spirit) or to
catastrophically call along with some sort of weak
cheese like T-T, J-J, or A-Q. After that, well, like the sign
says, "Someone's going to emergency, someone's going
to jail." Against any other player it would be what
Slaughter called "situational luck": the chance to cloak
the strength of his hand behind what would seem to be
needle-induced tilt. Against any other player, Hal would
play the hand that way, hope he got action, and hope
his aces held up. But he didn't want action from Dragic.
He wanted a long, unmolested look at Dark Mark's play.
For that, he needed to paint a picture of himself as
timid, passive, scared: a nonentity at this table. He had
to disappear.

Could he fold aces? Could he really do that?

Well, what might he do instead? Reraise all in? Dragic
would have to fold. But what if he didn't? He had Hal
slightly outchipped, and the hand would end with either Dragic crippled or Hal busted. Again, not what Hal
wanted—not here, not now.

Maybe Hal should play the hand trappy, just call
along and see what happened. By this plan, he might be
able to get Dragic to bet into the best hand (assuming
Hal's aces remained the best hand) and blow off a
chunk of his stack. This would show Hal capable of dragging a big hand, and probably slow down Dragic's aggression against him. But Hal didn't want to show himself
capable of that or anything else. He didn't want Dragic
thinking about him at all.

He knew he had to fold. Any other action, any attempt to engage Dragic in this pot or any pot was just
his ego talking, and while both his ego and his chip stack
might be thus served (especially in this case, where he
had the harmonic convergence of plausible tilt and hid-

den strength), that's not why he was here. Hard as it was
to quell his competitiveness—and his desire to punish
Dragic, who simply made his bile rise—he now told himself with unspoken words, *You're not in it to win it. Not this
time.*

So, then, fold aces? *Really?* Guess so. He cocked his
wrist and spun his cards toward the muck.

Slaughter had told Hal early on that in poker the
body can manifest the conflicting desires of the mind.
Someone uncertain whether he wants to be called, for
example, will toss in his chips differently from someone
clear about the outcome he seeks. Slaughter had taught
Hal how to glean tells from such indecision, and taught
him also to handle his own chips in a consistent manner, so as to give away nothing about his own state of
mind. But that discussion had dealt strictly with chips
and bets. Hal couldn't imagine body conflict impacting
the way he handled his cards. A fold is a fold is a fold,
right? Just now, though, Hal found it—literally—difficult to let go of those sticky aces, and his misfiring muscle instruction caused an unexpected hitch in his
release. His cards came out of his hand at an odd angle,
caught a corner on the felt, and cartwheeled, landing
faceup for all the world to see.

"What the fuck?" blurted Dragic. "What the fucking
fuck?"

They F-bombed him, of course. Twenty minutes away
from the table.

Dragic spent his penalty period glaring at Hal from
behind the rail trying to figure him out. Could Hal be
that scared of him? Scared enough to fold aces? No, he
decided, no one's that scared. He must have something
else in his mind. Was it a sophisticated image play? Muck
the aces, exposing them "accidentally on purpose," to
just basically mind fuck everyone? If that was Hal's in-

tent, Dragic had to admit it had worked. But it didn't ring true. How does a total poker novice get that tricky that fast? Either there was more to this Hal Harris than met the eye, or much less. In any case, Dragic was now on guard and determined to give Hal the full measure of his attention.

In this, then, Hal ended up subverting his own intent. Bent on keeping a low profile, he'd now announced himself as the guy who folded aces. A guy like that, who knows what else he's capable of? The situation called for damage control, and Hal wished for Slaughter's help, but Slaughter was tables away, caught up in clashes of his own. Besides, with so many eyes on him now (especially Dragic's), the last thing Hal needed was to underscore his connection with Slaughter Johnson. *So then what?* he asked himself. *Walk away from the table? Sing a song? Order drinks?* He'd dealt himself the ultimate madman's image; perhaps the best thing to do was just to press it so much that it became background noise. *Pay no attention to him—he's just that guy who mucked the aces. He's off his queefing rocker.*

Slaughter believed—and so Hal was inclined also to believe—that a poker player's best image was one that harmonized with his real personality. If you weren't fearsome by nature, for instance, you probably couldn't sell a fearsome image. But there was always *something* you could sell: playful, fearful, friendly, frisky, tight, loose, clueless, whatever. "Images are like hats," Slaughter said. "You have to find the one that fits." ("Images are like Jimmy hats," said Skip. "One size fits all.") Hal was most at home with what he had come to think of as his image of "accountancy authority." He presented himself as someone so fully in control of poker's numbers that his every move was mathematically justified, and therefore whatever countermove you had in mind would necessarily not be. Sometimes he played android, and that worked, too. The other end of the spectrum—so-called cartoon images like gambler, gangster, maniac, hotshot—those hats did not fit him well.

As for this jester's cap, well . . . nothing to do but wear it. As Guy used to say, "They can't figure out your strategy if you don't have one." So Hal leaned into his new image. He jacked up his unpredictability. Bought pots with massive overbets. Made outrageous bluffs, and showed them. Pushed all-in blind. Ignored pot odds. Sized his bets by random handfuls. As so often happens with a maniac at the table, several of the other players became completely unglued by Hal's antics. They abandoned their starting requirements and let Hal suck them into loose calls, ill-timed bluffs, and similar mistakes. Only Dragic remained immune: even after he returned to the table, he spent most of his time with his head propped up on his fists studying Hal as if Hal were some odd animal species or, more appropriately, representative of a lost and primitive culture under an anthropologist's scrutiny for the first time in history.

Hal's stack rose and fell in steep waves. One moment he'd be down to the felt; the next, a chip leader. Then back to the felt again, then back to dizzying heights. Everyone assumed it was only a matter of time until someone woke up with a real hand and crushed and eliminated Hal. Hal assumed this as well, but he didn't care. He was so free, so uncharacteristically *out there,* that he found himself becoming giddy, stimulated. . . . Hal was high. He watched himself as if from a great distance, amazed that he was able to play poker with such wild abandon. He didn't feel like himself at all.

He felt like Guy.

And it struck him with the force of revelation that he finally knew why, really, Guy had played poker. It was for this, for the chance to be free, to exist in the pure and perfect now, a now you could control on a whim if you wanted. This wasn't just fun; this was power—power, it seemed to Hal, over life itself.

And though he thought his antics would kill any chance of spotting the hack, his image so floodlit the table that certain other players (though not Dragic, Hal noticed) felt safe in the shadows and became more overt and explicit in the information they passed. Or maybe Hal was just riding his revelation to a heightened sense of perception. In any case, he started picking off code all over the place. A player drank from his water bottle in syncopated sips: one, two, three, four, five, his Adam's apple bobbing up and down. Another reviewed movies he'd seen. This one got five stars, that one four; could anything be more obvious? A third marked cards. Hal saw him do it, and knew he wasn't seen in the seeing. This bright, vivid image of his had rendered him, strangely, utterly invisible.

Hal finished the tournament in third place, busting out when he flopped top two pair and lost to bottom set. It was an unremarkable hand of hold'em—at the end of a truly remarkable run of play. This new Hal, this "organized chaos" Hal, was a potent force at the table, and though everyone agreed that folding aces was the most mirplo of plays, you had to acknowledge that Hal had turned the mishap to his advantage—or maybe it was no mishap to begin with. Marko Dragic, in particular, came to view Hal in a new light. Clearly there was plenty of cowboy in Hal.

Was there, he wondered, some outlaw as well?

17 Post Mortem

The cadaverous bald man who called everyone "Sport," and so was called Sport in return, had been caught with his pants down. While no one could prove anything—maybe in folding his ace-high flush to Mouse Skowron's straight flush he'd simply made the world's most inspired laydown—he knew he'd become the talk of the Mini. (Along with the guy who folded aces, and what the hell was up with that?) Still, he didn't think he'd done any serious harm, either to Dragic's plan for the Poker Apocalypse, or to his own part in it. He'd made a mistake, that's all. Like every mistake in poker, you do your best to learn from it, put it behind you, and move on.

So when a man came to his house the next day and offered him a lift to Dark Mark's post mortem on the Mini, he was only too happy to accept, even though he hadn't heard anything about a post mortem and was vaguely surprised that Dragic knew where he lived. But these days, with the internet and all, you can pretty much find out anything about anybody, right? At the end of the day, he was willing to do almost anything to improve the quality of the hack.

Okay, maybe not die.

In a sense, he did help refine the hack, post—as it were—mortem: by reducing by one the number of incompetent fuckwits involved. That's why Dragic organized the dry run in the first place, to test the hackers, not the hack. The Mini was a cull, wheat from the chaff, like. As for the mechanics of the gaff, Dragic already knew they wouldn't work.

Interestingly, Hal knew it, too. "I've done the math," he said, cloistered with the others in the kitchen of Vinny's town house, "and it doesn't add up."

"How so?" asked Vinny, sitting on the travertine floor with Minty McGinty's massive head filling her lap. She rubbed and massaged the big dog's scalp. He purred like a cat.

"What's the largest number of players Dragic could have involved in this?"

"Can't be too many," said Slaughter. "Loose lips and all."

"So let's be generous. Let's say he's got ten percent of the field."

"Two hundred and fifty?" protested Vinny. "That's ridiculous."

"Let it be," said Hal. "Let there be an average of one Team Dragic at every table to start. Who are they going to be able to collude with? On average, no one."

"To start with, maybe," said Skip. "But the field shrinks."

"And the team shrinks with it. Until they're sharing tables, they've got no edge."

"Skill edge?"

"Not enough," said Hal. "Check me on this, Slaughter, but in a big-time tournament like this, wouldn't the difference between the best and worst players be pretty much fractional?"

Slaughter nodded. "At that, they'd have to survive coin flips, bad beats, and traps, just like everybody else."

"So the chances are remote you'll get much more than an average number of them lasting long enough in the tournament to bunch up at the same tables. And if they do, there still isn't much edge."

"Sure there is," said Skip. "They'd know extra cards. That's huge."

"Most of the time not," said Hal. "I've got crap, you've got crap, we both know it, so what? We still have to catch playable hands. Otherwise, we fold. No play, no edge."

"We'd know if our draws are live."

"To the tune of one out more or two outs less," said Slaughter. He shook his head. "Hal's right. Just not enough edge."

"Crooked dealers?" asked Skip.

"I've been dealing for ten years," said Vinny. "I've met maybe three dealers who could cool a deck with any kind of consistency. And that's parlor trick shit, not heat of combat."

"Plus, again, the paths have to cross," said Slaughter. "Bent dealer plus bent player. Too slim a chance. Too small an impact."

Skip was persistent. "Counterfeit chips, then. Just give your guys big stacks. There's your fucking impact."

"Cameras," said Slaughter. "You have to get your bad chips into play."

"Plus RFID," added Vinny.

"RFID?" asked Hal.

"Radio frequency identifiers, built in. Special for the Apocalypse. Numbered, sequenced, and embedded in microchips."

"Well, fuck," said Skip. "So then there's no conspiracy."

"But there is," said Hal. "The Mini proved that."

"Maybe it didn't," said Slaughter. "Maybe it was all just confirmation bias."

"I don't buy that," said Hal. "I saw what I saw."

"So what we've got," said Skip, "is a code we can't crack on a hack that can't work."

Vinny stood up, much to Minty's dismay. "I'm starting to wonder why we're wasting our time."

"What I'm starting to wonder," said Hal, "is why is Dragic wasting his?"

The question plagued Hal through the rest of the day and into the evening. He didn't know Dark Mark well, but nothing about the man struck him as either frivolous or dumb. He couldn't see Dragic willfully organizing a fruitless hack on the Apocalypse; nor could he see him so badly misgauging his chance of success. Either Dragic had a hidden angle, one not revealed at the Mini, or else Hal, Vinny, Skip, and Slaughter had all seen something that simply wasn't there.

Feeling restless and agitated—*vexed,* that was the word for it—Hal borrowed Skip's van (he'd long since returned the Song Serenade) and drove to the Cortland. He went straight to the cardroom and put himself on the list for $25–$50 blind no limit. He was astounded that so big a game didn't faze him. It was a measure of how far he'd come in so short a time—not just that he could play high, but that he could hold his own in the Darwinian stew of big-bet poker. He wondered if Guy would have been proud of him—and felt a twinge of regret at having discovered the game too late to share it with his brother. Now that he knew poker, he knew what he'd missed: the chance to sit and kibitz with Guy, to tease him about weak leads and busted bluffs. He would love to have bluffed Guy, if only to see the look on his face when he turned over his ragged hand. He wouldn't mind having been bluffed by Guy in return. He was confident Guy could play rings around him, but just the same . . . *If I knew then what I know now, oh well.*

While waiting for a seat, Hal walked across the casino (its layout no longer perplexed him, another measure of how far he'd come) and took the escalator up to the ballroom on the second floor. This was a vast expanse, far bigger than the Adirondack Ballroom next door at Grossinger's, with space for three hundred tables and room to spare. It had long since been retrofitted for tournament poker, with superior lighting, security cameras, sign-up boards, and a permanent cashier's cage. Hal walked in and stood just inside the door, marveling at the hum of activity, for tomorrow would mark the start of the Poker Apocalypse, and last-minute preparations were in full swing.

Maintenance crews swarmed through the hall, setting up tables and chairs. Boom camera operators practiced their swooping moves. A covey of dealers confabbed in the corner, working out their break and brush protocols. Men in hard hats stood atop thirty-foot-high scissor lifts, hanging cameras, spotlights, and banners. The banners in particular caught Hal's eye. He couldn't believe how many different official sponsors Kai Cortland had lined up. Pokerismyaeroplane.com, the official online partner. Buzzzzzzz, the official energy drink. Dog's Nose, the official beer ("When I want something cold and wet, I reach for a Dog's Nose"). Litespēd, the official computer. Flatland, the official plasma-screen TV. And on and on and on.

Hal had never met Kai Cortland, knew him only by reputation, and by his often stated belief, "Anything that's worth doing is worth overdoing." Hence the stretch Bentley limousine in signature Cortland celadon and crimson. Hence the run for governor (broken off when allegations—unproven—of underage girlfriends emerged). Hence the helicopter. Hence the several sports franchises.

Hence the Poker Apocalypse with its unprecedented entry fee, mind-boggling prize pool, four-wall sponsorship, RFID chips, and front-to-back television coverage.

Television coverage . . . Hal wondered how they were going to swing that. Granted, there were dozens of camera platforms scattered throughout the hall, giving excellent lines of sight to every seat at every table. Dozens more handheld operators would certainly be running the floor, scurrying to scenes of action or drama as they unfolded. Hal noticed also that each dealer's chair sported tiny cameras atop vertical aluminum shafts, offering an over-the-shoulder view of every flop, turn, and river. These, no doubt, would be remotely joysticked from some distant control room, and one could only imagine what a Missile Command operation that must be. But still, something nagged at Hal. He got it that the final table would feature lipstick cameras, so that the TV audience could see the players' hole cards. The tiny rail-embedded lenses were standard operating procedure these days. Nothing new there. And that's what bugged him. For someone as over the top as Kai Cortland, it hardly seemed credible that he'd save the lipstick cam only for the final table. Where was the innovation? Where was the excess?

Hal strolled to the nearest table. As with everything Cortland built or bought, it was first rate: spacious and sturdy, its smooth celadon felt emblazoned with the Cortland Casino logo, a pair of highly stylized *C*'s in gold gilt. Hal ran his hand along the padded rail, thinking that Cortland had perhaps miniaturized the lipstick cam down to a pinhole. But he found no evidence of that, just an unbroken run of butter-soft, luscious red leather. He sat for a moment in one of the plush players' chairs. These, too, were top shelf: swiveling, fully adjustable, deeply upholstered. The padded armrests had built-in cup holders, and even little fold-out trays for snacks, notes, or iPods. Clearly, Cortland hadn't missed a trick.

Except the lipstick cams, thought Hal. *I wonder what—*

"Hey, buddy!" Hal looked up to see a Cortland security guard closing in. "This room is closed. You can't be in here now."

Hal stood quickly. "Sorry," he said. "I was just checking it out."

"Pretty special, isn't it?" said the guard.

"Yes," agreed Hal. "Yes, it is."

"You playing? Got your ticket punched?" Hal nodded. The security guard essayed a low, reverent whistle. "Wow. Won your way into a hundred-thousand-dollar tournament. You must be pretty damn good."

Hal didn't know what to say. His story was too complex to reduce or explain, so, "Just lucky," he said and walked himself out of the hall.

Hal took the escalator back downstairs, but he no longer had the urge to play poker. The sight of the tournament room had taken the wind out of his sails. It was a natural reaction. The contemplation of a full-field poker tournament can assault any player's confidence, make him feel outnumbered and overmatched. That's why so many top players considered it vital tournament strategy to "just play the table you're at." They kept their heads down, kept focused on the task at hand: these foes, these cards, these decisions here. *Play right now,* they told themselves. If you thought too hard about the tournament as a whole, it was easy to get overwhelmed, like standing at the foot of Mount Everest and thinking, *I'm gonna climb fucking that?*

The security guard had lauded Hal's poker skills, but at that moment Hal didn't feel "pretty damn good." He just felt lost. He wasn't even sure he wanted to play in the tournament anymore. With Dragic's hack apparently gone to hell, there didn't seem to be much point. Maybe he'd give his tournament entry chip to Slaughter or Skip. Sell it to Lanh Tran or some other hopeful striver.

Chuck it in Lake Mead.

Hal walked on, past a brewpub that proclaimed itself, "The Hoppiest Place on Earth." As he walked by, a booming voice called out his name. Surprised, Hal peered into the gloom and saw Big Mo standing at the bar with a small knot of friends. Mo beckoned Hal in with an enthusiastic wave.

"Hal Harris, ladies and gentlemen," said Mo, introducing him around. "He's kind of a big deal."

"Do you use that line on everyone?" asked Hal.

"Only the big deals. Hey, what're you drinking?"

"That's okay, I can get it."

"Nonsense! This is my bar. Well, technically not mine, but I've invested heavily enough in it . . . you know, one drink at a time." Hal yielded to the big man's insistence. It struck him that Mo's larger-than-life persona was in some sense a defense mechanism. Clearly, he couldn't stand not to be noticed. Hal thought about his own defense mechanisms. What could he not stand to be? *Out of control*, he thought. *I can't stand to be out of control.*

Hal stood silently for a few minutes listening in on Mo's conversation with his friends, several of whom had won seats in the Apocalypse. With good natured banter and ribbing, they were negotiating for shares of one another and setting the odds for various proposition wagers. Hal wondered what was the point of a $100 last-longer bet in the context of a $70 million first prize, but this was clearly their microculture, a culture Hal had not been in poker long enough to come to understand.

When a lull allowed, Hal said to Mo, "How about that play yesterday?"

"Which one?"

Hal laughed. "Which one? The guy who folded his nut flush."

"Oh, yeah, that," said Mo. He thought about it for a moment and said, "He probably just misread his hand."

"Really? You didn't seem to think so at the time."

"Nah," said Mo, jovially. "He was just folding out of turn, that's all. I hate when that happens. I'm kind of a stickler for the rules."

Was this guy on the level? Did he really think Sport had made an innocent mistake? "So why'd you wink at me?" Hal asked.

Mo regarded Hal with a carefully neutral expression. "Did I wink? I don't remember." He snaked a thick arm around Hal's shoulders and leaned in close. "Maybe I was hitting on you." Then, before Hal could react, Mo slapped him on the back, laughed effusively at his own joke, and turned his attention back to his friends.

With that, Hal was marginalized from the conversation; dismissed. He drained his drink as quickly as courtesy allowed, enduring a long, awkward silence with Mo's friends when the big man stepped aside to take and make a couple of cell phone calls. "What's he doing?" Hal asked, for lack of a better question.

"Ordering hookers," said one of Mo's claque. Hal assumed his chain was being yanked, and his discomfort ratcheted up a notch. There was more to being a poker player, he realized, than just playing poker. You had to inhabit the scene. Guy was always good at this; Hal figured he never would be.

When Mo returned, Hal thanked him for the drink and departed, suddenly wanting to go home as quickly as possible. His encounter with Big Mo had left a bad taste in his mouth. As with Dragic, there was something about the guy that abraded him. Maybe Hal just didn't like poker players all that much.

He hadn't gone far when he felt a tapping touch at the small of his back. He turned around and looked down to see Mouse Skowron standing there. "Hey, bud," said Mouse, "you wanna talk to Dark Mark? He wants to talk to you."

Mouse grinned a sardonic, gap-toothed grin, and Hal realized that here was yet another poker player who rubbed him the wrong way.

18 Free Lunch

Hal's first thought was to run. After all, what could Mouse do? Chase him down and tackle him? But then, as good poker players will do, Hal viewed the situation through the other guy's eyes. If Dragic wanted to see him, there must be a reason—a reason related, in all likelihood, to Hal's outburst of image at the Mini. And if Mouse was his emissary—Mouse whom Hal knew to be in on the hack—then Mark must be willing to acknowledge, at least, that such a conspiracy existed. How Mouse knew where to find him was an open question—a question that suddenly closed with a beer-flavored burp: Big Mo hadn't been ordering hookers after all. Hal gave Mouse a modest nod and said, "Let's go."

Mouse led Hal back toward the heart of the casino. Hal assumed they were making for the Aquarium, but Mouse vectored well away from the cardroom and arrived instead at a private salon called Kai's Highs, where the minimum bet at the table games was $1,000. "Wait here," said Mouse, then departed. Hal parked himself on a stool in front of a slot machine. The reels looked the same as any other pull toy's—cherry; bar; lucky seven—but the coin accepter indicated that it took only hundred-dollar tokens. Hal couldn't begin to imagine paying a C-note just to watch the reels go 'round.

There was but one gambler in the room, a fat man in a lavender track suit playing blackjack for $50,000 a hand while his arm candy wobbled atop stiletto heels and plucked dejectedly at the hem of her size zero cock-tail dress. She couldn't have looked more bored. Nor did the fat man seem to be getting much of a thrill from his wagers, which he regarded with blank equanimity, win or lose. Hal understood the nature of addiction—how it takes an addict progressively more to achieve the same level of stimulation—but he couldn't fathom build-ing up such a tolerance to risk that even fifty grand a hand didn't ignite a buzz. *How rich must that guy be?* won-dered Hal. *And how good must he be for the casino that they've got a whole room and staff here just for him?* That, of course, was just the tip of the amenities iceberg for this whale. On his frequent forays into Las Vegas, the Cort-land provided him with penthouse accommodation, companionship (the aforementioned arm candy), fine dining, show tickets, invitations to exclusive parties, spa, massage, anything his heart desired—though all his heart really desired was to fucking *feel something,* which he hadn't done in years. But he spent enough and lost enough to get the full whale treatment, and that made him feel respected, at least—though at fifty grand a hand, it was respect dearly bought.

Hal recalled a cartoon he'd seen once of a sheep standing outside a bar that bore the sign FREE LUNCH. The sheep was blissfully unaware that the bar was full of wolves. The caption read, "Edgar's about to discover there's no such thing as a free lunch." The high roller was being devoured, knew he was being devoured, and didn't seem to care. Win or lose, he was past the point of pain.

"Walk with me," said a graceless voice that Hal instantly recognized as Dark Mark's. Like a puppet on a string (and hating himself for being so easily voice commanded), he popped up from his stool and fell in beside Dragic, who strode into the deep recesses of the high-roller salon, aiming ultimately for some velour easy chairs (in celadon, inevitably, with crimson piping and pillows) far back against the back wall. Signaling for a cocktail waitress, Dragic recommended that Hal try the house Scotch, for it came from Cortland's own distillery—on Cortland's own island—off the Hebrides coast of Scotland. Hal declined. He didn't reckon that this conversation called for alcohol, and he wasn't particularly concerned that Dragic might be offended. In fact, as before when they'd met, he felt his blood starting to boil.

Dragic must have had a sense of this, for he said, "First off, let's not call anyone queef now, huh? That's behind us."

Hal supposed this was intended as an olive branch of sorts, though in his state of heightened chariness he wasn't inclined to take it at face value. Rather, he considered Dragic's overture to be the opening bet in a hand of poker, an attempt to establish position or glean information. He thought about raising, with some sort of snarky riposte, but instead just said, "Fine. No more queefs." Dragic considered Hal's response, and Hal knew that Dark Mark was playing this as poker, too, measuring every aspect of Hal's demeanor for clues to his state of mind.

The waitress brought Dragic's drink, naked Scotch in a snifter. He rotated the spirit slowly in the bowl, as if studying it was more important than actually drinking it. "Satisfy my curiosity," he said at last. "What kind of poker player folds aces preflop?"

Hal quickly considered his range of possible replies, from an inscrutable demure to the truth to an extravagant lie. Opting for a middle ground, he shrugged and said, "Unconventional?"

"That's a word for it." Dragic sipped his whiskey. "Well, you said you'd get game, and you did."

"I'm a quick learner," said Hal, flippantly, immediately regretting the insecurity his tone betrayed. *That's called overplaying your hand.*

"I'm thinking," said Dragic carefully, "that you've learned one or two things besides poker."

Hal read this as a not terribly veiled reference to the hack and was surprised, for it seemed to give much away for no good reason. Then he recalled Dragic's use of Mouse as emissary and realized that this admission had already, tacitly, been made. Dragic wasn't being coy; he was gauging how coy Hal chose to be. Hal decided to do a little gauging of his own. "You asked what kind of player folds pocket aces. I would ask what kind of player folds the nut flush."

"Someone who knows something," said Dragic. "But you already know that."

"So tell me something I don't know."

Surprisingly, Dragic did.

Over the next quarter hour, and with an amazing degree of candor, he sketched out his efforts to recruit and train team members for a collaborative assault on the Apocalypse, especially the delicate matter of finding players with the right combination of poker skill and, as he put it, "flexible ethics." He talked about the trade-off between team size and team control. Described the use of counterspies (like Big Mo, Hal now realized) tasked to act as suspicious outsiders, for he needed to know who could handle the pressure and who would crack. Finally, Dragic shared with a flatly flabbergasted Hal his conclusion—the same one Hal had reached—that normal approaches to collusion, even all of them taken together and expertly executed, wouldn't get the job done. "What I learned at the Mini," said Dragic, "is that dog don't hunt."

"Why are you telling me this?" asked Hal.

"Obviously, I want you to join my team." Hal was on the point of asking, with frank incredulity, why Dragic would want that, but he thought he already knew the answer. Per Sun Tzu, *Keep your friends close, and your enemies closer.* With this in mind, he concluded that this new, frank, accessible Marco Dragic was just another level of deception.

So he put out a blocking bet of sorts. "I'm not that good a player."

"You weren't before. You are now."

"What, just because I folded aces?"

Dragic laughed, that same grating, hawking laugh that had once set Hal's teeth on edge. "Of course not. Because of how you worked your image afterward. That was inspired. That was art."

"Okay," said Hal, "so I'm an artist. What good does it do if that dog don't hunt?"

"There's more than one dog. There's lots and lots of dogs."

"What kind of dogs are we talking about?"

Dragic shook his head. "Not till you come on board."

Hal considered the carrot being dangled. He wondered about the stick. "I don't know," he said slowly. "I'm not sure I've got those flexible ethics you need."

Dragic hid a wince at Hal's assumption of moral superiority. But he kept an agreeable tone as he said, "Yeah, take the night to decide. Maybe you'll change your mind." He drained his Scotch at a gulp. Color rose to his cheeks. "But let me just say this: if you don't play for me, it might be better if you didn't play at all." *Ah, the stick.* "Can't have cowboys going around folding aces."

Dragic left. Hal watched him go, thinking, *Edgar's about to discover there's no such thing as a free lunch.* After a moment, he stood up and walked out of the high-rollers' lounge, leaving the lone whale to his forlorn pursuit of the buzz at fifty grand a hand.

Hal went to the self-park garage and made his way back to Skip's van. As he turned the key in the lock, a figure stepped out from behind the van. Hal recognized him instantly by his mop of dyed blond hair: it was Larry "Lanh" Tran, paying him another van-side visit.

Only this time . . . with a gun.

"Okay," said Lanh, "let's have it."

"It? What it?"

"Don't get cute," said Lanh. "The tournament entry chip. I want it right now and I'm not fucking around."

"Why on earth," asked Hal, "would I be walking around with the tournament entry chip? How stupid do you think I am?" In fact, Hal was inwardly chiding himself for being exactly that stupid: he had the chip tucked in the right front coin pocket of his pants; had kept it there almost fetishistically since it had first come into his possession.

"Get on your knees," said Lanh. "Put out your hands." Lanh produced a roll of duct tape.

A sense of unreality swept over Hal, a lightness of spirit that prompted him to ask—taunt, really—"So, never could win a satellite, huh?"

"Shut up," said Lanh. "What do you care?"

"Larry—"

"Lanh!"

"Whatever. Look, suppose you got my chip. You

think I can just let you take it and play it without a word?"

"You can if you're dead."

"Oh, now you're gonna kill me?"

"Dead as disco."

"Disco is only dead in the hearts of the unforgiving." Hal had no idea why he said this. Though he was facing a (presumably) loaded weapon, he seemed to be having trouble taking the moment seriously.

Lanh cocked the gun. "Get down." Hal dropped to his knees. Something about Lanh struck Hal as new and different. *He's got the courage of his convictions,* thought Hal. *What does he know now that he didn't know before?* Lanh stepped forward, peeling off a skein of duct tape with his teeth while keeping the gun trained on Hal. Again, Hal was struck by a feeling of . . . well, you'd have to call it whimsy. He started whistling the flatted first bars of Beethoven's Fifth.

"Oh no, you don't!" said Lanh, looking around wildly in anticipation of a charge by Minty McGinty. "I swear to God, I'll shoot that miserable—" Hal lunged forward, sweeping Lanh's ankles out from under him. Lanh fell backward and landed on his ass with a grunt. Hal scooped up the gun. Adrenaline surged through him. He kicked the roll of tape to Lanh and said, "Bind your wrists." Lanh stared at him dully. "Do it!" Stunned by the sudden reversal, Lanh complied, awkwardly wrapping pieces of duct tape around his own hands. Once Lanh's fists were somewhat immobilized, Hal stuck the gun in his belt and finished the job, taping Lanh securely from his hands to his elbows.

A young couple passed by, draped in souvenir beads and giggling over some shared intimacy. They paused to stare at the tableau of Hal and Lanh. Hal grinned expansively and said, by way of explanation, "Fraternity prank." He could have said, "Anthrax attack" for all the inclination they had to get involved, but it occurred to Hal that the next passersby might not be so disinterested, so he hustled Lanh into the back of the van, climbed in after him, and shut the door.

"Now," he said, "tell me if you can, in as simple and clear a way as possible, why you decided to fuck with me again."

Lanh wouldn't say a word. Hal sat with him for an hour trying to cajole something out of him, but Lanh stayed mum. Hal's problem, he realized, was that he was trying to run a totally transparent bluff. Though he held a gun, he had no temperament to use it, and this Lanh knew. So all his earnest questioning and veiled and unveiled threats were met with blank resistance that Hal simply couldn't penetrate. At last, exasperated, he leaned back on the palms of his hands and said, "Man, what am I going to do with you?" He knew he couldn't just let Lanh go, for if Hal had no credibility as a stone killer, Lanh equally had no credibility as someone who could be trusted to walk away and stay walked away. They had both lost their image equity and had therefore arrived at a certain standoff.

It had been almost a month since he and Lanh had last crossed paths. Had the young Asian been stalking him all this time, waiting for a chance to strike? That didn't seem likely, for if he'd remained bent all along on hijacking Hal's TEC, why wait until the night before the Apocalypse? Too dicey a play, Hal decided. It wasn't in Lanh's nature.

So what had changed? What had moved Lanh off the sideline? Had he squandered every satellite attempt, such that Hal became his Hobson's choice? Hal doubted it. Lanh didn't seem that well heeled: how many satellite shots did he have in his bankroll? No, if he'd wanted to come after Hal, that would have been his first option, not his last. So then . . . what had changed?

Something Dark Mark said came back to him just then. *There's more than one dog.* What did this mean? Other, more reliable hacks? If that was the case, and if Lanh was aware of it, he might have become more urgently motivated to separate Hal from his tournament entry chip. After all, there are limits to what a man will do for a *shot* at millions . . . but a *lock* for millions?

Hal regarded Lanh silently, wondering if he should share any of these thoughts, and by sharing maybe get some salient thoughts in return. *It's like showing cards,* thought Hal. *Sometimes the information you get is worth more than the information you give.* In this instance, though, Hal didn't think so. All Lanh could do, after all, was confirm Hal's suspicions—a confirmation, of course, not to be trusted. *All these damn poker players,* thought Hal. *I'm getting so sick of these damn lying liars.*

Thus, the two of them sat in the back of Skip Loder's van, not talking, barely moving. And the night slipped away and the hour of the Apocalypse approached.

PART THREE

A Chimp in a Chair

The universe is there to sort you out.

19 I Am the Cheese

The Apocalypse has played deep into day two. Blinds are now, like, $1,000–$2,000 with a $300 ante. There are eight players at my table, so that's $5,400 in the pot preflop. I have an average-size stack and pick up pocket eights in the cutoff seat. The chip leader is on the button, to my immediate left, with about twice what I have. Behind him, the blinds are short- and medium-stacked, respectively. It's folded around to me. The button has been playing bully, betting and raising with a wide range of hands as he attempts to reinforce his image as the straw that stirs the drink. My image is selective-aggressive. I don't think people think I'm getting out of line at all—at least not those who are paying attention. But this guy on my left is not paying attention, and as such he's capable of anything. I'd like to shut him out of this hand with a raise, try to win the blinds or, at worst, take the best of a coin flip against the short stack, who will probably go all the way here with any good ace or even two wheelhouse cards like K-Q or K-J. I'm not worried about the big blind; he's a Tighty Tighterson, doomed to ante and blind himself to death. But the button is crafty enough to put me on a move, and bold enough to put me to a hard choice.

If I flat call, he might raise to isolate the blinds. If they both folded, I could smack him with a limp reraise and take the pot away, but if the big blind calls I'll probably have to muck. Maybe I should lead into him after all, represent my strength, and take the pot while the taking is good. Of course, I could always fold, but that seems like a weak play with a semistrong hand. If someone reraises I can reconsider, but right now I have no reason to believe I'm not ahead. I need to make a quick decision, though, for the longer I linger over this, the more I give the impression that I'm on, well, exactly the sort of iffy hand I'm on. I look left, trying to pick off some tells, but none of the others have looked at their hands yet. Curse them for good card hygiene! It's my turn to act. I have to act. I . . . I . . . I . . .

"I have to take a leak," said Lanh.

Hal snapped out of his reverie. As he did quite frequently these days, he had fallen into a poker fantasy, projecting himself into an artificially constructed game situation and trying to devise the best plan for the hand. This was not a trick he'd learned from Slaughter or Skip or anyone else, but something he'd developed on his own, a productive means of thinking about poker away from the table. It had become second nature to Hal so fast and so fully that he could no longer remember a time when he didn't think that way.

"What?"

He looked at Lanh Tran, who sat with his back against the van's rear doors scratching his nose awkwardly with the ball of duct tape encasing his hands. "Unless you want me to piss my pants and stink up your van." Lanh gave the interior of the van a speculative sniff. "Not that anyone would notice."

Hal looked at his watch. It was nearly five a.m. The Apocalypse would start at noon. This was certainly not the preferred way to prepare for a major tournament, and he was afraid—no, he *knew*—that all his productive poker fantasy would be a poor substitute for sleep later today.

He really had to do something about Lanh Tran. He thought about turning him over to the police, but on what charge? Assault? Kidnapping? Tran was the one with his hands bound, not Hal. He also considered taking him out to Slaughter's Airstream and stashing him there till the tournament was over. But that really *would* be kidnapping, and, despite the threat that Lanh represented, Hal couldn't bring himself to cross that line. It briefly crossed his mind to give Lanh the damn tournament chip and be done with it, but that was just surrender, and Hal was not prepared to surrender. Not yet. Not while all his questions remained unanswered.

Had Lanh killed Guy? Lahn insisted not, but what else would he say? Likewise Dragic, the prime suspect . . . but where was the proof? Guy had laid the crime on some big ugly fucker who wanted his tournament entry chip, but could even Guy's account be trusted? Though Guy had no reason to lie, his sense of the dramatic had been known to outstrip his grasp of reality. And how accurately does any victim of a fatal assault process the details? Maybe Detective Ding had been right in the first place. Random act of violence; shit happens. *Maybe . . . maybe . . . maybe . . . raise . . . call . . . fold . . .* Hal was foundering in doubt.

And Lanh had to pee.

Hal crawled between the front seats of the van and let himself out through the passenger-side door. Circling around back, he opened the rear doors for Lanh, who spilled out and stretched the stiffness out of his legs. They walked together to a nearby concrete pillar. Hal waited for Lanh to pee, but Lanh just stood there.

"Come on, man," said Hal. "If you're gonna go, go."

Lanh raised his hands. "Like I can unzip," he said.

Hal sighed. *I'm crap at this criminal stuff,* he thought as he bent down to undo Lanh's pants. He was just on the point of realizing that he'd have to pull out Lanh's junk, too, when Lanh brought both fists down on the back of Hal's head as hard as he could. *I'm* really *crap at this criminal stuff,* Hal thought as he fell down. The wad of duct tape had softened the blow, but the next shot, a brutal boot to the ribs, was cushioned not at all. Hal felt something crack and through stars of sudden agony saw Lanh Tran running away.

Then he passed out a little.

When he woke a few minutes later, he immediately reached to see if his tournament entry chip was still there. A bolt of searing pain sliced through him like a Ginsu knife through a radiator hose. He fell back on the concrete floor of the parking garage and almost passed out again. He tried to steady himself by breathing deeply, but each breath was a new living hell. Slowly, careful not to jostle his ribs again, he moved his hand to his pants pocket and patted it speculatively. Yes, the chip was still there.

But now what?

A certain clock was ticking, Hal knew, for Lanh would be back as soon as he got the duct tape off, and Hal was in no condition to defend himself. He had to get out of there, pain or no pain. Gritting his teeth, he dragged himself to the van and pulled himself up into the driver's seat. He fired up the engine, and not a moment too soon, for here came Lanh at a dead run, his hands freed from their sticky prison, and now holding what looked like a length of rebar. Hal gunned the van backward out of its angled parking space. Every movement was torture, but now adrenaline kicked in, helping to mask the pain. He threw the van in drive and headed straight for Lanh, who leapt aside and tomahawked the rebar against the driver's-side window. Hal ducked as the window shattered, spraying him with pebbles of tempered glass. He drove on, entering the parking structure's spiraled access ramp. Lanh gave chase down the tight curves of the descent as Hal careened heedlessly off the retaining walls, bashing in both sides of the van. Reaching the ground floor, he hit the gas hard and sped away. Lanh fell behind. In desperation, he hurled the rebar at the van, but it landed short. Hal took one last screeching turn, clipping a parked rented Song Serenade and totaling it instantly. He bounced over a series of speed bumps, each impact sending fresh shards of molten agony through his chest. A minute later he was out on the street.

Five minutes later, he was on the highway, blinking back tears.

Twenty minutes later, he was in Vinny's town house, passed out on the foyer floor.

"Hal? Honey, can you hear me?"

Hal's eyes fluttered open. He lay on his back in bed. The room was dark, but he could see daylight peeking around the edges of the drawn shades. He dropped his chin to his chest and saw thick swaths of Ace bandages holding packs of frozen peas against his rib cage. Minty McGinty's huge head lay flopped up on the end of the bed. He looked at Hal with soulful, sorrowful eyes, and Hal was sure the dog could feel his pain. Vinny and Skip stood on either side of the bed. "Hey, bud," said Skip. "How ya doing?"

Hal took a breath, bracing himself for the pain . . . that didn't come. "I don't hurt," he marveled.

"That's the Dilaudid," said Skip.

"Dilaudid?"

"Hydromorphone hydrochloride to you." Skip grinned, apparently quite pleased with himself. "Yup, nothing like a good opioid agonist to cure what ails you. You're lucky I had some lying around."

"How—?"

"Overseas pharmacy. Friendly dentist. Won it in a poker game. That's really not the issue now. Dude, what happened?"

Hal filled them in. The words spilled out in a surprising torrent. The Dilaudid had parked Hal on a fluffy pink cloud, where not only was pain eradicated, but also all confusion and doubt. By the time he'd run through everything, he felt a fire rising in his belly. He wasn't going to let little things like cracked ribs, death threats, or conspiracy keep him from the Apocalypse. He was going to enter the tournament with his head held high and—

"Yeah, that's gonna be a problem," said Skip.

"Why?"

"It's already four o'clock."

"What?! We have to go!"

Hal sat up quickly. An Exocet missile slammed into his chest, knocking him back on the bed. "Take it easy," said Skip. "That's just drugs, you know, not the waters at Lourdes."

There ensued a short, spirited debate over whether Hal was in any condition to play in the Apocalypse. (He certainly was in no condition to drive or operate heavy machinery.) Vinny wanted to take him for X-rays, but Hal couldn't see the point. "What will X-rays show?" he asked. "That I've got a busted rib?"

"Or *some* busted ribs."

"I know that. That's not news." Something about the word *news* struck him as funny. He said it again, stretching out the vowel so that it sounded to his ringing ears like *noooooooooze*. Melodic. Wonderful. "Look," he said, "I'll probably bust out in an hour anyway. Then you can take me to the airport."

"Hospital."

"Hospital, yeah." Words were giving Hal some trouble.

But in the end, he prevailed. It was, after all, his decision to make.

As they eased him toward Vinny's station wagon, it occurred to Hal that someone was missing. "Where's Slaughter?" he asked. Skip and Vinny exchanged looks. "Where?" Hal repeated, more forcefully.

"He's playing in the Apocalypse," said Vinny.

The news filtered down through fluffy pillows of pain occlusion, finally landing in the part of Hal's brain that registered shock. "He toke my tooken—uhm, took my token?"

"Of course not," said Vinny. "He . . . well, he had one all along."

"What?"

"He won one of the first satellites."

"Guy never knew?"

Vinny shook her head. "At first it was going to be a surprise for him. Slaughter was going to let him play his entry. Then Guy got all obsessed about winning on his own and . . . I don't know . . . that got Dad's back up. Then, well, you know the rest.

"You had yours. He didn't see much point in mentioning his."

Hal thought he should be offended by this somehow, but the drugs had robbed his ability to feel all hurt, including emotional. He did manage to voice this thought: "So I show up with my crap kicked in and he goes off to play poker?"

"He doesn't know," said Vinny. "He stayed at his place

last night and went straight to the tournament from there. I didn't tell him about you. I knew he'd bail."

"Yeah, he would, the mirplo," said Skip. He threw a convivial arm around Hal. "I love you like a brother, man, but if you were lying in a ditch bleeding from many wounds, I would step over you to play for seventy million."

Hal appreciated Skip's honesty. It smelled like tangerines.

They drove to the Cortland, where huge banners hung from its crimson towers announcing the start of the Poker Apocalypse. A hundred-foot-high blow-up balloon of Kai Cortland stood guard over the main entrance. TV news crews loitered, enjoying the catered spread Cortland had laid out for their benefit.

Vinny dropped Hal and Skip off and went to park the car. She kissed Hal gingerly and said, "Try not to bust out before I get there." Hal grinned. Such an outcome seemed simply impossible, for his mind was alive with confidence and poker moves. He felt like he'd never seen the game with more clarity, and though Skip had to guide him to keep him from walking into people (or walls), he strode with a resolute sense of purpose to the registration table outside the tournament hall.

Hal handed over his tournament entry chip with some reluctance, for that slick silver disk had owned his life for the past month. By relinquishing it now was he surrendering his touchstone? This was an existential question he completely lacked the cognitive skills to process at the moment. All he could think was, *This smells like tangerines.* As for the bored casino employee who signed him in, her contribution to his existential crisis was a critically voiced, "You're late." That, too, smelled like tangerines. Hal didn't have the word for it, but he was suffering from synesthesia, a confusion of the senses.

Should he have encountered a real tangerine at that moment, he likely would have thought, *This feels like gravel* or *This sounds like harps*.

"He likes to make an entrance," offered Skip. "Thinks he's Phil fucking Hellmuth."

The woman made a moue at Skip's language and handed Hal his seat card. "Good luck," she said, but she didn't really mean it.

They stepped away from the table. Skip reached into his pocket and pulled out a plastic pill bottle containing two dozen tablets about the size and color of children's aspirin. "The key," said Skip, "is to stay ahead of the pain."

"Stay ahead of the pain," repeated Hal. He grasped for the bottle; missed by a fairly wide margin; then watched, slackjawed, as Skip put it in his hand. He turned and headed off, feeling cool, calm, and grandly alive. *I am the cheese!* thought Hal. He had no idea what that meant, but with bold, self-assured strides, he marched down the hallway outside the ballroom and stopped in front of a door. Beyond that door, he knew, laid greatness.

He started to go through.

Skip grabbed him by the elbow. "That's the ladies', man." He brought Hal across to the real ballroom entrance, and there turned him loose on the world.

20 A Pair of Oakley Thumps

Guy had been the altered statesman of the family and had pursued recreational chemistry with an avid enthusiasm from an early age. "Drugs is not the answer," he used to say. "*More* drugs, that's the answer." In his time he had sampled just about everything: grass; shrooms; X; nitrous; even a nameless capsule that, he said with a certain perverse pride, flatlined him for forty-eight hours and put him on a first-name basis with God. He was no Hunter Thompson, but on a peyote-driven spirit quest or an all-night absinthe bender he could certainly hold his own. Hal, on the other hand, had no experience with, nor any interest in, what Guy called peeling back the corner of the carpet of the mind. He'd never so much as smoked pot—not even a cigarette—and rarely drank. "You should have a tattoo," Guy used to chide him, " 'Born to designated drive.' "

The painkillers Skip gave him, then, were literally the strongest medicine he'd taken in his life, and they affected him in uncharacteristic ways. Where the typical opiate user tends to mellow out and slow down, Hal felt wired, edgy, hyperaware. His fingertips tingled with the simple pleasure of touch; rubbing them together, he heard an emery rasp. As he searched through the ballroom for his tournament table, everything he looked at took on the aspect of a 3-D Magic Eye stereogram, fraught with hidden pictures and, indeed, meaning. Was it his imagination, or were an unusually large number of players wearing those new Oakley Super Thumps, the ones in rainbow colors with the built-in Bluetooth receiver? At one point, he thought he spotted Slaughter, but when he went to greet his friend and mentor, it turned out to be a transgender semipro named Chaundra Kelly, who looked about as much like Slaughter as a moose looks like the surface of the sun. *The mind plays tricks,* Hal warned himself. The caution brought him no small amusement—but then, so did his beard, which he thought he could actually hear growing.

Kai Cortland, in a smirking nod to the poker tournament he intended to render irrelevant and obsolete, had structured the Apocalypse to mirror exactly the main event of the World Series of Poker: same blinds, same level-lengths, same starting stacks of $10,000 in tournament chips. The only thing different was the huge buy-in. This was not so much an homage as a kiss goodbye, a genial "fuck you" to an institution that Cortland had no real beef with, except that it wasn't his; it didn't bear his stamp. So although Hal had been blinded off in absentia, thanks to starting blinds of $25 and $50 and leisurely two-hour rounds of play, by the time he finally settled into his seat, he still had over $8,000 in chips. He still had plenty of room to move.

And move he did.

In fact, he took his table by storm.

A story is told of Pittsburgh Pirates pitcher Dock Ellis, who hurled the game of his career against the San

Diego Padres on June 12, 1970. According to Ellis's own account, he thought he wasn't scheduled to pitch that night and, in a move not at all untypical for the times, decided to make the most of his day off by dropping acid. Upon discovering that he was, in fact, tabbed for the start, he hustled to the ballpark and threw a wild (eight walks) but winning complete game no-hitter. Said Ellis after the fact, "The ball was small sometimes; the ball was large sometimes; sometimes I saw the catcher; sometimes I didn't." And while LSD can hardly be considered a performance-enhancing drug, for that one time, at least, it seemed to work.

Similarly, from his first hand forward, Hal viewed the tournament through a filter of poker completely foreign to his experience. Good hands looked like bad hands; bad ones looked like good ones; stone bluffs looked like pocket aces; and his foes, for a while at least, all looked completely transparent. Right or wrong, Hal thought he could read minds, and since confidence is so much a part of success in poker, the confidence he felt quickly gave him command of the table. It may have been the reductio ad absurdum of "they can't figure out your strategy if you don't have one," but, as with Dock Ellis and the magic shrinking baseball, it seemed to work.

The dealer tossed Hal his first hand: 8♠7♠. Slaughter Johnson called this holding a "package hand," because he routinely added it to his package of raising hands once he had established a suitably tight-aggressive table image. The logic of the package hand was clear: if his foes expected him to be in there raising only with top drawer hands like A-A, K-K, or A-K, they would willingly surrender to high flops like A-K-x but pay off middling flops that connected with the hidden strength of the package holding.

For Hal to use this as a package hand without first establishing a tight image was completely incorrect.

As he was stoned out of his gourd, he didn't much care.

With blinds at $100 and $200, Hal raised under the gun with his 8♠7♠, making it $1,000 to go. He had actually intended to raise to $600, but poor motor control ended up slopping four extra $100 chips into the pot. Such an out-of-position raise from a player arriving well after a tournament's start usually represents one of two things: either the new blood is playing caballero, attempting to stroke a bully image right away, or else he lucked into a major holding on his first hand. Since most players follow Slaughter's notion of "kosher until proven tricky," most players would assume that Hal had a big hand here, particularly considering the size of the overbet. Everyone folded around to the player in the big blind, an endomorph in a flower-print muumuu and matching floppy hat. She did indeed put Hal on a high pair but figured she held just the hand to slay such a pair:

8♥7♥.

She called.

Hal's head was spinning. He looked at the big blind, trying to gauge her strength, but he had trouble pulling focus. *Her nostrils are flaring*, thought Hal. *All three of them. I wonder what that means.* Her dress caught his eye, its pink and purple bougainvillea assaulting the tweaked cone cells in his retina. "That's a nice muumuu," he said, the words oozing out of his mouth like chocolate syrup. "Muumuu," he repeated. "Mooooomooooo," like a cow.

The big blind smiled sardonically, watched the flop come down, and knuckled the felt. "Action's on you," said the dealer. Hal shook his head to clear it and examined the flop. Against long odds, it had hit them both: 8♣7♣6♦. He knew that a continuation bet was

called for here, assumed that his foe knew this too, and
so saw no reason not to bet. *If she thinks I'm just making a
play at the pot, she'll pay me at least once.* He bet $1,200 into
a pot of $2,100. At this point, Hal experienced a weird
bifurcation of mind. On one hand, he felt clear and crisp
in his analysis, despite the fuzzy coating on his neurons
and axons. On the other hand, he couldn't stop saying,
"Mooooomooooo, mooooomooooo," and he knew that
must seem odd.

Odder still, the big blind hadn't made the expected
call. Instead, she saw his bet and raised him back, an ad-
ditional $2,000. Hal sat back in his chair, startled. He
ran his fingers through his hair. It felt like seaweed. He
was pretty sure he smelled kelp.

"Think things through," Slaughter had always told
him, but it was hard to think things through with all the
chatter in his head, a noise like sand in a gearbox. Still,
he tried his best to piece it together. *She called an overbet
out of position against a new player, and then check-raised
into a board that didn't figure to have hit the original bettor.
Could she have called pre-flop with T-9, 9-5, or 5-4, and now
be sitting on a straight?* Hal had no reason to think so, but
he couldn't be sure. Such is the risk of making strong
moves early in a poker session or tournament: you
don't know your foes; don't know what sort of craziness
they're capable of. Of course, neither do they know that
about you.

Hal decided to call the raise and see what happened
on the turn. He was now sweating profusely and wondered if this would be interpreted as a tell. Also, his
hands were shaking, and he tried to tranquilize them by
shuffling some chips, but only succeeded in knocking
over his stack. The dealer burned and turned, placing
the A♠ on the board. Again the big blind checked. Hal
tried to figure out where he was in the hand. If she'd

called preflop with a good ace, say A-K or A-Q, she probably thought she just hit good, and Hal was in position to do stealth damage to her stack. If, however, she started with something like A-8 or A-7, then he was in considerable shit.

"When in doubt," Slaughter had once told him, "keep the pot small." That way, at least, your doubt will cost you less. So Hal checked. The dealer placed the river card: 6♥. As usual, Hal was not looking at the board, for Slaughter had also taught him always to watch his foes and not the board when the cards came down. "The cards'll still be there," Slaughter said, "but your enemy's reaction won't." Savvy opponents, Hal knew, gave little away; however, it never hurt to look, if for no other reason than to avoid giving away any information of his own. Normally, Hal liked to focus on the other guy's jaw muscles. He had found that players would clench their jaw if they hit, but relax if they missed. It made sense: either disappointment or the certain knowledge that they're done with the hand will cause unguarded players to release their stored tension. In his addled state, though, Hal found himself looking not at the woman's jaw, but rather at her rather substantial rack, which rose and fell beneath her muumuu. *Her boobs are talking to me!* thought Hal. He marveled at the revelation. Breasts, as far as he knew, had never talked to him before, but these spoke to him quite clearly, and they said that the six had killed her hand.

The big blind checked, putting the action on Hal. *If she thought I had an ace . . . ,* he mused, *then now I've got two pair.*

Two pair bigger than hers!

And he knew beyond the shadow of a doubt that they held the same hand. She had hit two pair, thought it was good enough to check-raise with on the flop, went for a check-raise again on the turn (which she didn't get), and was now prepared to surrender to any bet on the river. To seal the deal, he ridiculously underbet the pot by firing just $1,000 into it, as if desperately trying to price her into a call. She gave him an "Oh, no you don't" look and slid her cards into the muck.

"Eight-seven?" asked Hal. She nodded reflexively before she could stop herself. "Me, too," he said, flipping over his cards. Hal was not a fan of showing cards—why give away information for free?—but in this instance he dimly figured there was a lot of image equity and tilt equity to be collected here, so he went for it. Sure enough, the woman glowered darkly at him; not long after, she got her money in bad with A-T against someone else's A-K and busted out. As she stood up to leave the table, her breasts once again spoke to Hal from behind their bougainvillea curtain, saying, *This is all your fault!* Hal could only shrug. *Talking breasts,* he thought. *Man, play poker long enough, you'll see everything.*

And it's true: Play poker long enough, eventually you will see everything. A royal flush on board. Quads-over-quads bad beats. Miracle one-outers. People stroking out or dying at the table. Snatch-and-grab thefts, an idiot move if ever there was one, for have these nimrods never heard of security cameras? That Hal and his foe started with the same hand may have seemed like a long-shot coincidence, but coincidence is really just the law of averages playing catch-up.

Twenty-five hundred players had started the Poker Apocalypse. That this number hit the over/under line exactly was less a matter of coincidence than of people who set betting lines being good at their job. Given that Hal knew maybe a dozen other players in the field, the odds were roughly 200 to 1 against someone he knew by name filling a vacant seat at his table.

The odds of this person being someone who had lately assaulted him were somewhat longer than that.

But coincidence is just the law of averages playing catch-up, so here came Lanh Tran, bringing his formidable chip stack, his bogus Vietnamese accent, and his Oakley Super Thumps (where were they all *coming* from?) to seat six at Hal's table.

Had Hal been a little more clearheaded (or even any clearheaded) he might have wondered how in hell Lanh had managed to land a seat in the Apocalypse at this late hour. Had he been in command of his speech center, he might have asked. Had he been in the mood for a confrontation, he could have blown the whistle on Lanh's fake Saigon drawl. Had he been at all compos mentis, he would've guessed that Lanh had somehow bridged the gap between himself and Team Dragic. As Hal was none of these things, it was actually a good fifteen minutes before he even noticed his own personal dyed blond bête noire in the seat beside him—and at that a mere moment before the cops came and hauled Lanh Tran away. . . .

Lanh had had an eventful morning. After futilely chasing Hal through the Cortland's parking garage, he had retreated to a casino men's room to scrape and rub the last vestiges of duct tape goo off his hands. The more he lathered, the more lathered he got, working himself into such high dudgeon that he became determined to play in the Apocalypse regardless of cost or consequence. Plan A (steal Hal's entry chip) having failed, he now turned to plan B, which was, basically, "Think of fucking *something!*" He didn't know what "fucking *something*" might be, but obsession had overwhelmed him, such that he was no longer burdened by the niceties of logic. The Elvis of his common sense, as it were, had left the building of his brain. Greed will do that to you, especially when it's backstopped by the certain knowledge that if you can just get in, you cannot lose.

So he removed himself to the tournament registration area, and there lurked, waiting for inspiration to strike.

It struck in the form of Mouse Skowron, who had a tournament entry chip, a pair of Oakley Super Thumps and—key, as it turned out—an unrelenting nicotine jones. Mouse signed in, collected his seating card, and made a beeline for the Cortland's smoking terrace. This elegantly appointed patio overlooked the Strip from several stories up, and when Lanh got Mouse alone out there he moved with the swift confidence of the truly deranged: pinning Mouse against the low retaining wall; relieving him of his seat card and his sunglasses; and then, without much thought or ceremony, bench-pressing the mere sixty-five pounds of Mouse and chucking him off the terrace to his death.

Nimrod. They've got security cameras out here, too.

Lanh had lost it. Lost it completely. There's no way he should have gotten away with even ten minutes of this masquerade—but the best bluff you run is the one where you don't believe you're bluffing. Lanh had been chasing the Apocalypse for so long that he actually felt like he'd earned his way in. And if what he'd heard about the Oakleys was true . . .

Lahn had put the shades on his face.

And suddenly everything had changed.

That it took the cops the better part of six hours to identify and locate Lanh is a testament to general human incompetence. That Detective Danny Ding was assigned to bring Lanh in was a measure of Ding's own personal incompetence; the detective had made such a hash of Guy's murder investigation that he'd been demoted to lackey fuckup, and tasked to such no-brainers as arresting murder suspects whose identity and location were positively known. He led a mixed team of plainclothes officers and Cortland security guards to Lanh Tran's table, where the furiously protesting Lanh was grabbed, cuffed, and hustled from the tournament hall.

Play the game long enough, you will see everything.

In the ruckus of Lanh's arrest, his Oakleys fell off his face and landed in Hal's lap. There they sat for a while before the fact of them traveled the distended limbic distance to his brain. Hal, a good citizen under even the most bizarre of circumstances, called out, "Hey, you forgot your Thumps!" But Lanh was long gone. Hal didn't know what to do with the shades. They looked expensive, and far more complex than Oakley's original Thumps, the first crude union of eyewear and music technology. He supposed he would hold on to them and deliver them to some sort of lost and found somewhere, though even in his demented state he figured it might be a while before Lanh could come back around to collect them.

Then Hal sneezed, and a searing bolt of agony shot through his chest, for broken ribs hate sneezes like a cat hates baths. *Stay ahead of the pain,* thought Hal. He hung the Oakleys from his shirt collar, knocked back a couple more Dilaudid, and returned to his peculiarly successful, stunningly off-kilter game.

21 WTF

Typically in poker tournaments, even in ones with big starting stacks and gently rising blinds, there come moments when a lot of players start to feel squeezed at the same time. The math of this is pretty straightforward. Say a hundred players each started with 100 chips and the blinds were 1 and 2. Everyone would have fifty times the big blind and none would feel particular need for rash action. Now fast forward a few levels. The blinds have climbed to 5 and 10, and the field has been trimmed by just ten percent. The ninety remaining players have an average not of fifty times the big blind, but instead a mere nine. That's called short-stacked and imperiled, and throughout the tournament field, players will be looking for chances to get their chips in good. With all-in confrontations breaking out like wartime flu, it's not uncommon to hear overlapping shouts of joy, dismay, disbelief, outright disgust. Some call this phase of a tournament "the hour of the outburst." It happens every time the average chip count sinks low compared to the size of the blinds, and it lasts until a fair number of competitors bust out. The remaining chips are then consolidated in relatively fewer hands; the average chip stack is once again large enough to stave off imminent danger; and a lull, of sorts, ensues. This lull lasts until the rising blinds exert renewed pressure on the field, and a new hour of the outburst rolls in.

The structure of the Poker Apocalypse was such that the first significant hour of the outburst came during the last level of play on day one. With antes of $50 and blinds of $200 and $400, each lap around a ten-person table cost $1,100 in chips—enough to put pressure on a wide swath of stacks. Fatigue was also a factor, affecting both judgment and playing style. Those who thought they needed to make moves were making them. Others with medium to large stacks tightened up, desperate for the closing bell, a good night's sleep, and a fresh start on day two. A few players turned hyperaggressive, applying pressure to the growing number of shrinking stacks.

Some just got rude; cranky and rude.

One such obnox, a certain Sully Fisher, occupied the two seat at Hal's table. A couple of bad beats had put Sully on tilt, and from the elevated platform of his own sour mood he started hurling insults and invective at everyone at the table. "You focking clowns," he growled. "How can I focking beat such focking bad play?"

"Dealer," said another player, "F-bomb?"

"Open your ears, dickweed," said Sully. "I'm saying 'focking,' not that other thing." He muttered under his breath, "Focking retards can't even focking hear."

"Look, buddy," said the other player, "even if you're not technically swearing, your language is abusive and—"

"Oh, you little girl," said Sully. "Why don't you just go cry?"

The dealer, a frail young Filipina, tried to cool him

out. "Sir, please—" But she didn't get any further than that.

"Don't you focking start with me," said Sully. "This is your focking fault in the first place. Put a decent damn river card down once in a while, why don't you?"

The player to Hal's right leaned over and whispered, "To an asshole, the whole world looks dark." Hal chuckled, which brought Sully's ire down on him.

"What are you laughing at, butthead? You're the worst focking clown I've ever seen." In Hal's normal frame of mind, Sully would not have troubled him; Hal would have simply and dispassionately devised a strategy for using Sully's tilt against him. In his current state, though, he found Sully's ranting impossible to take. *I can't listen to this,* thought Hal. If he'd been more practiced in the ways of self-medication, he would have known the reason why: Sully was harshing his mellow, shackling his buzz. As it was, Sully's voice, filtered through the throes of synesthesia, tasted like dead snakes in Hal's mouth and made him sick to his stomach. He found himself wishing for the analgesic refuge of headphones. And then realized he had some. He put on Lanh's Oakley Super Thumps, powered them up, and sighed with sweet relief as the sound of music filled his head. He didn't recognize the tunes; didn't care. The sound blotted out Sully's voice, and that's all that mattered.

The dealer dished him his cards. As he looked down, he glimpsed a pair of card and suit symbols, the 9♥ and J♠, hanging there on the periphery of the Thumps' left lens. He looked left, trying to center the image, but it disappeared the moment he lifted his head. *Huh,* he thought, *trick glasses.* He looked back down at his cards— and saw it again: the 9♥ and J♠ floating in his field of vision like instrument readouts in a heads-up display. Hal looked up and shook his head, and once more the symbols vanished. He had never hallucinated before—never so much as a déjà vu—but he realized that that must be what this was, a drug-induced delusion. He found the sensation odd, but not unpleasant. He looked down once more, and the symbols reappeared. *Talking breasts are one thing . . . ,* he thought. *I assume this wears off eventually.* He went to lift up his cards, carefully cupping them in his tented fingers and peeling back the corners with his thumb.

The nine of hearts and jack of spades.

"What the fuck?" he said out loud and got himself a twenty-minute time-out.

Sully sniggered as Hal got up from his seat. "Focking potty mouth," he said. Hal didn't hear him. Apart from the music still pouring into his ears, a combination of shock and pharmaceuticals had kicked Hal into an altered reality. *Did I see what I saw?* he wondered as he staggered away from the table. *What the hell is going on?*

He spotted Slaughter Johnson nearby, locked in confrontation with a well-known young internet pro whose screen name, bigfatsmellycat, belied his schoolboy look and demeanor. The two were heads up in a pot of substantial size, with a board that showed A♥3♥7♣9♦ as they waited for the river card to come. Hal crept up behind Slaughter and looked down at his cards. The A♠ and 7♦ symbols appeared in his heads-up display. Hal began to tremble. He looked toward the other end of the table, focusing his vision on bigfatsmellycat's cards. The A♠7♦ faded out, and two new cards appeared: K♥ and Q♥. Hal swallowed hard. *This can't be happening,* he thought. He looked away; the card symbols disappeared. He looked back; they returned. He looked at the deck in the dealer's hand; nothing. The dealer burned and turned, and placed the 7♥ on board.

Slaughter was first to act. He leaned back in his chair, noticing but not acknowledging Hal as he studied his foe. After a long moment, he silently rapped his knuckles on the felt: check. His Adam's apple bobbed up and down, and Hal thought, *What is he afraid of?* Then he realized that of course Slaughter wasn't afraid. He was just selling fear to induce a bet from a lesser hand or even a naked bluff. At that, he was pretty damn convincing. *I bought it,* thought Hal, *and I know what he's got.*

Then: *How do I know what he's got?!*

Hal didn't linger to see how the hand played out. He knew Slaughter would win either a big pot or a huge pot and, given his current stack size, finish the day's play among the chip leaders. As for Hal's own stack, the twenty-minute penalty would keep him away from the table almost till the end of the level—not necessarily a bad thing, considering his turbulent state of mind—and leave him somewhere in the middle of the pack going into day two.

Hal lurched to the perimeter of the room, where spectators stood behind velvet ropes (spirals of celadon and crimson—was there *anything* in the casino not color branded?) and craned their necks to follow the action. He located Skip and Vinny and went to stand next to them.

"Nice Thumps," said Skip.

Vinny looked around the tournament area. From where she stood, she could see a dozen or more players wearing similar glasses. "They seem to be pretty popular," she said.

"They have some special qualities," said Hal, his voice quivering badly. They both looked at him.

"You okay, man?" asked Skip.

"High as a kite," said Hal. "But apart from that . . ." He handed Skip the glasses. "Go look at some hands.

Tell me what you see." Skip put on the Super Thumps and stepped over the rope. "Skip," Hal added, "be cool."

"When am I not?" asked Skip as he walked away.

"What's going on?" asked Vinny.

"Me not going crazy, I hope." She looked at him for a long moment, then wordlessly took his hand in a gesture of such affection that Hal's heart just melted. He thought back to their first meeting, that first drive out to Slaughter's place in the desert, when she had been so guarded and close. They'd come a long way since then, and though he recognized that there were doors to Vinny he'd never have the key to, he felt like he wouldn't mind spending his life trying the locks. "I might have to marry you," he said lightly. "'Course, that's just the drugs talking."

Vinny smiled a Mona Lisa smile. "Keep talking, drugs."

Skip came back. His face was pale as pasteboard. "WTF?" he said with elaborate simplicity.

"What the fuck, indeed," Hal agreed. He handed the glasses to Vinny. "Check it out." She put the Thumps on top of her head and walked out across the tournament floor. Hal followed her with his eyes as she paused beside a table at random and flipped down the glasses. He saw her knees buckle, and she grabbed the back of a player's chair to keep from falling down. The player shot her an irritated look. She offered a wan, apologetic smile and returned to the boys, stopping to view a couple more tables on the way.

"What do you think?" asked Hal.

Vinny took off the Thumps and handed them back to Hal. "I think Oakley's got some explaining to do."

Hal counted down the clock of his twenty-minute penalty and returned to his table in time to take one last hand before the close of play. He didn't wear the Oakleys. Didn't play the hand, either; felt too rattled to attempt it. He just waited for the hand to conclude, then counted his chips and bagged them. Then he sealed the heavy plastic bag and wrote his name, seat number, and chip count on the outside: $21,025; not a monster, but not too shabby. He slid the bag across the table to the dealer.

As he slid his hand back, he palmed a card.

With some difficulty, and no small amount of pain, Hal then bent down to tie a shoe. Glancing at the underside of the table, he noted a rat's nest of wiring and small black boxes, one at each seat position. He nodded to himself, slipped the card into his jacket pocket, rose, and walked away.

By the time they all got back to Vinny's place, the Dilaudid had worn off, and Hal's chest was a throbbing gong of pain. As he opened the door, he could hear Minty McGinty thundering down the stairs and braced himself for the onslaught. But Minty skidded to a stop at the bottom of the stairs, padded over to Hal, and greeted him with a gentle lick on the hand, his tongue like bubble gum wrapped in sandpaper. He was, and continued to be, as Guy had advertised him: one smart fucking dog.

Hal was mortally weary. The one-two punch of sleep debt and opiate crash had brought him to the brink of exhaustion. But he couldn't let go of the day just yet. First . . .

He pulled out the card he'd palmed, a completely ordinary deuce of spades with the Cortland's logo and the words *Poker Apocalypse* on the back. He bent it, bowed it, held it up to his ear, and gave it a speculative thwack. Then he handed it to Skip, who did the same. "Seems normal," shrugged Skip, who then put on the Oakleys and looked at the card. "Nothing," he reported.

"There wouldn't be," said Hal. "They'd pull the signal from the card reader, not the card." He told them about the equipment he'd noticed beneath the table. He guessed that the black boxes were beaming card values from the table to some back office, where it was all sorted and stored for TV postproduction.

"But that's hundreds of thousands of hands," protested Vinny. "That's way too much data!"

"Not if it's time coded," mused Slaughter. "The cameras capture an interesting hand—they're time coded, too—and then postproduction just goes and grabs what they need."

"Meanwhile, the Oakleys grab it first."

Again Skip thwacked the deuce of spades. "But the card's just a card," he said. "How does the reader know which one it is?"

"RFID," said Vinny. "They have them in the chips. Why not the cards?"

Skip felt the smooth, flat surface of the card. "They'd have to be incredibly fucking tiny," he said.

"Get a razor blade," said Hal. "Let's find out."

Vinny found an X-Acto knife and went to work on the card. At first it seemed to be a typical Kem or Copag playing card, a solid piece of flexible, durable plastic. As Vinny teased at the corner with the knife, though, it revealed itself to be two ultrathin sheets seamlessly laminated together. She prized the layers apart, and there, a quarter of an inch in from the edge, found a tiny metallic sliver no bigger than an eyelash.

"That?" asked Skip.

"That," said Hal.

"Kids," said Slaughter, "it looks like we've found the hack."

22 His Own Stupid Stupidity

On day two of the Poker Apocalypse, Hal decided to give the Dilaudid a miss. The pain in his chest still raged, but he knew that masking it would have to catch up to him eventually. He'd been lucky yesterday: his altered consciousness had given him unique approaches to the play of hands and unusual insight into his foes; but also he hadn't been in many difficult or dicey situations. Today would be different, with the dead money having been swept from the field, and chips consolidated in the hands of capable and dangerous foes. Plus, he'd be using the Oakleys. As they weren't his, it was only a matter of time before someone noticed him wearing and using them. He was crashing a certain party. Best to keep his wits, such as they were, about him.

Over breakfast in the town house, while Skip messed around with the Oakleys, Vinny, Hal, and Slaughter discussed how to use them most effectively. It wasn't simply a matter of looking at everyone's hand, measuring them against your own, and bulling ahead on the strength of your known edge. For one thing, deception was called for. Make too many radical moves based on hidden knowledge, and you start to call attention to yourself. People wonder how you got so smart. Nor could you necessarily count on others being appropriately smart in return. Say you hold pocket jacks and your foe is on a low straight draw. If you overbet the pot, there's no way your opponent is getting the right price to call—but also there's no law that says you won't get a call anyway. Just one suckout later, you're riding the rail, magic glasses and all.

At one point Slaughter said to Hal, "It doesn't bother you that you're cheating?" In fact, it bothered Hal quite a lot. There were, he realized, two contests being played now: the Poker Apocalypse, and his own cat-and-mouse game with Dragic. He was using the former to leverage the latter. That made everyone else in the tournament innocent victims. They had all entered the event with the expectation of a level playing field. To that extent, he was stealing their money, potentially quite a lot of it, and though he essayed a certain "end justifies the means" argument in his mind, his conscience remained unclear. Still . . .

"What would Guy have done, do you think?" Hal asked.

Skip looked up from the Oakleys. "Fuck the motherfucker up," he said.

And on that cheery note, they headed out.

By the time they reached the Cortland, the corridor outside the ballroom was packed with players waiting for the hall to open. The crowd buzzed with speculation about Mouse's murder and Lanh's arrest. To the casual ear, reasons ranged from Mouse sleeping with Kai Cortland's trophy wife to Lanh settling debts for a Vietnamese triad. Truly, rumors are almost as rampant in poker circles as outright lies.

Seats had been redrawn for day two, and a printout

taped to a wall listed chip counts and new seat assign-
ments. Dragic, Skip noted, had only an average stack.
Hal suspected that he was laying back, letting his stalking horses do his work. He was on the point of voicing
this thought when Big Mo strode up. "Hal Harris, everyone!" bellowed Mo. "How you running, champ?" He
jovially aimed a mock punch at Hal. Hal flinched, gri-
macing as shock waves of pain coursed through his sternum.

Skip moved to interpose himself between Mo and
Hal—a gesture long on bravado but short on common
sense, for he gave away seven inches and a hundred
pounds to Big Mo, who seemed merely amused by Skip's
pugnacity. "Relax, little dude. I'm just horsing around."
He turned to Hal. "You okay, slick? You look a little shaky."

"I'm fine," mustered Hal.

"Well, good. Wouldn't want anything to hurt your
game. They say you were really playing above the rim
yesterday. Caught a lot of eyes." Hal essayed a wan smile.
There really wasn't anything to say. "Well . . . take care,"
said Mo, aiming a mock punch at Skip, who, to his credit,
did not flinch.

Mo wandered off into the crowd, glad-handing other
players like a politician working a pancake breakfast.
Vinny watched him go and asked, "What was that about?"

"I'm thinking warning shot across the bow," said Hal,
his voice quavery with pain.

Slaughter looked at him with concern. "It's not too
late, you know," he said. "You can still bail."

Hal managed a weak smile. "Never leave money lying
on the table."

Skip, meanwhile, continued his love affair with the
Oakleys. "These are wild," he said.

"Yeah, no duh," said Hal.

"No, I mean, seriously"—Skip tapped various parts of

the glasses' frames, stems, and lenses—"they've got it all. MP3, flash drive, voice memo, camera. I think there's a phone in there somewhere." Skip handed Hal the glasses. "I put a music mix on for you, something to keep you awake." He patted Hal gingerly on the back. "Shred 'em, Hal. Swoop and pummel."

"Swoop and pummel," agreed Hal.

Just then, the ballroom doors spilled open with a pneumatic whoosh, and the tide of players streamed into the tournament hall. Hal and Slaughter entered the roped-off table area, while Vinny and Skip moved to a spectators' place along the rail. Hal made his way to his assigned seat, an altogether easier proposition today than yesterday. Thinking about how impaired he'd been, Hal marveled that he had survived the day's play. He wondered if there was such a thing as instinct in poker, and whether he wouldn't be better off just letting it guide him now. Of course, now he had the glasses, but even these gave him pause. Should he use them on every hand? Only in big pots? As a tool for analysis, to deduce other players' strategies from their cards? At this last thought, Hal had to laugh, for what need of deduction when all is laid bare?

Might as well listen to some music, at least. See what Skip's cooked up. He turned on the Super Thumps and flipped the earpieces into place. The greasy guitars and chunky drums of uptempo country rock filled his ears. He didn't recognize the tune, nor any that followed, but he found them all compellingly catchy. They stimulated him and energized him for the task at hand.

Play began with a certain amount of cautious parry and thrust, as the seat redraw put players together in new and untested combinations. Through carefully calibrated bets and raises they felt each other out, probing to see who would come on strong and who was content to play at a more measured pace. For a long time, Hal had no need of the Oakleys, for his cards made him a series of offers he couldn't accept: 7-2, 8-3, 6-2, 7-4. *Fold, fold, fold, fold. Poker is easy when your decisions are automatic.* However, Hal was aware that if he went too long without seeing good cards he ran the risk of loosening up his starting requirements and getting involved—possibly disastrously overinvolved—with a questionable holding like K-Q or A-J. This was not a matter of sound tournament strategy, of moving his stack before it became too short and lost all fold equity: the power to make the other guy lay down. Rather, it was what Slaughter called "raisitis," a disease of subjective reality such that the hands you folded an hour ago are the ones you raise with now, just because your brain craves action.

Hal realized he could be at risk for this even while knowing what cards the other guy had. He might be holding pocket eights against someone's A-K and be about a 5 to 4 favorite. Should he go? Granted, he'd have the statistical edge, but would he want to commit a lot of chips on, essentially, a coin flip?

Only if he lost the plot.

Of course, Hal had the luxury of seeing flops with hands like these, and then betting with confidence if his opponent missed. Even at that, though, there were pitfalls. Say he called a raise from that A-K and caught a favorable flop like 7-4-2 rainbow. His pocket eights would be way ahead . . . but how should he play the hand? Let his foe bluff into him? Lead out and try to take the pot away? It wasn't inconceivable that the other guy would put him on a steal and play back at him for all his chips. Then what? With that flop, his 8-8 would stand up against A-K about three-quarters of the time. But do you bet it all with even that big an edge? One time out of four, it's gonna go against you. With magic glasses, you should be able to get your money in with mortal locks, shouldn't you?

Well, shouldn't you?

After a long slog through a card desert, where the best hand Hal saw was T-T (and had to let it go because the big blind had J-J), he finally picked up two red aces in early position. Looking at each player in turn, he saw that no one had much of anything: the best hand out against him was K♠Q♠, a more than 4-to-1 underdog to his pocket aces. The player holding this hand was a former (and very rich) heavyweight boxer who had lately turned his attention to poker. For someone in his tax bracket, buying into the Apocalypse was probably not much different from that whale the other night who played blackjack at $50K a hand. Some people have more money than common sense. In this instance, the boxer—they'd called him the Bludgeon back in the day— had shown a willingness to mix it up with a wide array of hands, and Hal felt that if he made a modest raise, he'd likely get a call. But did he want one? As Guy used to say, "Slowplay aces, go to hell." He decided to content himself with winning the antes and blinds, or else invite someone to make a very bad mistake by calling. So he bet big, $2,500 into a pot of $1,650, telegraphing real card strength. As predicted, everyone folded.

Everyone except the Bludgeon, who made a very bad mistake.

They both had about $20,000 in chips, so neither was yet terribly deeply committed to this pot, but when the flop came J♥T♥T♠, Hal wondered if he had a problem on his hands. He knew that his opponent had only four true outs, the four nines in the deck, but figured the Bludgeon would assume that aces were clean guts, and possibly kings and queens as well. An optimistic reading of his situation could give the boxer as many as fourteen outs—more if he wanted to invest a particle of faith in a runner-runner flush or full house. With better than a 50/50 shot of getting there—at least in the Bludgeon's mind—there was a good chance he'd call a reasonable bet. Did Hal want that? True, the boxer was drawing slim—but drawing slim is not the same as drawing dead, and what would Hal do if a nine came on the turn?

At this point, Hal paused to view the situation as if he didn't know what his foe held. How would he play his aces then? Check-calling was an option, for he might be facing J-T, J-J or T-x, but he'd more likely bet to protect his hand against the wide range of other holdings his foe might have. For the sake of keeping his actions organic, then, Hal fired off a pot-sized bet and hoped he wouldn't have to see a turn card. This made him feel strange—uncharacteristically timid. Did he really not want his opponent calling with so much the worst of it? His X-ray specs, he realized, were actually inhibiting his play. Since the odds were so great that he'd have pure lock situations downstream, he hated to leave open even the slightest possibility of a suckout.

Especially when the Bludgeon raised all in.

With certain knowledge of his foe's hand, Hal knew this play to be pure kamikaze, though from the other guy's point of view, it certainly made some sense. By betting huge with his (presumably) huge draw, he leveraged his fold equity to the maximum. Someone like Hal, who had raised preflop and then made a standard continuation bet on the flop, might very well be in there with something like pocket eights or pocket nines and now be forced to release his hand to the Bludgeon's big semibluff.

Hal had the Bludgeon covered by about $2,000. If he called and won, he'd be up over $40K, within shouting distance of the chip leaders. If he called and lost, he'd be down to the felt, in a hole so deep that maybe not even X-ray specs could dig him out. What to do? Take the extremely favorable proposition he was being offered, or get away from the hand with his medium stack intact? In the back of his mind he found himself shocked (and a little amused in a perverse sort of way) to discover that knowing the other guy's cards could be such a double-edged sword.

Hal took off the glasses. Leaned back in his seat. Templed his fingers. Noted, again with wry amusement, the camera crews swarming in to capture this showdown. He could imagine some later commentators in postproduction saying, "He's got a real dilemma on his hands here." They didn't know the half of it.

He kept coming back to the odds. There were only four nines in the deck. The Bludgeon had about a 16 percent chance of catching up.

Then he remembered: *There aren't four nines in the deck! There's only three! Seat one folded a nine preflop!* This reduced the Bludgeon's odds to just under 10 percent. Nine times out of ten he wouldn't catch a nine on the turn or the river. *Christ,* thought Hal, *how can I not accept a nine-to-one edge?* He moved his hands to his chips and started pushing them toward the betting line, the white stripe on the green felt that served as every bettor's Rubicon. Hal thought about how sick he'd feel if a nine came down. Then: *Wait! Fuck! That math's not right! His odds aren't four in forty-five twice! That's what they'd be if I didn't know any other cards. But I know seventeen other cards!* Hal did some fast math in his head. The Bludgeon had a 3-in-29 chance of hitting on the turn, and then a 3-in-28 chance of hitting on the river. All told, he was . . . *My God, I'm only a four-to-one favorite!* Hal stopped his hand.

Too late!

His chips were already over the line!

And the Bludgeon called him on it. Either he thought Hal was calling with an underpair (and all of Hal's sweaty indecision could certainly have led him to think so) or else he just had the gamble in him and wanted to play the hand out; in any case, he called for the tournament director, who correctly ruled that Hal's chips had crossed the line and were committed to the pot.

Now Hal's fate was out of his hands. Both players turned over their cards. The others at the table admired the Bludgeon's gutsy raise—and wondered about the wisdom of Hal's call. Granted he had pocket aces, but wasn't he afraid of pocket jacks or any ten? He sure as shit should have been.

The dealer burned and turned.

The nine of hearts struck Hal like a dagger in the gut.

How could I be so stupid? How could I make that call? I didn't have to gamble! With these damn glasses, I should never have to gamble! I should be playing small pots to the river and then betting for value or else bluffing when I know the other guy can't call. Christ, I can't even cheat right! At that moment, Hal wasn't thinking about the hack or the glasses or Dark Mark or Guy's murder or anything. He was just thinking, as any tournament player would, that his own stupid stupidity had cost him the main chance. Hal's heart sank.

But speaking of hearts . . .

The dealer burned and turned, placing the 3♥ on board beside the J♥T♥T♠9♥. The other players at the table gasped. The Bludgeon smacked his fist against the felt and shouted, "No!!!" (The TV cameras caught this, delighting the director in the production truck, who knew he could play that particular clip—the KO of a heavyweight—to death.) It took Hal a moment to realize what had happened. He'd made a runner-runner flush to stay alive.

Not just stay alive, but double through.

Not just double through, but survive his own stupid stupidity.

Hal swallowed hard and wiped the sweat from his forehead. He couldn't believe what had happened. A lucky cardfall had snatched him back from the brink of catastrophe. He'd been given a crucial second chance—and he'd damn well better make the most of it. From now on, he'd use the glasses judiciously, circumspectly. In poker, he reminded himself, you're rarely a lock—even if you know what the other guy has. Luck will always be a factor.

He had to make it as small a factor as possible.

Hal got up from the table and took a slow walk around, missing several hands before returning to his seat. He had temporarily lost his footing, lost the plot, nearly lost his tournament life. He took the time he needed to right himself. When he finally sat back down at the table, he puffed out his cheeks and shook his head. *Wow*, he thought. *What did I almost step in?*

23 Here's What's What

As the hours of the Apocalypse wore on, Hal had better success. He started picking his spots, measuring small edges against huge ones against locks. He eliminated one player in a set-over-set confrontation when his opponent's case quad card was gone, and got someone else drawing dead with a made straight against his made flush. He started to get the hang of the Oakleys and, after his near disaster against the Bludgeon, was not imperiled for the rest of the day.

Pangs of guilt pinged him, though, as he eliminated one earnest striver after another. They all had such hope—and reasonable expectation—that their luck and skill would carry them to a high-money finish in the world's biggest poker tournament . . . maybe all the way to the top of the $70 million mountain. But Hal's glasses, once he mastered their use, trumped both luck and skill. It was like playing darts with a blind man; it just wasn't fair.

At intervals, Hal got up and walked around the tournament floor. He spotted a dozen or more players wearing Oakleys. Not surprisingly, all had amassed huge mounds of chips. Though many, many tournament players wore sunglasses, long-billed caps, low-riding visors, translucent shields, and other esoteric eyewear and headwear, the stylish Super Thumps were apparently delivering a competitive edge—an edge that everyone would assume came from nothing more than the confidence of looking sharp or the convenience of having all your entertainment options built right into your shades. Hal could imagine the marketing department at Oakley geeking out over this: *Oakley—Sunglass of Champions.*

Unless, of course, the truth came out.

A thought was growing within Hal, a thought spawned in guilt but fed by sheer cussed-mindedness. He hadn't asked to be part of Dragic's crew, yet here he was, using their tools, tarred with their brush. He considered his actions to be reprehensible, and the deeper he went into the tournament, the stronger that feeling became. Ultimately, he decided, his despicable behavior must not be in vain. The only thing that could make this whole nasty episode worthwhile was . . .

Justice.

But how to get it? What play can I make? What tools do I have at my disposal but a pair of funky sunglasses?

The day gave way to evening. They had reached the last level of play before dinner break, with antes of $200 and blinds of $500 and $1,000. The field had been trimmed to under 500. With the money bubble set to pop at 250, it would yet be several hours before players would start to cash—though at the rate Team Dragic was mowing down the competition, that time would come sooner rather than later.

Hal was weary, sweaty, and sore. He had taped his

chest, and while the constricting support minimized in-
cidental shots of pain, the bandages were starting to
chafe; he could feel a rash rising. Beyond that, he was
having increasing difficulty keeping his focus. His mind
boiled with rage, furtiveness, uncertainty. More and more,
he relied on his glasses to guide him through hands;
more and more, he was becoming reckless in their use.
Pocket eights versus pocket sevens? *Raise!* A-K versus
A-Q? *Raise! Let the sucker suck out on me—I don't care anymore!* Though Hal was blessed with a natural emotional
equilibrium, the special circumstances of this tournament were testing him . . . oppressing him, almost. He
was tilting, and in the nature of players on tilt he didn't
even know it.

Music blasted in his ears. Skip had programmed an
audio roller coaster segueing from rock to jazz to reg-
gae to rap, with odd detours into . . . what? Pan pipes?
Melodeon? Hal didn't know what he was listening to,
but he hadn't tuned out in hours. He had become as
habituated to the music as he was to the heads-up display. No two ways about it, Hal Harris was a mess.

And then, things got a whole lot worse.

He was sitting in the big blind with K-8 offsuit, scoping
out the table as usual, scanning from left to right, col-
lecting data as he went. *J-2, 7-3, 8-6 . . . no hands there . . .
4-4, might play . . . 7-6 . . . What the—?* Hal tapped his left
ear, then his right, for the music had suddenly drained
away. He continued surveilling the table—but his HUD
had gone dark. The player in the cutoff seat limped
into the pot, and for the first time all day, Hal had no
idea where he was in the hand. Suddenly and explo-
sively adrift, he watched the button and small blind
fold, and reflexively checked.

The flop came down K♥3♦2♣. Again Hal checked,

though it wasn't in his nature to let top pair go unbet heads up. He took off the Oakleys and gave them a vigorous shake. He put them back on and looked down at his cards. The glimmer of a K-8 appeared in his peripheral vision, but when he went to inspect his foe's holding, the image died and did not return. He was on his own. A certain crutch had been kicked out from under him, and Hal stumbled. The cutoff made a pot-size bet, and Hal called without thinking. *What are you* doing *?!* he heard himself inwardly scream, but the chips went in the pot just the same. The turn was the A♠, and Hal started thinking maybe he could dodge this bullet, for his check-call on the flop could possibly have represented something like A-3; maybe his foe would slow down, and he could stagger to the river for free. Again he checked, but he tried to put some verbal topspin on it, a "power check," intended to indicate strength.

The cutoff didn't go for it. He bet the pot again.

Now Hal was—oh, there's no pretty way to say it— fucked up. He took it into his head that the cutoff was on something like middle pair, or maybe even real trash like middle suited connectors. His heart told him that a big reraise right here could take this pot away . . . but his head didn't have the heart for it, and he just flat-called again, the weakest way on earth to play the hand. With anticipation and trepidation, he waited for the river to come down, praying for an eight to fall and bail him out of this mess, for he'd finally figured out that the cutoff was on a better king. *God forbid he's on A-K.* The river was an utterly unhelpful nine of spades. There was no straight or flush to represent; in his wildest imagining, he thought about betting as if the nine had given him trips, but common sense—or sheer timidity—prevailed. He checked. His foe hesitated, then made a modest bet of about $5,000. It was a Hoover bet, designed to suck him into a call. Hal knew it. The rest of the table knew it. Life on other planets knew it. Somehow, though, Hal convinced himself that this was not a textbook tease bet, but rather a weak attempt at a hopeless bluff. And with the pot up over $30K, how could he *not* call?

He called. The cutoff showed A-K. Hal nodded and mucked his hand. Was there ever any doubt?

Good God! he thought, looking down at his diminished stack. *What happened to my chips?!*

The next few hands passed in a blur. He managed to fold in the small blind, but when it was folded around to his button, he raised in position with some crap hand only to face a monster reraise from the big blind. Thankfully, he had the presence of mind to surrender, but there was no doubt now about where Hal was at: he was a cork bobbing on the sea of poker.

He was, quite literally, saved by the bell—the digital chime indicating the end of the round and the start of the dinner break.

Hal stood up quickly, panic bringing perspiration to his pits and upper lip. He saw Slaughter vectoring toward him from another table, but couldn't look his mentor in the eye. Instead, he stumbled out of the tournament hall, lurched to the bathroom, and locked himself in a stall until the rush of bathroom traffic subsided—ten long minutes—and he could have the cool, quiet porcelain hell to himself. He went to the sink and splashed some water on his face. He couldn't even meet his own eyes in the mirror, so humiliated was he by the way he'd played that last hand. It was a low point in Hal's brief poker career, and it was only his natural gift for the game that made the moment so unfamiliar; lesser players get there all the time.

Emerging from the men's room at last, Hal found the others waiting for him. He gave them a brief account of the disastrous hand, and while he tried to cast his actions in a positive light, there was no doubt in anybody's mind that Hal had managed to mirplo away half his stack, X-ray specs completely notwithstanding. Hal gave the offending glasses a vigorous shake but, as before, they showed no sign of life.

"They're broken!" said Hal. "Fucking pieces of shit are broken."

"Let me see 'em," said Skip. He plucked the Oakleys from Hal's hand, checked them out for a moment; and then, with a hangdog expression, said, "Oh, this is my bad."

"What do you mean?" asked Vinny.

Skip turned to Hal. "You loved my music mix, didn't you?" Hal nodded dully. "Yeah, I should be a fucking DJ." Hal still didn't get it and looked at Skip blankly. "Nimrod, the batteries are shot." Skip tucked the glasses in his pocket. "I'll get some new ones." He loped off toward the escalator. Not bothering with the metal steps, he slid down the black banister and disappeared in the noise and confusion of the casino floor.

Vinny said to Hal, "Come on, let's go get something to eat."

"You two go," said Hal. "I just really want to be alone."

Said Slaughter, "Son, everybody makes mistakes."

"It's not about the hand, Slaughter. I . . ." Hal paused, at a loss for words. "I just have to sort things out."

"Can we bring you something?" asked Vinny.

"Sure. Sandwich. Anything. Go." He watched them depart down the escalator and into the casino. It looked like they were being sucked into a netherworld.

Hal was not having a good day.

Nor did his mood improve when a beefy hand landed on the back of his neck. Though the gesture could be interpreted as friendly, there was a bit of a grip to it. "Your friends go off to dinner?" asked Big Mo. Hal nodded. Mo kneaded Hal's neck, maybe 10 percent too vigorously to be considered massage. "It's good to have friends," he said. "Even when your friends borrow things without permission." At this, Hal tried to break free of Mo's grasp, but the hand just tightened on the scruff of Hal's neck, sending referred pain down through his rib cage. "Here's what's what," said Mo, a chill coming into his voice. "If you're wearing our glasses, you're on our team. You can play it any way you like—so long as you know who you're playing for."

"Dra—"

Mo cut him off with a squeeze. "No need to say it. Just tell me you understand what has to be done."

"Chip dump," said Hal.

"Yes, that's right. Are you up for that?"

"Why wouldn't I be?"

"I don't know, you know. The kind of equipment you've got, people start to get independent minded. That's not gonna happen to you, is it?"

"No."

"Good news. 'Cause speaking of friends, you know, mine know who yours are."

Hal had to get outside, breathe some air that didn't stink of cigarettes and slot tokens. He spent the rest of the dinner break walking the casino grounds: past the giant convention center, through the overblown botanical garden, and out around the pool. This was a serpentine affair that covered acres. In the waning daylight, couples smooched under artificial waterfalls; kids splashed in the shallows; and clots of revelers sat around plastic tables, enjoying the last of the day's drinks, or the first of the evening's, or both. They all seemed so carefree. Hal could not recall the last time he felt that way. It must have been before he came to Vegas, when he was still a drone in an office doing a job that required little of him and tested him less. Had he been happy then? He honestly couldn't remember.

And since? Certainly there had been moments during his journey through poker when he'd been so consumed and transported that he momentarily forgot everything else, for such is the narcotic effect of the game. And making love to Vinny . . . well, that was narcotic, too. But always over everything had hung the Apocalypse, when all his questions would be answered—or not. Now things were coming to a head. With the words of Big Mo still echoing in his ears, he wondered if there was any path through this hand except dumping his chips to Dragic, cutting his losses, and walking away. Smart poker players know how to do that: leave a game they can't beat. Hal didn't know if he could be that smart.

He tried ghosting Dragic. What did the man want? What price was he prepared to pay? Clearly, money alone wasn't the issue; if it were, then a single pair of pimped Oakleys would have assured him at least a high-money finish, with no risk of exposure—which risk, of course, multiplied with a larger team. For that matter, how much must it have cost to develop those glasses, and bribe or compromise the necessary people in Cortland's organization or on the TV side to make sure they worked? It was a massive undertaking, and one that didn't make sense for a man who, let's face it, didn't need the money in the first place.

Well, then, what did Dragic need? What did he not have and couldn't live without? Fame. *Acclaim.* Hal knew this must be true, but it baffled him that renown could be so potent a drug, for he wasn't wired that way. But Dragic was, and since he was, Hal realized that he might have a path through the hand after all.

He went back inside the casino and found that his contemplation of need had heightened his awareness of the stuff. He could see it plainly in everyone he met, as if they all wore flashing neon signs. The pit boss who needed a day off. The craps player who needed a hot roll. The cocktail waitress who needed to get off her feet. The bride-to-be who needed to believe that bright lights and *mojitos* could substitute for romance. It was the true knack of mind reading, coming plain to Hal at last: ninety percent of everything everyone thinks is the same stuff, so if you can read your own mind openly and honestly, then it's no great leap to read others', especially when you focus your insight through a vivid and precise filter like need.

Vinny and Slaughter were waiting for him outside the tournament hall. Vinny handed him a sandwich. "Are you all right?" she asked. "We were worried."

"I'm fine," he said, "but look, we've got to watch our backs now." He told them about Big Mo and the not-so-veiled threat. "From now on, no one goes anywhere alone. Where's Skip?"

"He's not back yet," said Slaughter. "The battery must've been harder to replace than he thought."

"Yeah," mused Hal. "I hope that's all."

"Hope what's all?" asked Skip, suddenly appearing in their midst. He was surprised to find himself greeted with a big hug from Vinny. "Whoa, mom. Back off." She kissed the top of his head, then filled him in on Hal's latest news. "Mayonnaise motherfuckers," muttered Skip. He handed Hal the Oakleys. "Here," he said. "You're good to go."

Hal took the glasses, but after a moment he returned them. "Hold on to them for now," he said. "I think they're just holding me back."

And before anyone could voice a word of protest, Hal Harris went back to the tournament floor, and back to work, with nothing to help him win but his own burning desire and his natural gift for the game.

24 Double or Done

The Oakleys, Hal realized, had enslaved him. They'd made him think he had something to lose. Liberated from them, and from their feeling of oppressive entitlement, he returned from the dinner break and went on an absolute tear. On his first hand back, he ran a sophisticated program, calling in late position, raising a continuation bet on the flop, checking behind on the turn, and pushing all in on the river—all on the stonest of bluffs. He was delighted, but not too surprised, to see how such a move put the others back on their heels. A player such as Hal, capable of doing anything at any time with any cards, became such a threat to players hoping to limp to the money bubble. More than a threat: a befuddlement, a—Guy's words came back to him and filled him with ineffable joy—*a rift in the fabric of space.*

After an hour or so, Hal got moved to Slaughter's table. Dialed in as he was, he had to resist the urge to show off for his mentor. *This isn't about ego,* he reminded himself. *It's not about shining. It's about playing perfect poker.* Mixing adept manipulation of his own image with keen awareness of his foes, he sliced through them with surgical precision. Apart from Slaughter, who knew better than to mess with Hal when he was in this zone, they all ended up leaning the wrong way, calling when they should fold, folding when they should raise, completely out of phase, and basically just hating life. In this way, Hal exploded through the money bubble and finished play for the day among the chip leaders.

Despite a good deal of looking over shoulders on the ride home, they made it back to Vinny's town house without incident. Minty greeted them with a mixture of affection and indignation, for while they'd been off frivolously wasting time (in a dog's opinion), he'd been cooped up in the house with no recreation more compelling than chewing on his own tail or harassing the odd wayward spider. Hal and Vinny took him out and let him romp the neighborhood while they strolled down deserted sidewalks in the midnight cool. At first, a frisson of wariness kept their senses on high alert, but it soon became clear that the night offered no threat. They walked arm in arm. It seemed they had always done so. Minty orbited through like some sort of crazy comet, his apogee extending to distant bushes and gopher holes, his perigee coming close enough to nip their heels as they walked along.

Hal reached over with his free hand and picked a piece of stray cotton fuzz off Vinny's shirt. "What are you doing?" she asked.

"Plucking fluff."

"Is that what we've come to?" asked Vinny. "Plucking fluff? What's next? Checking each other for lice?"

"I'd check you for lice."

"I bet you would."

They paused to kiss in the moonlight.

And didn't notice the dark sedan rolling slowly by.

Hal slept well that night, as the pain in his ribs subsided along with the turmoil in his mind. In the morning, over coffee, he and Slaughter discussed strategy for
the day ahead. Some 150 contenders remained, and play
would last until the final table was set. Once again there
would be a redraw for seats, this time with the tables set
at nine players instead of ten. Hal knew this would have
little impact at first, for the difference between what's
playable ten-handed and what's playable nine-handed
was only incremental. But today the hour of the outburst would last all day, and there would be many times
when they'd be playing eight-handed or seven-handed—
occasionally even six-handed—as players busted out faster
than the tournament directors could fill their seats or
consolidate tables. Slaughter reminded Hal that many
of his opponents wouldn't know how to adjust for short-
handed play. "That's the time to turn up the heat," he
said. "Even under the gun, you're not that far from late
position."

Another factor today—the critical one—would be the
impact of the Oakley players. So far, Hal had not played
a single hand against a wired foe. Slaughter had shared
a table with one; however, being in the know, he was able
to avoid any direct confrontations with the man. Today,
they agreed, Team Dragic's edge would start to amplify.
A few dozen Oakley players spread out over a field of
2,500 was a far cry from a dozen squeezed into the fin-
ishing sprint.

"We're gonna have to play 'em at some point," said
Hal. "What are we gonna do?"

"Think along with them. Remember, they'll be acting on exactly the hand you have, which, in a sense, will make them more predictable. Plus, Hal, you know what it's like: It's such a valuable tool, they'll be afraid to screw up with it. Most of the time they won't have a lock, and they may back down even if they're on the right side of the odds. Look how many have busted out already."

Hal shook his head. "I wonder what kind of game poker would be if everyone played their cards face up."

Slaughter laughed. "It'd cut down on bluffing."

"That it would," said Hal.

After he drained his coffee, Slaughter made one final point. "Just don't let 'em get to the river for cheap. They'll kill you at the river."

Hal mused upon this on the ride in to the Cortland. He contemplated what he would do with something like top pair, medium kicker, if he was at the river against one of the wired players and faced an all-in bet. Would his foe be betting a better hand, or betting that Hal wouldn't have the bottle to call? Hal knew that if the pot was big enough, even the Oakley players would be constrained to bet into a hand they couldn't beat. How else could they win the pot? So even if Hal knew the other guy knew his hand, he still might be able to call and snap off a desperation bluff. Hal tucked this awareness away. He hoped the situation wouldn't come up, but he resolved to keep his nerve if it did. Recalling Guy's words, "To win, you can't be afraid to lose," he was determined to be not afraid.

The mood in the tournament hall had shifted overnight. Where on prior days the air had crackled with the bright kinetic energy of stored hope—hope magnified and multiplied by the critical mass of 2,500 earnest entrants—today a deadly calm settled on the remaining competitors and their modest entourages. Today the money would start to get serious, with $170,000 in cash for the day's first eliminations, and a staggering $2 million for the tenth place finisher—the TV table bubble boy. The knowledge of the money now within reach weighed heavily on the players and brought a sepulchral chill to the room, a chill reinforced by air-conditioning originally set to offset the cumulative body temperature of thousands but presently doing arctic overkill on the few hundred participants and fans who inadequately filled the cavernous hall.

A gallery had been set up, an elbow of bleachers from which spectators could watch the action at the remaining tables—seventeen of them now, though that number would rapidly shrink through the day. Vinny and Skip had front-row seats—unfortunately, directly beneath a giant A/C vent.

"It's freezing in here," said Vinny. "I'm gonna go get my jacket."

"I'll come with you," said Skip.

Vinny looked at the line of spectators waiting to pounce on any vacant seat in the bleachers. "No, stay here," she said. "Save our places."

"Hal said we shouldn't go anywhere alone."

"I'm just going to the car. I'll be fine."

While Vinny headed to her car, Hal settled in at his table. As if to even out the law of averages (or regress to some sort of perverse mean), he now found himself facing not one but three players wearing Oakley Super Thumps. It was interesting to see them dance around each other, and Hal half wished he was wearing his Oakleys just to correlate their actions with the hands they held, for it was clear that none wanted to engage the others directly. This certainly made sense, since each would know if his hand was dominated. Then again, they had to clash at some point, if for no other reason than to consolidate their chips. It occurred to Hal that with the right hand at the right time he could crash their chip dump and ship their chips to his stack instead.

In the meantime, though, the three wired players were evenly spread around the table, occupying the two, five, and nine seats while Hal camped out in the seven. At no time did he have position on all three, so he never had the luxury of acting after all of them had folded. At best—when he was on the button or in the cutoff seat—he had two acting before him with just one yet to act in the blind. In that instance, his better-than-average hands had some equity—but how much equity did he have, really, against a foe who knew exactly what cards he held?

Fortunately, all three proved predictably timid in their play. They didn't want to squander their edge on coin flips and, accordingly, adopted the strategy Hal himself had arrived at—keeping pots small and hoping to get to the river with a mortal lock. Hal's counterstrategy was simple: put pressure on them during the early betting rounds, and bank on them not having the cards or the nerve for a big confrontation. Accordingly, he pushed hard with medium pairs and high unpaired cards and hoped they didn't wake up with pocket aces or kings at the wrong time.

Vinny, meanwhile, had made her way out to the Cortland parking garage. She was thinking about all Hal had been through there: his search for Minty McGinty; his encounters with Lanh Tran. So lost was she in this musing that she was practically on top of her car before she realized something was wrong with it.

Someone was trying to break in!

A thick slab of a man towered over the driver's side

window, poking around with a Slim Jim and muttering obscenities under his breath. So startled was Vinny by this that at first she just stood there gawking. The man became aware of her presence and turned to face her. His face was a moonscape of acne craters, his bulbous nose a riot of exploded capillaries *à la* W. C. Fields. His malformed ears were—there's no other word for it— grotesque, as if they'd been attacked by a flesh-eating virus or chewed upon by rats. A thin, greasy mat of hair covered his scabby bald head in an ineffectual comb-over. A port-wine stain ran from his neck to his chest. The skin of his arms was mottled with lesions, welts, and scars. His beer gut flopped over his belt like the marsupial pouch of some mutant kangaroo.

This is one fugly dude, thought Vinny. She was almost feeling sorry for him, when he suddenly launched himself at her and started whacking her with the Slim Jim. As this was merely a flexible metal wand, it more annoyed than hurt her. She couldn't imagine what he hoped to accomplish by this unless he expected her to become hysterical and collapse in a weepy heap, "the way women do." In that he would be sorely disappointed, for Vinny Barlow was her father's daughter and took no shit from anyone.

She timed a duck so that Fugly's next blow sliced through open air; then she rose and hammered hard at his wrist. He dropped the Slim Jim and reflexively stooped to retrieve it. Vinny brought her knee up to meet his face. It hit him square in the nose, causing it to gush blood. With a feral growl, he rushed at her, but Vinny was quicker and much more nimble. She darted around to the far side of her station wagon and had no trouble keeping the bulk of it between them.

After a moment's futile chasing, Fugly became winded

and stopped. "Look, girly-girl," he said, "we can do this the easy way or the hard way."

"What's the hard way?" she asked.

He grinned, revealing rotten teeth and evidence of gum disease. Then he pulled out a gun: a subcompact Beretta Tomcat that fit neatly in the palm of his hand.

Are you shitting me? thought Vinny. She was in no sense a meek woman, and in no mood to lie down for this creep, gun or no gun. She knew what it meant to be a woman in a man's world, a continual target of abuse, invective, innuendo. But she also knew what men expected of women in a man's world. So she did the expected thing. Letting terror bloom on her face, she quivered her lip and threw her hands up in surrender. Her breathing became heavy and labored (a classic false tell if you recognize such things). Fugly walked slowly around the car, smiling in triumph. By the time he got close, Vinny was apparently hyperventilating.

Then she "fainted" and fell toward him.

And when he reflexively reached out to catch her— "the way men do" for a damsel in distress—she reached between his legs, grabbed his ball sack, and gave it a vicious twist. His legs buckled. He and Vinny went down together in a heap. He tried to flail at her with the gun, but two swift rabbit punches to his scrotum took the fight out of him. One thing a woman in a man's world learns: men's weak spot. She got up and stood over the man, now reduced to a whimpering pile of fugly.

Vinny opened the car door and grabbed her jacket— after all, that's what she'd come for. Then she leaned on the horn and stayed on it till two security guards showed up. She explained to them how Fugly had tried to rape her.

"Looks like it didn't work out," said one of the guards.

"Yeah," said Vinny. She shrugged into her jacket. "Not so much."

Some setbacks on day two had Slaughter starting day three near the back of the pack. In the early going, with antes at $400 and blinds at $1,500 and $3,000, he had pushed all in on successive hands with pocket kings and pocket jacks. No one called, and collecting two quick rounds of antes and blinds gave him some breathing room. But with aggressive chip leaders at his table, plus an Oakley player who had been moved into a seat on his left, it was all Slaughter could do to stay ahead of the rising price of poker. He wasn't about to commit the cardinal sin of tournament poker and let himself get blinded off. Before that happened, he'd find a hand and make a stand.

He had about $35,000 in chips. At the current level, he was not quite in dire straits, for he still had more than ten times the big blind, a stack yet big enough to make others think twice about calling him down. In a few minutes, though, the level would end. There would be a break while they removed the $100 chips from play. After that, action would resume with antes of $500 and blinds of $2K and $4K. That jump in blinds would devalue his stack and kick him below the critical 10x big-blind line. Then he'd be forced to move with any half-decent hand, and he couldn't count on having enough fold equity to drive other half-decent hands into the muck. Moreover, he realized, there was a shifting metric for the Team Dragic player to his left. While she might be unwilling to gamble against stacks equal to her own, there was no reason for her not to take coin flips—or better—against shorter stacks like his. If she got unlucky, she could just tighten up and go back to waiting for lock opportunities. But if the odds held true, she'd eliminate another player and move that much closer to the final table.

All in all, it would be best if Slaughter could find something to work with now, before the blinds went up.

In other circumstances, he would pounce on any unopened pot and move all in with even so ragged a hand as J-9 suited. He'd be hoping that no one would call, but counting on at least having two live undercards if someone did. Even against A-K, he'd only be a 3-to-2 dog. Not the worst situation in the world.

But that damn Oakley player! J-9 suited doesn't look so good if the gal on your left is holding, say, J-Q. Normally there's no way someone can call with a J-Q, but if they know you've got J-9 . . .

Still, desperate times call for desperate measures, and Slaughter's situation was trending toward desperate with every passing hand. With a lap around the table now costing more than $6,000 in chips, and due to jump above $8K soon, he simply could not afford to wait. He'd have to push soon, and if the Oakley player—or anyone—happened to look him up, well, then it would be up to the poker gods to decide his fate.

One thing he had going for him was a nifty tell on the player to his left, who was in the habit of looking at her cards as soon as she got them, rather than waiting for her turn to act. Horrible card hygiene—but her Oakley edge evidently made her cocky and sloppy. In any event, Slaughter had determined that she only ever bothered capping her cards with a protective chip when she intended to be involved; otherwise, she just held them in her hand, preparing to muck.

The dealer pitched the cards around the table. Slaughter glanced left. His foe looked at her cards—and held on to them. Now Slaughter checked out his own hand, and found K♦Q♦. Not the best hand in the world, and not a favorite against any A-x, but, again, desperate times . . .

Double or done, thought Slaughter as he pushed his chips forward and announced, "All in."

The Oakley player folded, as did the players to her left, all the way around to the button, who gave Slaughter the extensive fish eye before finally releasing his hand. That left only the small and big blinds. The small blind pitched immediately. The big blind . . . paused to chat.

"I know you," he said. "You're that *Swoop and Pummel* guy. I read your book. You're all 'go big or go home.' "

"Yes, and?" said Slaughter. He knew that his foe was trying to get a read on the strength of his hand. He knew also that silence on his part would be read as tension; a bluff. He figured if the big blind had much of a hand he'd already have called by now, and so probably had a weak ace or a modest pair. Slaughter didn't figure to be a favorite, didn't really want a call, but reckoned he'd get one, for he had outlined exactly this play in exactly this situation in his book. *Damn book!*

"And the blinds are about to go up and you're getting worried. I think you're on a steal. I call." He flipped over his hand. K♠J♦. Slaughter was a little surprised. Against any other hand in his opponent's calling distribution, Slaughter would have been an underdog; against this one, he was a 3-to-1 favorite.

Well, thought Slaughter, *I can't ask for much better than that.*

As long as my hand holds up.

The dealer knuckled the table and laid out a flop reasonably favorable for Slaughter's cards: 2♠3♥3♠. But the turn was the 7♠, and Slaughter got a sinki͟n͟g feeling in his gut. A runner-runner flush ca͟t͟c͟h͟ likely, a 23-to-1 shot; however, once that third spade hits, the odds drop to 4 to 1 against the flush getting made.

The dealer burned and turned. Q♠.

"Damn," said the big blind, thinking Slaughter had hit his kicker for a pair. Then, as the fact of the flush sank in, he let out a whoop. Slaughter, meanwhile, just shook his head. He had started the hand as a 3-to-1 favorite, but 3-to-1 favorites get shot down every day. He stood with measured dignity and started away. Two tables over, Hal was still ducking confrontations with the three Oakley players he faced. He lifted his eyes to Slaughter, who essayed a wry smile as he passed.

"The first thing you need to know about poker tournaments," Slaughter had written in *Swoop and Pummel,* "is that most people lose most of the time. If you can't stand disappointment, you don't stand a chance."

I can stand disappointment, thought Slaughter.

That doesn't mean I have to like it.

25 Tweedledee and Tweedlestupid

Day three wore on. Hal was still comfortably chipped, thanks largely to doing largely nothing for long stretches of time, but he knew he couldn't sit on the sideline forever. His stack was trapped at the table, frozen by three players who always knew exactly what he had. Like hyenas, they avoided direct attacks, contenting themselves to go after his blinds, which he couldn't defend without a powerhouse—and of course if he had a powerhouse they wouldn't attack. His own snugness, he knew, was encouraging them to bluff, but until he started drawing some stronger starting hands, there was nothing he could do but masquerade as a timid Timmy trying desperately to climb a few places higher in the pay table before his luck or his chips ran out. It would have been helpful for his table to break, potentially shifting him to a better setting, but the luck of the draw had placed him at one of the tournament's center tables. Unless he got plucked from his big blind and moved to the big blind at a short-handed table, he'd be here until the tournament got down to twenty-seven players and the last four tables were combined into three. He also considered resorting to his own Oakleys—fighting fire with fire—but knew this would really only result in a game of high-stakes chicken, where someone would eventually blink and decide to take a coin flip. Hal didn't want to put his fate in the hands of luck. He just didn't.

During the first break, Vinny had told him about the clash in the parking garage. He hadn't liked that one bit, had almost become angry with her for going off by herself. She had told him, politely but firmly, to "get that macho bullshit out of my face," and Hal remembered what he knew to be true: that Vinny was her own woman. Which was why he loved her, of course. Still, he asked—*asked*—her to be more cautious from here on out, and she promised she would. He suspected that the incident had rattled her more than she let on.

What intrigued Hal was Vinny's description of her assailant, for it correlated with Guy's take on his killer: "big; beer gut; fucking ugly." There was no doubt in Hal's mind that this was Big Mo's "friend," and Marco Dragic's hench. Presumably, the man was now in custody, but Hal didn't imagine that Marco Dragic had only one strong sidewheel on his team.

Said Skip, "Look, why don't we just rat these assholes out? We've got the Oakleys. Plus there's surveillance tape. I'm sure the cops can make a case."

"A case for what?" asked Hal. "Trying to fix a poker tournament? I don't see anyone doing hard time for that. Anyway, that's not what I want."

"Well, what the fuck do you want?" Skip asked.

"A confrontation. A chance to know the truth."

But hours later, thanks to these three mayonnaise motherfuckers in Oakley Super Thumps, he was no closer to his goal. By picking his spots—and he picked them with meticulous care—he'd managed to maintain a slight chip lead over them, but his situation was fragile, and the rising blinds were starting to make themselves felt even on his relatively healthy stack.

Time to iron out the slackjaws, thought Hal.

Hal picked up A♠K♠ in middle position. The Oakley in the five seat had already folded. The other two, button and big blind, respectively, would get to act after Hal. He knew that if he pushed all in, they could really only call him with A-A or K-K. Anything else would be a coin flip or worse, and this pair—Hal had mentally tagged them Tweedledee and Tweedlestupid—had shown no stomach for such gambles. Given the long odds against their having aces or kings, he had the option to push.

But that was a mook's game, the all-in push. Russian roulette. He could do it all day and they could afford to wait until they hit the hand they needed to beat him. He had to do better than that, engage them in some pots, maybe catch them in a bluff. Even a player who knows your hand can still make a mistake. So Hal made his standard raise to slightly less than the sum of antes and blinds in play, in this case $11K. The button looked at his cards and then at the big blind. This downstream glance, of course, is what any thoughtful player would do before taking any action, though Hal knew Tweedledee wouldn't have to settle for tells and inference. He'd know for a fact what Tweedlestupid held.

Which is why it struck Hal as odd when the man's whole upper body gave a tiny jerk. The big blind seemed likewise surprised by what he saw in the button's cards. Hal had to wonder: What could each have that caught the other so off guard?

Unlikely holding of some kind, he thought.

They both called. They were ganging up on him in a sense, but Hal didn't even bother to feel outrage at the implicit collusion. In the circumstance, that was the least of his problems. *The question is,* he thought, *what sort of hands gang up well against A-K suited? They can't both have pocket aces or pocket kings, though one could have aces and the other kings. Highly unlikely, but still . . . If that's the case, I'm crushed. I'll win, like, ten percent of the time.* Then he smiled inwardly. *But if that's the case, the one with kings would pass, because* that *hand wins only ten percent of the time, too.*

So then it's not huge pairs in both hands, and it's not any kind of unpaired undercards in both hands, because why bother?

Maybe they both have underpairs.

Hal did the math quickly in his head. If he was facing something like T-T and Q-Q, they were a cumulative 3-to-2 favorite to beat him between here and the river—a tad better than that if they controlled a couple of his spades. It was certainly possible that they'd call along, hoping to flop a set, or just bet him off the pot on the flop.

So what is it? What hands could they have that would make them both flinch in surprise, and yet both play?

The dealer put down the flop: J♠6♣7♦. Tweedle-stupid checked, and the action was on Hal, who asked for time. The dealer nodded his assent, and Hal processed his choices: not really thinking consciously about the hand at all, but just letting all the known, deduced, and guessed factors spin in his mind like tumblers spinning on a combination lock. *Not aces . . . not unpaired undercards . . . maybe underpairs, but where's the flinch in that?* Suddenly, the dials clicked into place. *One has A-K suited,* he thought, *and the other has . . . A-K suited!* These three hands would split the pot 90 percent of the time.

There was no reason to get excited and start throwing raises around, but then again there was no reason to throw away any equity. That logic held up for the big blind, who had some chips invested in the pot. But why did Tweedledee call? All he stood to make on this pot was one-third of the antes and blinds. Still, that's not nothing.

Plus, each of these holdings would make a flush about 5 percent of the time, which meant that they had a cumulative 10 percent chance of taking the pot from Hal. If they worked the whipsaw, they could build up quite a pot and essentially be freerolling at a chance to eliminate Hal. They would make this move, of course, only if the flop didn't come heavy in spades; if that was the case, they could get away from their hands if need be.

But let's look at this flop a little more closely. One spade, one club, one diamond. I have spades, which means there's a two-third's chance that one of them is drawing dead to anything but a tie. I have a five percent chance to make a runner-runner flush. At least one of them does, too—but the other might not.

That edge—razor thin, to be sure—was enough to motivate Hal's next action. He wasn't going to let them see the turn for free, wait for it to come nonspade and then whipsaw his ass or drive him from the pot. Instead, he pushed all in. Almost all of the time, he knew, this play would be profit neutral. But if one of them folded, he'd win half the pot instead of just a third. And if one called without a flush draw, then that was a mistake, and a tiny bit of extra (at least theoretical) equity for Hal. He was, he knew, pushing the slimmest of edges, *but when you're up against foes who know your cards, what other kind of edges are there?*

So he pushed. They both called so fast that Hal suspected they hadn't bothered to think things through, as he had. To their minds, the hand was virtually a tie, so why not call?

Because, well, *virtually* a tie and *actually* a tie are two very different things.

And when the turn came the T♠, Hal was drawing live not just to a flush but a royal, not that that mattered. The others' shoulders sagged as they realized the unlikely trap they had stumbled into.

Hours earlier, Slaughter Johnson had been eliminated by a runner-runner flush, the queen of spades delivering the killing blow to his tournament chances. It was neither the hand of fate nor some mythical poker god's love of irony that controlled the river card in this hand. Rather, it was math, a simple fraction: the 1-in-42 chance of the queen of spades coming off the deck.

And here it came. Giving Hal a royal flush and sending Tweedledee and Tweedlestupid to the rail. Hal could see the blood drain from their faces as the rest of the table erupted in the characteristic hoopla that greets unlikely events in a poker game. Players at other tables craned their necks to see what was going on. Including Dragic—who watched, stone-faced, as two members of his team walked away from their table in shock.

Hal was now the prohibitive chip leader at his table—indeed among the six tables remaining in play. As such, he could play bully, and he played it to perfection. He made frequent raises in position, of course, but also made resteal reraises in position, or else just called behind and took pots away on the flop. He attacked the big blind from the small blind, with or without a hand. He made flop-dependent bluffs, banging away at every coordinated board as if he owned it. About the only move he couldn't make was to open raise in very early position, for the remaining Oakley player, sitting two seats to his right, would be in the blind on those hands and would know if Hal was on a steal. No great loss. With so many other weapons now at his disposal, Hal could afford to forgo the out-of-position steal attempt. Then again, it didn't look like the Oakley player was much in the mood for a fight. He seemed, in fact, totally spooked, for he had just seen Hal knock out two players on the same hand *when they both knew what cards he held*. No wonder he turned turtle. He didn't even attack Hal's blind from the button.

Hal was having a field day. Not normally loquacious at the table, he now became quite the talker, goading foes into ill-advised calls, raises, or folds. No matter what he told them, even if he told them the God's honest truth, they seemed to draw the wrong conclusion, make the wrong decision. As he had at the end of day two, Hal fell into his zone, and in a perfect storm of cards, image, and insight, he ran over the table until it broke, then ran over the next table and the one after that.

Shortly before two in the morning, Hal pushed pocket jacks against a desperately short-stacked player's A-9 suited. When the board came all small, the Poker Apocalypse had its tenth-place finisher, and the final table was set. Tomorrow, nine players would face off under the unblinking eye of the television camera. Marko Dragic was one, sitting on a chip stack of $4 million. Big Mo and another Oakley player held about $3 million between them, ready to be dumped to Dragic, no doubt. Five players were nonfactors, dead men walking. And the ninth player, the tournament leader with over $7M in chips, was none other than Hal Harris, the former Pittsburgh accountant and current poker powerhouse.

Leaving the ballroom, Hal had to fight his way through a considerable crowd of rail stoats. He was astounded at how many new best friends he had—how many earnest fans were there to assure him that they'd noticed him back on day one, and had been pulling hard for him since the tournament began. Hal remembered Guy commenting on this phenomenon, and while Hal had won a few tournaments, he'd not experienced anything like this. He knew it was just the mooks' self-serving attempts to position themselves for a handout, and though not nearly naïve enough to take their adulation at face value, he couldn't deny the emotional impact. *So this is how celebrity feels,* he thought. It was a buzz, no doubt about it.

Hal saw Marko Dragic working his way through a similar swarm of well-wishers. He didn't imagine that Dragic bought their act any more than Hal did, but he noticed Dragic basking just the same. If something met your need, Hal supposed, it didn't matter whether it was authentic or not.

Outside the ballroom, Hal met up with Vinny, Skip, and Slaughter, and became aware of a much different sensation. Until that moment, his run through the tournament hadn't seemed tangible, like it was happening to someone else. Now, among his friends, seeing himself through their eyes and glowing in the warmth of their support, he felt the whole thing becoming real for the first time. It struck him with the force of revelation that this was the single most intensely felt moment of his life so far—made so only by the fact that he had friends to share it with. *The things in your life don't exist,* he realized, *until they exist for the people you love.*

A production assistant from the TV broadcast came to collect him. There were biographical sheets to fill out, releases to sign. He followed the PA to a small production office in the Cortland's back of house. The other final tablists were there as well, including Marko Dragic, who said nothing to him, but kept watching him with cold and chary eyes.

When Hal finished and left the office, Dragic fell in beside him and paced him all the way down the long, empty hallway that led back to the tournament area.

"I'm worried," said Dragic under his breath.

"About what?"

"About maybe you forgetting why you're here."

"No, no," said Hal. "I remember."

"Then why haven't you moved your chips?"

"Come on, man, you can't deny me the final table, can you? There'll be plenty of time for that tomorrow."

"I'm just saying," muttered Dragic, "I've come too far and risked too much to let you stop me now."

They reached the hallway outside the ballroom, an area still clotted with fellow travelers and hangers-on. "Relax, will you?" said Hal. "I'm just a chimp in a chair." He patted Dragic on the back, a wholly inappropriate gesture that sent a visible shiver through the man. Then he announced in a booming voice, "Marko Dragic, everyone!" He grinned at Dragic. "He's kind of a big deal."

And Hal walked off, leaving Dark Mark in the middle of an impromptu autograph session that he didn't seem to be enjoying nearly as much as he wanted to.

26 Where's Minty?

"You shouldn't play him so fast and loose," said Vinny. "He's still a dangerous guy."

"I know," said Hal, "but if you don't show strength, they'll run all over you, right?" They were having this conversation in the kitchen of Vinny's town house, waiting for Skip and Slaughter to come downstairs and join them so they could roll out together to the Cortland. Despite Hal's bravado, he insisted that they travel in a pack. And, in truth, he had spent the night second-guessing whether it had been right to give Dragic the needle. There would come a point today when he would have to sell a certain image, the image of overweening pride. He hoped he'd set up the image play last night.

He hoped he hadn't gone too far.

Slaughter and Skip walked in. Hal asked Skip for the Oakleys.

"I thought you weren't going that route," said Skip.

"TV lights," shrugged Hal. "I might just want some shades."

Skip went to get them. Hal thought about the remarkable Super Thumps—truly the Swiss Army Knife of sunglasses. Of course, they couldn't do everything. At that thought, he reflexively patted the small, weighty item in his back pocket.

Vinny, meanwhile, looked around and asked, "Where's Minty?"

"I let him out earlier," said Hal. He went to the front door and gave the Beethoven whistle. After a minute, Minty came loping up, panting from the effort of his morning walkabout, his breath a pungent testament to something dead for breakfast. Seeing the others squaring up to leave the house, Minty took up station at the door, enthusiastically ready to come along for the ride—but his expression turned to one of reproach as Hal left him locked in the house. He whimpered as they walked to the car. "How can you betray a dog by taking care of him?" Hal asked. "That's what I want to know."

As Vinny piloted to the Cortland and Minty settled down to a day of lying on his paws, the man known to Vinny as Fugly—and to the rest of the world as Carl Ott—was getting kicked from jail. Due to a glitch in the Cortland's parking garage surveillance system, there had been no footage of Ott attacking Vinny. A male judge, viscerally sympathetic to the assault on Ott's junk, had decided that, absent a statement from the complainant (indeed, absent a complainant), he had no reason to hold Ott, not even on a gun charge, for the Beretta Tomcat never was found. He ordered Ott's release.

From Ott's point of view, not a moment too soon.

When Hal got to the Cortland, he was whisked away to a brightly lit room where they ran him through hair and makeup, videotaped some b-roll footage, and sent him out to the tournament floor. He found the place transformed. What had yesterday been a nondescript hotel ballroom was today a glittering TV set. The final table sat on a raised platform, framed by a cube of aluminum risers and girders that provided anchor points for the many multicolored lights. Plush stadium seating had replaced yesterday's bleachers, with plenty of room for the hundreds of fans eager to see the culmination of "the biggest poker tournament in the history of ever." TV techs swarmed around the stage, checking everything from the players' chairs to the tiny lipstick cameras embedded at each competitor's playing position. The cameras in particular caught Hal's eye. He wondered if they'd caused the wrinkle he predicted.

Dragic and Big Mo came in, as did the other final table players. The seat draw had placed Hal in seat eight, out on the starboard wing. Dragic was in the four seat, at the other end of the table. Big Mo sat immediately to Dragic's right. The third remaining member of Team Dragic, a flamboyant young hotshot who called himself Plume, and only Plume, occupied the six seat, two places to Hal's right. Plume wore a vacant, autopilot expression, and Hal wondered if the kid regretted mortgaging his glory to Dark Mark. Of course, without Dragic's hacks and help, it was unlikely that he'd be here at all. Just the same, how many times do you come this close to a $70 million score?

All of a sudden, a bombastic orchestral theme boomed out through giant overhead speakers. The stage lights flickered and flashed. A dry-ice machine coughed to life, filling the set with colored smoke. Into this scene of high drama strode the one and only Kai Cortland. A natural showman, he instantly commanded the crowd's attention as he thanked everyone for being there; thanked the players for competing so hard; and, at length and in detail, thanked himself for being so wonderful. Then he uttered the iconic words, "Shuffle up and deal," and, with no small reluctance, surrendered center stage to the game.

Mo, Dragic, and Plume immediately put on their Oakleys—and immediately looked perplexed. Smiling inwardly, Hal slid his own Oakleys into place and looked down at the cards he'd been dealt. Nothing. No image in the heads-up display—not of his cards nor anyone's. Hal had anticipated this, for since the final table was fitted with lipstick cams, there was no reason to use the special RFID playing cards. They had today been replaced with decks bearing the logo of Largesse, the male enhancement drug sponsoring the broadcast. It was to be expected, really. Cortland had sold the naming rights to everything else; why not the cards?

Of course, the Oakleys were just one tool at Dragic's disposal. He still had a viable chip-dump strategy and no doubt a working set of hand signals, too—subtle, effective ones tested and perfected during the run-up to the Apocalypse. Dragic, Hal noticed, spent a lot of time obsessively stacking and restacking his chips. This could have been an innocuous expression of nervous energy; however, it was somewhat uncharacteristic for Dragic, who preferred to play his poker behind a mask of lassitude. Mo, meanwhile, was hitting his chat button very hard, and while this was typical of his table demeanor, his choice of subjects rang tinny to Hal. Much of what he said seemed unmotivated and random, even for a yacker like Big Mo.

Hal couldn't break their code, but he knew what they'd be looking for: a plausible pair of hands with justifiable lines of play, but also no risk of an unexpected outcome. They wouldn't want to get all the money in, for example, with pair over pair, or even an overpair against undercards. In the latter scenario, the overpair is almost a 9-to-1 favorite—but what if that longshot came in? The dump would fail, and Dragic would be crippled. As before with the glasses, they'd want something better than a huge favorite. They'd want a mortal lock.

It took them a couple of tries to get it right.

On the first attempt, with antes at $3K and blinds at $10K and $20K, Mo raised to $70K from middle position, and Dragic called behind. Everyone else folded, including Hal, who mucked pocket eights. He knew that a subsequent TV audience would either applaud him for his discipline or excoriate his weak play, and while Hal seemed to be agonizing over his decision, he was really just coffeehousing. He didn't want to interfere with the dump, and he didn't want it to fail. At the end of the day, he wanted Dragic all to himself.

The flop came 2♥Q♥J♦. Mo led out, betting $150K into a pot of almost $200K. Dragic called. The turn was the 9♠. Mo bet $400K, a little more than half his remaining stack. *There's the dump,* thought Hal, for he knew that by halving his stack, Mo had basically committed himself to either a crying call or a desperation bluff on the river. When he lost, he would appear blameless, the victim of a self-inflicted brain fart on the turn. Dragic flat-called Mo's turn bet, and this, too, made sense, for they'd want to see a completely safe river card before consummating the dump.

The river card, the 2♣, looked safe enough, but Hal detected hesitation in Mo—and disgust in Dragic. They didn't like that card at all.

Hal assumed that Mo had opened the pot with rags, figuring to isolate himself against Dragic, and dump his chips on "a bluff gone wrong." The flop must have hit Dragic in some sense, or he would have aborted the play by folding to Mo's flop bet. And the turn must have helped him a lot, for that's when Mo committed his chips. But what happened on the river? How did that turn things around?

They're gonna check it down, Hal realized. *This hand has gone south.*

Mo stewed, agonized, called for time, stewed and agonized some more, then finally checked. Dragic checked behind. Mo turned over his hand: 2♠9♦. He had turned a naked bluff into a baby full house. Dragic mucked without showing, but Hal figured he must have made a straight on the turn, or else Mo's two pair at that point would have driven him from the hand.

"Couldn't get you to bite, huh?" said Mo.

"I'm not betting your hand for you," said Marko. "You want something done right, you've got to do it yourself." This attempt at banter rang laughably false, for Dragic was not the bantering kind. Nor, however, was he the type of player to miss a value bet on the river, which confirmed to Hal that Mo had managed to communicate his exact holding. That deuce on the river had really screwed them. Now, against forecast and intent, Mo actually had more chips than Dragic. He was going to have to work a little harder to eliminate himself from play.

He went right at it. Masquerading as someone trying to manufacture a rush, Mo allowed himself to get out ahead of several hands, making big opening moves, only to fold with overwrought agony when Dragic came over the top. In short order, he'd managed to "misplay" himself down under a million in chips. He looked for all the world like a man on tilt, hell-bent on giving his chips away.

Funny how only Dragic benefited from his generosity.

Mo's demise came on a flop of K-6-2, when he pushed with K-J and got called by Dragic's A-K. Mo essayed dig-

nity and disappointment as he stood up to leave, but to
Hal's jaundiced eye, he managed to sell neither with
much success, for dignity was a stance that simply es-
caped the big man, and as for disappointment, well,
$3.3 million softens a lot of blows.

A few hands later, Plume managed to slip his chips to
Dragic, too. After that, it was a matter of Hal and Dragic
carving up the remaining smaller stacks like hege-
monist Spain and Portugal carving up South America.
Between them, they managed to eliminate three more
players, the third going down just as level twenty-five
came to an end. After a twenty-minute break, play would
resume with antes of $5K and blinds of $20K and $40K.
Chip counts would show Dragic at $8M and change;
Hal at $10M; a deftly clever amateur named Billy Trux-
ton at $3M; and one of the world's top women players,
Aimee Ortega, at $4M. Though the stacks seemed quite
deep relative to the blinds, Hal knew the tournament
would likely last only one or two levels more, for at this
point it was stack size, not blind size, that dictated the
action. Though it's possible to play deep-stack short-
handed poker with circumspection, it usually didn't
happen that way. Small bets simply have no impact on
big stacks, so there's not much point in making them.
When confrontations brew, they blow up fast into monster pots.

As far as Hal could tell, Truxton and Ortega were
playing on the square, though after all his hours and
days of poker play, he was no longer sure he could trust
his own perspective. Hal was mentally fatigued, damn near
drained, suffering from what Guy used to call "oxygen-
debt stupidity," a state of mind where you become so
tired you don't even know how tired you are. You can
see things that aren't there.

Or fail to overlook the obvious.

Hal spent half the break tracking down a cup of coffee at one of the casino's many coffee kiosks. He pimped it out with sugar and cream and drank it down in three quick gulps. Even this, he knew, was a delicate dance, for he ran the risk of a sugar crash or caffeine overload. But what else could he do? Take Dilaudid?

His path back to the escalator took him through a labyrinth of quarter slot machines, low-roller specials long on bells and whistles and short on favorable payouts. Hal marveled at how oblivious the punters were to everything except the spinning reels before them. Right here in this building, the last act of the world's biggest poker tournament was being played out, but that was of no moment to the tourists and degenerates who poured their money and psychic energy into the pull toys in hopes of hitting—oh, let's be bold and dare to dream—a thousand-dollar jackpot. *Truly,* thought Hal, *each of us is the center of our own universe.*

And we're of astoundingly little interest to the universe next door.

He turned a corner and encountered the jarring sight of Marco Dragic sitting at a slot machine, feeding coins in with one hand and fingering a cell phone with the other. He looked up at Hal, not at all surprised, and Hal realized that Dragic had been waiting for him. He started to walk past, but Dragic swiveled around and threw a leg out to block Hal's path. Hal stopped and regarded him coolly. "You don't strike me," said Hal, "as the slot-machine type."

"And you," said Dragic, "don't strike me as the sort of person who honors commitment."

"Hey," said Hal, "I told you I'd dump and I'll dump."

"Yes, but when? You're running out of time."

"Well, I mean, sometime in the next level, for sure."

"How sure?"

"Absolutely sure."

"Yeah, you are," said Dragic. "Let me show you why." He handed his cell phone to Hal. Hal looked at the display screen, and what he saw via streaming video made his heart sink.

It was Minty.

Leashed to a tie-down cleat in the back of a pickup truck.

Only that was no collar around his neck.

It was a noose.

Hal's blood ran cold. In the background of the shot he could see the front of a building he thought he recognized, but that didn't really register. All that registered was the enormity of Dragic's act—and the deflating awareness of how badly Hal had let himself get outplayed. "You wouldn't," was all he could manage to croak.

"The question is: Would you?" Dragic smiled crookedly. "How much, really, is a dog's life worth?"

"Look, I told you I'd—"

"Shut the fuck up. I know what you told me. Poker players are a bunch of damn liars, but what are you gonna do?" Dragic stood up. "So, now, do we go upstairs and end this, or do I tell my guy to take your dog for his last walk?"

"When I dump," said Hal, "how will I know Minty is safe?"

"Oh, he's close," said Dragic. "We'll bring him right in here."

Close? thought Hal, and a certain penny dropped. He looked at the phone screen again for a minute, sadly shaking his head. "All right," he said. "I fold."

27 Ub-Gub-Gub-Guh-Gub

Hal went to the bathroom before returning to the table. He sat in a stall for a moment and composed a short note, which he slipped to Skip in a handshake. Returning to his seat at the table, he glanced over his shoulder and saw Skip, eyes wide, sharing the note with Vinny and Slaughter. After a moment, Skip and Slaughter departed, leaving Vinny sitting alone in the spectators' bullpen, fretting. He wanted to smile at her, reassure her, but he knew Dragic's eyes were on him, so he kept his face a mask.

Inwardly, he felt himself returning to equilibrium. By happy accident, Hal had recognized the façade of Foxxy's, the bar he'd gone to the night after Guy's murder—the very place where he had decided to set off down the path that led . . . well, as it turned out, right here. Whether Skip and Slaughter would be able to spring Minty remained to be seen, but that was down to them. For his part, Hal just needed to stall, give them time to work.

Stalling had its effect: With every passing hand, Dragic

became more incensed. He was looking for Hal to dump his chips—had mortally twisted his arm to ensure it—but still Hal stuck to his game plan of playing strong but snug and avoiding big clashes with Dragic. Dragic was cooking; Hal could see it. Still he refused to engage. Thanks to eliminations in the five, six, and seven seats, the two were now effectively adjacent, with Hal holding position on Dragic on every three hands out of four. This should have given Hal an exploitable edge, free rein to attack Dragic's blinds in position, or raise from the big blind if Dragic limped from the small. But Hal had no intention of building pots for Dragic. If he didn't have good hands, he simply refused to give action. This, of course, made him easy to read when he did have big tickets, killing any action he might have gotten in return. Thus, they achieved a rough equilibrium, and though Hal knew he couldn't continue this rope-a-dope approach forever, he imagined it was cracking both Dragic's patience and his confidence. After all, how well did Dragic really know his foe? Could he be sure that Hal hadn't changed his mind and decided that a dog's life was, in fact, worth $70 million? How could he be certain that Hal would be dumping, not trapping? In this, then, Hal had managed to wrest psychological control of the match away from Dark Mark.

It was a start.

Aimee Ortega eliminated Billy Truxton in a confrontation that saw Truxton holding pocket queens against Ortega's pocket jacks. Ortega called a preflop raise, and all the money went in the middle on a flop of J-Q-7. Another jack on the turn killed Truxton with kindness: it gave him the nut full house but gave Ortega quad jacks. Truxton cashed $15 million, disappointed to have finished only fourth, and never aware of how well he'd managed to do in a field so fully gaffed.

Even after adding Truxton's chips to her stack, Ortega remained deeply mired in third place, holding about $4M in chips, against Hal's and Dragic's $11M and $10M, respectively. She entertained the hope of one busting the other in a big pot, so that she could back into second place, but with Hal playing so tight, she had to modify her strategy. She started limping into more pots in an effort to create three-way action and catch a favorable flop. This plan backfired—and spelled her demise—when she called the $40K big blind from the button holding 7♦6♦. Dragic completed the small blind, and Hal checked, as usual, from the big.

The flop came 3♦8♦5♥, giving Ortega fifteen outs, assuming neither of the others was drawing to a better flush. With about a 60 percent chance to complete one or the other of her draws, she had the right side of the odds, and when both men checked to her, she led at the pot for $100K. This created a dilemma for Dragic. He held pocket tens and very much wanted to tease Hal into the pot, should Hal be holding A-8 or A-5. But Ortega's smallish bet screamed "draw" to Dragic, and he needed to protect his current lead in the hand. Caught between this rock and hard place, he chose a middle course, making a minimum raise, hoping Hal would call and Ortega would come over the top with her draw.

It only half worked. Hal folded. In fact, he folded Q-8, not because he thought he was beaten but just because he refused to let Dragic draw him in. Ortega, on the other hand, immediately went all in, pushing her semi-bluff to the hilt. Dragic weighed the pros and cons of a call. To fold would be to sacrifice minimal equity, leaving the three players' relative positions essentially unchanged. Calling might result in eliminating Ortega and getting heads up with Hal—or it could get Ortega well and make her a real factor in the match. His gut told him to fold, play it safe, but impatience had rasped away at his discipline, leaving it ragged and raw. He wanted Hal heads up.

Heads up, Hal would have nowhere to hide.

Dragic called. The board bricked out, and Aimee Ortega finished in third place, cashing $30 million, and instantly becoming poker's all-time top female money winner. She found this to be cold comfort but, again, had no idea how many hidden hurdles she had actually overcome.

With just two players left, it was time for the presentation of the winner's trophy and money prize, so the tournament clock was stopped while these things were brought in.

The trophy was appropriately egomaniacal, a bust of Kai Cortland—though it was an open question as to who, apart from Cortland, would want a bust of Cortland gracing their trophy case.

As for the prize, well . . .

In the early days of the World Series of Poker, they'd tote in the winner's cash in a cardboard box and dump it on the table. As the prize pool increased, this required more boxes, more $5,000 bricks of Franklins, more space. Eventually the cash outgrew the final table, and they added a whole separate table just for it. Later they dispensed with the cash and presented a big dummy check instead.

Kai Cortland was having none of that. His tournament paid the winner $70 million, and he was determined to show the world what $70 million looked like.

Couldn't do it with cash, though, for 700,000 Big Bens was more than even Cortland could assemble and present. Bundle them in bricks and you're looking at a tower more than a hundred feet high. Just not practical. Cortland investigated higher-denomination notes, such as the $1,000 Grover Clevelands and $5,000 James

Madisons, but these bills hadn't been printed in half a century, and even through well-heeled collectors there simply weren't enough of them to make the nut.

He thought of using higher-denomination bills of some foreign currency, but the notion stuck in his craw. He didn't want his grand statement of American ostentation to pay off in alien dough. He was jingoistic like that.

Gold, then? A hundred thousand ounces or so? Not unless they moved the event to Fort Knox. Cortland toyed with diamonds, even put together a sample box of them, but they failed to impress. To the untrained eye, $70 million in diamonds would look pretty much like $7,000 in zircons. Plus, diamonds were iffy. They traded more like a collectible than a commodity, their value pegged not by the market but by what a buyer was willing to pay.

Eventually Cortland found what he was looking for: rhodium. Expensive big brother to platinum and palladium, it sold at five grand an ounce. Hell, he'd only need eight hundred and something pounds of the stuff—no trick for a man of his resources, though there were parts of South Africa that would now never be the same. In practically the only understated gesture of his career, Cortland had the rhodium fashioned into a simple cube, silver-white, perfectly smooth and polished, with just the casino's monogram engraved on each face. Cortland himself drove it to the final table on a motorized hand truck, flanked by a phalanx of armed security guards. When the TV lights struck the cube, it was just beautiful—awe inspiring, really. *To own a thing like that,* thought Hal, *you might just take a pass on the cash.*

With that, it finally sunk in to Hal that, win or lose, he was guaranteed at least $40 million . . . life-changing money, and then some. When this was over, he realized, he'd have some serious decisions to make about how he intended to go forward from here. Would he want to play more poker? Go back to taxes? Move to Alaska and open a bar? The world lay at his feet. Who could have anticipated that?

But first . . . one last slackjaw to iron out.

Hal knew he could beat Dragic heads up: it would be a small matter to hoist him by the petard of his need and goad him into a fatal blunder. But Hal had needs of his own. Merely beating Dragic wouldn't suffice. So he had cooked up a program, a plan for the hand that he thought (well, hoped) would take him where he had to go.

Standard procedure for heads-up play has the small blind on the button, first to act preflop, with the choice of completing the blind, folding, or raising. The big blind thus has the option of checking or raising in position preflop but must then act first on later betting rounds. This structure gives tremendous advantage to the small blind, who gets to see flops in position and at a discount if he so chooses and the big blind cooperates. Another approach is to raise promiscuously from the small blind, with the intent to leverage position advantage on subsequent streets. Dragic, holding a narrow chip lead, chose to go this route, hammering away from the small bind on hand after hand. Further, when Hal didn't show the same initiative on his own button, Dragic started raising from the big blind as well, responding to Hal's passive play with ever more aggressive forays of his own.

Hal let Dragic control the action completely, and to almost everyone watching—the people in the TV truck were especially disdainful—this seemed a blatant mistake. Granted, Hal was ridiculously deep-stacked. He had some $10M in chips, and with the blinds at $20K and

$40K, with $5K antes, he could afford to be patient. But if he didn't engage Dragic in a fair number of hands, he had no hope of trapping him in a big one, for his strong holdings would have no cover. Hal was engaged in a war of attrition, though he was keenly aware that at this point the attrition was all one-way. He knew he couldn't keep it up forever. Fortunately, he didn't have to.

Because just then a cell phone rang.

It was Vinny's; Hal recognized her ringtone, Ponchielli's "Dance of the Hours." She answered self-consciously, for cell phone use was banned during the TV taping. Wilting under the tournament director's glare, she muttered, "Sorry, my bad," switched off her phone, and stashed it deep in her purse.

A moment later, she whistled.

The opening bars of Beethoven's Fifth.

It was a pretty crude code, but that was okay. It only had to work once.

Hal swallowed a sigh of relief. He folded his hand preflop (pocket jacks, and boy did the boys in production laugh at that) and asked the dealer for time. Then he turned to Dark Mark and said, "I want to make a deal."

Slaughter and Skip caught lucky. They had, of course, wasted no time getting over to Foxxy's, but even at that they almost missed Carl Ott, who was just driving away in his pickup truck when they rolled up. Seeing Minty tied in back, his neck at the mercy of every pothole and hard swerve, Skip had wanted to broadside the motherfucker, but Slaughter's cooler head prevailed. They fell in behind and followed Ott to a convenience store about a mile away. "So what's the play?" asked Skip.

"Can you fake a seizure?"

"Are you kidding? That's my Halloween costume."

They rolled past the convenience store and parked in the lot of an office building next door. Skip hopped a low retaining wall and headed toward the convenience store. Minty caught sight of him but seemed to sense that this was no time for a barky outburst. He remained still and silent, his massive head resting on his paws, as he regarded Skip with doleful eyes.

Skip sauntered into the store. He spotted Ott in back, grabbing several tall boys from the beer racks of a walk-in cooler. As Ott moved from there to the snack food aisle, Skip vectored to intercept. He picked up a bag of pork rinds and asked, "How are these, man? Pretty good?"

"The fuck should I know?"

Ott started to push past Skip, who suddenly shouted, "Oh, God!" and grabbed his head with both hands in evident agony. He grabbed Ott's shirtfront. Ott shook him off and watched with detached curiosity as Skip fell to the floor, his body in full spasm. "Help me," pleaded Skip as his eyes rolled up in his head and a string of drool seeped from his mouth. But Ott just stepped over him and started away.

Well, fuck that, thought Skip. His hand snaked out and grabbed Ott's ankle. The big man toppled to the floor. One of the tall boys rolled away under a display case. The other splooshed open on impact, soaking Ott in a spray of foam.

"What the hell?" said Ott. "Let go!"

"Ub-gub-gub-guh-gub," replied Skip. He clamped his other hand on Ott's ankle and held on for dear life as he jerked and flopped around on the floor like a hooked ono. Ott tried to pry himself free, but Skip's soi-disant seizure gave him a grip of steel.

The store clerk came running over. "What's going on?"

"The guy's freaking out," said Ott. Skip continued to writhe and shake, knocking jars and bags off the shelf. Then he seemed to pass out, his hands holding a death grip on Ott's ankles. It took Ott and the clerk a good two minutes to pry them free. By the time Ott got back to his truck, there was nothing but a tatter of cut ropes where the dog had been. Realizing he'd been mooked, Ott raced back into the store. Skip was gone. "Where's the kid?!" he shouted.

"He went out the back," said the clerk. "I've never seen anyone recover so fast from a—"

Ott shoved him aside and ran out the back door. No Skip. Ott circled the building. He checked the parking lot and the adjacent lots, even looked up on the roof, as if maybe Santa and his eight tiny reindeer had snatched the dog. Nothing. Ott jumped into his truck and tore out of there, jetting down the street in hope of catching sight of the dog.

He knew it wouldn't happen.

In his heart, he knew he was fucked.

Back in the store, the clerk went to work cleaning up the mess. After a few minutes, Skip emerged from the walk-in cooler. "Thanks, man," he told the clerk, handing him a Big Ben. "Best practical joke ever."

He pulled out his cell phone and dialed Vinny's number. Then he grabbed a cab to the Cortland, hoping it wouldn't all be over before he got there.

28 Goodbye, Queef

The tournament director didn't like it. The producer of the TV shoot didn't like it, either. The crowd didn't like it at all, for what were they supposed to look at, an empty table? But players had the right to negotiate a deal, so Hal led Dragic off the tournament floor and into the service corridors behind the ballroom, looking for a place where they might talk in private. He found a small utility closet and gestured Dragic inside. Dragic looked around the small space with a "what the hell" expression. "No cameras," said Hal, by way of answering Dragic's unasked question. "We can talk freely."

"About exactly fucking what?"

Hal found himself fiddling nervously with his Oakleys. Now that he was finally making the pitch, he supposed he was edgier than he would have expected, even though he had ghosted himself through this moment many times. "Well, a deal, you know. A reasonable distribution of assets."

Dragic sneered. "We already have a deal. You dump, I don't kill your dog."

"Yeah, no," said Hal. "We're gonna need a new deal."

"I knew it. You sold out your mutt."

"Not in a million years," said Hal. "Call your guy."

Dragic's eyes narrowed. What bullshit was this? Nevertheless, he punched up Ott's cell phone number. When Ott answered, the connection was thick with background noise. Said Dragic, "What's going on?"

"What do you mean?" asked Ott, his voice a transparent attempt at casual innocence.

"Show me the dog," said Dragic.

"What show you the dog?"

"Switch to video and show me the dog."

"Can't do it," said Ott. "Video's broke."

"What the fuck?"

Suddenly a loud roar blasted through the phone. "Can't talk," said Ott, and the line went dead.

Said Hal, "I don't know, you know, but that sounded like the airport to me. Is your guy taking a trip?"

Running away, more like, thought Dragic. He switched off his phone in disgust. "Okay," he said. "That was plan A. Plan B is maybe I just kick the shit out of you right here, right now."

"You could," said Hal, fiddling with the shades again, "but that won't get you what you want." Dragic said nothing, but Hal read the lust in his eyes. "But you can still have it, you know."

"In exchange for what?"

Hal swallowed hard. *Here goes nothing.* "Just the answer to one question. Why'd you kill Guy?"

"Are you out of your fucking—"

"Come on, man, cut me a break. Look where we are." Hal waved a hand vaguely around the service closet. "Just satisfy my curiosity. Who's ever gonna know?"

Dragic shook his head in disgust. He reached for the

door handle. "I think I'll just beat your ass fair and square."

"Sure, you might," said Hal, "but what if I catch lucky?" He essayed an ingenuous shrug. "Well, anyway, lots of people remember who finishes second, right? Though after everything you went through to get here . . ."

"You are a fucking pain in the ass, you know that? Just like your brother."

"It runs in the family, yeah. Mutant genes, something, I don't know." Hal paused for a beat, then pressed on. "Look, I want what I want, you want what you want. We can hook each other up."

Dragic crossed his arms. He stared at Hal levelly. "Fucking dipshit," he said. "Where the hell do you get off?"

"I'm an open book, man. You know exactly where I'm at." Hal was so nervous he couldn't stop messing with the Oakleys.

At last, Dragic said slowly, "It won't do you any good, you know. The guy who did your brother's on the next plane out."

"Figured so," said Hal. "But you sent him, and that's what I don't get. You've dealt with all these other mayonnaise motherfuckers. Why did Guy get special treatment?"

"He cracked the gaff," said Dragic. "Threatened to take me down. Said there was the integrity of poker to protect. Can you believe that shit?"

"So you killed him to . . ."

"Keep him fucking quiet."

"And tried to steal his entry chip because . . . ?"

"Because why the fuck not. Because he was an asshole who didn't know to keep his nose out of other people's business, and I guess that runs in the family, too.

So, yeah, I had him killed." Dragic sneered. "What are you gonna do about it? Ott's in the wind. And like you said"—Dragic banged a wall of the utility closet—"we're away from prying eyes."

"Yeah, we are," said Hal. "So you've got deniability." He slid the Oakleys back in his pocket. "And I got what I want. So let's go win you a tournament. I'll just call myself to death—how's that sound? You bet the flops and turns, I fold the rivers." Then he added, "But listen, I can't do it on every hand. If I'm calling along with just nothing, it's gonna smell bad. So I'll call with middle pairs or draws and then, you know, lose my nerve. Once you get me down to about a quarter of the chips, I'll donk off the rest on a suicide bluff. Code word: rascal. Yeah?"

"Yeah, I got a code word for you, too," said Dragic. "If this doesn't work . . ."

"I know," said Hal somberly. "It's not just my tournament life on the line."

They went back to the ballroom and play resumed. The TV announcers speculated on what kind of agreement they'd reached. The assumption was that they'd saved something like $50M each, and were playing for the remaining $10M and the trophy. (Though maybe the loser gets the trophy, one announcer joked.) Now that a deal had apparently been made, everyone expected play to loosen up. Sure enough, Hal started calling more than folding, creating a series of pots in the $1M to $2M range. Dragic seemed to be winning them all, though, as Hal evidently didn't have the cards or the courage to call key bets. If Hal continued to play this way, Dragic seemed a lock to win. In anticipation of this, and seeing Hal so smoothly taking his dive, Dragic became expansive and talkative. He was having a party, playing to the cameras and joking it up. He was on the verge of his dream come true, the end of a twisted path that began more than twenty years before with the death of Tall Paul Rogers.

Hal imagined that Dragic was already conducting his postmatch interview in his mind.

After a few more hands, Dragic had acquired about $18.5M in chips. He was now looking to pick off Hal's suicide bluff but knew he'd need at least half a hand to do so. On the next deal, he raised to $100,000 from the small blind. Hal threw in another $60K to call. The flop came Q-6-4 rainbow. Dragic pushed out two stacks of $5,000 chips: $200,000. Hal counted out enough chips to call, and it looked to be yet another weak, loose, bad play on the part of the rookie who obviously had no clue how to play endgame tournament poker. But then . . .

Hal essayed a wry smile. "All in, you rascal," he said. "Call if you don't like assignable-value pieces of plastic." Dragic studied his adversary. After all this time and all this deception, he had to be leery of the double cross. Suppose Hal had hit two pair. He'd expect Dragic to call with top pair, top kicker, or even just naked top pair. After all, hadn't he given the code word? But Dragic wasn't nearly so credulous. Code or no code, he wouldn't have called with anything less than a monster here.

As it happened, he had a set of sixes.

Which, as it happened, was no match for Hal's trip queens.

Dragic seemed to take the setback in stride. He clamped a veneer of calm on his face as he shipped $6.5M in chips to Hal. Then he placidly got up from his seat; walked around to Hal's side of the table; and muttered in a low, flat voice, "We need to refine our deal."

"Of course," said Hal. They stepped off to the side, well out of range of the ambient microphones hanging above the table.

"What do you think you're doing?" said Dragic in a hissed whisper.

"Sorry, man. Autopilot. I flopped top set. I couldn't lay it down."

"You fucking set me up!"

Hal regarded him levelly. "You think?" Then, "You know what? I guess I did." He laughed, a conscious imitation of Dragic's grating honk. "Got your confession, too."

"You *heard* my confession."

"No," said Hal. "I *have* your confession." He pulled out the Oakleys and tapped them against his teeth. "Does the phrase 'voice memo function' mean anything to you?" Dragic immediately snatched the glasses, threw them to the floor, and crushed them under his foot. The tournament director took a worried step forward, but Hal waved him back. "It's okay," he said. "We're negotiating." Then he turned to Dragic and whispered calmly, in a voice thick with disdain, "Bluetooth, dude. You don't think I already e-mailed that file?"

Dragic's hands clenched into fists. "Easy," said Hal. "Everyone's watching." With great difficulty, Dragic relaxed his hands. "Bad news," Hal continued, his voice pitched low so that only Dragic could hear. "I don't dump for anyone."

"I will fucking kill you," whispered Dragic.

"Do you want the tournament win or not?" Dragic's eye twitched as he glared at Hal. He nodded imperceptibly. "Then come and get it."

On the first deal back, Hal completed the blind, Dragic raised, and Hal reraised him all in. He knew Dragic couldn't call, for his raise had certainly been inspired by rage, not cards, and he simply wouldn't be ready to risk losing now. Sure enough, Dragic folded, increasing Hal's modest chip lead.

But Dragic had reached the tipping point, and Hal knew it. Considering how much time, energy, and money Dragic had put into the hack only to find himself having to play on the square for his personal grail, Hal figured Dragic would overplay the first big hand he held. If Hal had a hand that matched up, he planned to call, because getting Dragic to tilt during the tournament was only half the battle. He had to get him to tilt after, too, and for that, he needed to strike before Dark Mark's ire could cool.

It's well known that no one wins a poker tournament without a little luck along the way, and those who think they managed on skill alone are just not paying attention. In fact, the landscape of any major event is littered with *woulda, shoulda, coulda* corpses, worthy competitors who played well enough to win, but just didn't get the right hand at the right time.

The *right* hand. Not necessarily a *big* hand.

Marko Dragic made a minimum raise from the small blind. This was the first min raise Dragic had made during their entire heads-up battle, and it shrieked to Hal of a big pocket pair. In such circumstances, cautious players will trust their read and fold. There's something to be said, certainly, for not giving one's foe the satisfaction of getting a big hand paid off.

But there's something else to be said for delivering the knockout blow. Hal looked down at his cards. He held the perfectly dreadful 6♣2♥. Against a big pocket pair it wins like 12, 13 percent of the time. But it has the power of deep deception, especially if it's disguised to look strong, too. So Hal reraised Dragic's min raise with a min raise of his own. This, he knew, would convey big tickets back to Dragic, and when Dragic flat-called, Hal was sure Dark Mark was looking to milk a monster.

That the flop came 6-2-9 rainbow was only a matter

of situational luck, the kind of luck you need to execute a plan for a hand like this. Hal didn't figure Dragic for pocket nines or pocket sixes, for he would have played those weakish pairs much more strongly preflop. In first position, Hal bet the pot. Using the strong-means-weak metric, he wanted Dragic to think that he was on something like pocket tens or pocket jacks, looking to take the pot away from the A-K or A-Q that Dragic had been trying to suggest with his preflop betting sequence. In fact, he was fairly sure that Dragic had aces or kings, and when Dragic smooth-called, he just knew it.

The turn was an 8, creating a straight possibility, but only if Dragic held 7-T or 7-5, and, again, these holdings were entirely inconsistent with the betting so far. Hal checked.

Dragic pushed his stacks across the line.

This wasn't a bluff, though Dragic tried to sell it as one. Dragic believed he had the best hand, and he wanted to cripple Hal *now*. Hal measured their stacks. It was close. He had Dragic covered by a hair. If he called and won, it would be all over. If he called and lost . . . he'd have a problem.

Hal replayed the hand in his mind one more time and reached the same conclusion: Dragic had aces and was drawing dead to two aces, three eights, and three nines. Eight outs. Hal was better than a 4-to-1 favorite. Was it enough? Should he wait for a better opportunity? Nope. Now was the time. "Call," said Hal. Dragic tabled his aces. When he saw Hal's 6-2, he simply couldn't believe the trap he'd fallen into.

The dealer burned . . .

And turned . . .

The jack of hearts.

Hal had won! He was the winner of the Poker Apocalypse!

Or, well, not quite.

When the dealer shipped Dragic's chips to Hal, she noticed that Dragic had inadvertently failed to put a lone $5,000 chip into the pot. Had he declared all in? No. He'd said nothing as he'd pushed in his chips. What about Hal? Had he raised, or himself said all in? No. So Dragic's $5,000 chip was still live.

The proverbial chip and a chair.

Hal's heart sank. He knew it was *virtually* impossible though not *entirely* impossible for Dragic to mount a comeback.

It actually never came to that.

Dragic had gone to another place. The place where Tall Paul's corpse lay, and that tourist from the Maxim.

Dragic picked up that one last chip . . .

Rolled it slowly over the back of his hand . . .

Flipped it into the air . . .

Caught it on the fly . . .

And winged it at Hal as hard as he could!

After that, things happened fast. Hal ducked the chip. In an instant, Dragic was on Hal, grabbing him in powerful arms and throwing him to the floor. A security guard raced over. Dragic decked him with a punch and grabbed his gun. He held it to Hal's temple. "Fucking goodbye, queef!" said Dragic with cold fury.

But this was the second part of Dragic's tilt. The part Hal had anticipated. The part he had known he had to trigger.

A single shot rang out.

The last thing that registered in Dark Mark's eyes was surprise. He fell down right on top of Hal, and it wasn't until Hal was able to wriggle out from underneath that everyone could see the Beretta Tomcat in Hal's hand. He set the gun on the floor and stood up, his hands in the air in surrender.

Hal had gotten Dragic's confession. Presumably there would have been a conviction. But Hal had no illusions about this. He knew that even in prison, Dragic could have been a threat to them all. So he had played a dangerous game, set himself up as the Tall Paul of the Apocalypse—equipped, though, to act in self-defense.

In poker, you don't play the cards; you play the player. You figure out where your foe's weaknesses are and you exploit them.

Technically, the tournament wasn't over, for Dragic still had that one chip left. Some time later, as a formality, they dealt one last round of cards and declared the hand, like the player, dead. So that was that with that.

Big Mo blew the whistle on the whole Dragic hack. He turned state's evidence, and all the conspirators were variously fined and barred, but, as expected, no one did time. Big Mo made a name for himself on the talk show circuit and ended up working as a casino security consultant. He was kind of a big deal.

Kai Cortland refunded everyone's buy-in. He barely felt the hit.

Carl Ott had had it in mind to go to Nicaragua, but when he landed in Houston he was arrested and shipped back to Nevada. Detective Danny Ding, despite an effort of mind numbing diffidence, found sufficient evidence to put Ott away. Lanh Tran was likewise convicted; even Ding couldn't screw up that case. He subsequently retired from the Las Vegas police department and devoted himself to vodka, keno, and escorts sent directly to his door.

Hal and Vinny were married the following spring. Slaughter gave the bride away. Skip was best man. Minty bore the ring in a velvet box clipped to his collar. He sat patiently through the ceremony, but Hal could tell he'd rather be off chasing squirrels.

It had been almost exactly a year since Guy had died in Hal's arms. Hal had settled his affairs in Pittsburgh and moved to Las Vegas. He didn't play a lot of poker—found that his fire for the game had been quenched. Every now and then, though, he, Vinny, Skip, and Slaughter would enter a small local tournament, or else take a cash game by storm, just to keep their hand in. It was fun. You never knew what the next two cards would bring.

Walk down the beach, Guy had said. *Pick up everything you find and turn it into a party hat.*

The justice of the peace asked Hal a question. He snapped out of his reverie and said, "I do." Then, per instruction, he kissed the bride.

He liked this party hat. He liked the way it fit.